# Unexpected Fall

*New York Times & USA Today* Bestselling Author

# KAYLEE RYAN

Cover Design: Sommer Stein, Perfect Pear Creative Covers
Cover Photography: Eric Battershell
Model: Corey Mortenson
Editing: Hot Tree Editing
Proofreading: Deaton Author Services
Formatting: Integrity Formatting

# Chapter 1

## Dawn

I make my way toward Mark with Reagan's words, *"He assumes you're his while you're standing here wondering if he's yours. Talk to him,"* bouncing around in my head. Does he really already think I'm his? Sure, I want to be, but like I told her, we've never talked about it. I'm not even sure how we ended up where we are. We just kind of started hanging out with everyone as a group, and before we knew it, we were hanging out just the two of us. Hell, we didn't even start sleeping together until a few months ago. Things are always easy and fun. I just assumed that's what we were. A good time. Now, I'm not so sure. I know what I want. What my heart wants. But Mark is one of those guys. You know the type. The one that every woman is drawn to. He has that "bad boy" vibe with his tattoos adorning his arms and back. He's not the type to stick with one woman. Then again, from what Kendall has told me, neither was Ridge or even Tyler for that matter. Now look at them.

Family men.

I can't help but smile as I think about Mark and his group of friends.

They're the poster image for badassery, but when it comes to the women and now kids in their lives, they're big softies. It's endearing.

It's sexy as hell.

I stop next to Mark, and he immediately slides his arm around my waist and pulls me close. "It's hard to believe she's already a year old," I say, observing as Everly laughs at Knox. He's dancing around being goofy, and she's loving every minute of it.

"Right, and those two,"—he points to Tyler and Reagan's twin boys—"they're going to be next. Time is passing us by." He laughs.

He's right. Time is flying by, and as I stand here watching our friends and their kids, I know that's what I want. I want kids of my own, and a husband. My gut twists because I don't know if he does. I need to just ask him. After all, communication is key to every relationship. Right?

Before I can reply, Knox makes a beeline for us and wraps his arms around my legs. I lift him into my arms and settle him on my hip. He rests his head on my shoulder and my heart melts. This little guy is so full of love.

"What are you doing, birthday girl?" Mark smiles down at Everly, who pulls on his pants leg. He lifts her effortlessly and holds her in his arms. "I think you need to tell your daddy it's time for cake," he whispers, loud enough for me to hear. He winks at me then addresses Knox. "Look at you moving in on my girl." He reaches out and tickles his belly, which causes Knox to wiggle in my arms.

"No." He chuckles. Mark eases up and Knox wriggles to get down. He rushes across the room to his dad, who swings him in his arms upside down, pulling a deep belly laugh from him before settling him on his hip.

"Are you tired, sweetie?" I ask Everly. Reaching over, I push her brown locks out of her eyes.

"I think we better get to the cake and presents before this little one passes out," Kendall says, appearing beside us. At the sound of her mom's voice, her eyes open a little wider and she turns toward the sound. She immediately holds her arms out for Kendall, who takes her from Mark after he kisses her on the cheek and whispers another "Happy Birthday" to her.

By the time Everly opens her gifts and smashes a handful of cake in her face as we sing "Happy Birthday," she's done. It's not just her. All the kids seem to be cranky and ready for a nap. When Everly rubs her eyes and gets cake in them, she starts to cry. Daddy to the rescue. Ridge scoops her up and cradles her in his arms.

"You ready to head out?" Mark asks, his voice low and only for me. All the kids are exhausted, and I'm sure Ridge and Kendall are ready to have their house to themselves.

"Yeah. We heading to my place?"

"Thought we could go to mine." He playfully wags his eyebrows and it's such a contrast from his usual intense stare. That's something I've noticed he saves for those closest to him.

"We can do that," I agree, stepping a little closer to him. "I was hoping we could talk."

His eyes, full of intensity, are back and focused on me. "Everything okay?" His concern is evident in the tone of his voice.

"Yes." I smile reassuringly.

"Oh, I get it." He smiles. "I like the way you think," he says with a wink. "Talking." He wags his eyebrows again. "Sounds like a grand idea."

Even though he's not even close, I can't help but smile at him. Mark is so laid-back, nothing seems to ruffle his feathers. That's why I'm not worried about breaking the news to him that me wanting to "talk" means I actually want to talk. Although, his double meaning has some merit as well. Maybe we can do my version of talking, and if all goes well, move onto his. That is if he still wants me around. He could have a different idea of where this is going, and once I tell him I want more, that I want it all, that could be the end of this.

The end of us.

"Let's make our rounds," he says, placing his hand on the small of my back and leading me around the room. We stop and say goodbye to Seth and Kent first, then make our way to Tyler, Reagan, and the twins.

"Uncle Mark has to go." He lifts Ben into his arms and hugs him close. And I know what he's thinking. We could have lost him.

"My turn," I say, reaching for Ben. He comes willingly into my arms, and just like Mark did, I snuggle him. I'm not related to these boys by blood, but I couldn't love him anymore if I were. "Aunt Dawn is going to miss you," I tell him, kissing his chubby little cheek.

"Hey, we want some of that," Mark taunts, holding Beck.

Leaning into them, I kiss Beck on the cheek, making him giggle. "I'll miss you too," I coo at him.

"What? Uncle Mark can't get any loving?" Mark teases.

Leaning in, I kiss his cheek. The twins laugh from the four of us being gathered so close together. Ben reaches out and tugs on Beck's shirt and they cackle with laughter. I'm not sure why they find that so funny, but baby laughter is infectious, especially from these two after the last few months of worrying about Ben and his heart condition.

"That'll do for now," Mark whispers huskily, once again just for me.

The combination of his words and the deep timbre of his voice in my ear causes a shiver to race through me. "All right, we'll see you soon." I give Ben another hug and tickle Beck's side before Mark and I pass them back to Tyler and Reagan.

"Hey, we're going to start poker night back up," Tyler tells Mark.

"And," Reagan chimes in, "we're starting a girls' night."

"Count me in. Just let me know when and where."

"What exactly does this girls' night consist of?" Tyler asks as we walk away.

"You leaving?" Kendall asks as we approach her.

"Yeah, this little cutie has had a big day." I run my hand over Everly's baby-fine hair where she's resting against her daddy's shoulder.

"Thanks for coming," Ridge says.

"No place we'd rather be, brother," Mark replies.

"Hey, buddy, can Aunt Dawn have a hug?" I ask Knox, who is watching us with tired eyes.

He holds his arms out for me and I take him from Kendall. He rests his head against my shoulder and snuggles close. I hold him a little tighter. He's growing up too fast. I glance at my best friend and her smile is wide as she watches her son in my arms.

Mark leans in close to Knox. "You moving in on my girl, little man?"

"Mine," Knox says, tucking his arms into himself.

Mark's eyes flash to me. "You're the only one I'm willing to share her with," he says, his voice strong. Confident.

4

The war that's been raging inside of me since my talk with Reagan calms a little. Sure, he could be saying that for Knox's benefit, but the intensity of his gaze tells me that's not the case.

"I'll see you later, buddy." I give Knox another gentle squeeze. "I'll give you back to Mommy." At the sound of me referring to her as a mommy, Kendall's eyes light up. It's as if she still can't believe that she holds that title for this little guy.

"Bump it." Mark holds his fist out for Knox, and he doesn't leave him hanging. He presents his little tightened fist to Mark, and they bump. "And you." Mark leans in and kisses Everly on the cheek. "Happy Birthday, Princess Everly." His voice is soft. When he backs away, I lean in and do the same.

The only girl of our tight-knit group and she has the guys wrapped around her little finger, and she has no idea. Although, they're soft for the boys as well.

"Thanks for coming," Kendall says again. "I'll see you at work Monday."

"Ugh," I groan and she laughs.

"Tell me about it. The weekends seem to fly by."

"I'll be there." With one last wave to everyone, we're out the door. Mark's arm settles around my waist as we make our way to his truck. He opens the door for me and I yelp in surprise when he grips my hips and lifts me into his truck.

I'm sitting sideways, and he steps in close. My thighs open for him, welcoming him closer. I want him as close to me as I can get him. All the time. His lips crash into mine in a searing kiss. The kiss is electric, not that I expect it to be otherwise. That's how it's always been between us. My mind swirls as all thoughts leave me, his kisses intoxicating. "Talking," he mumbles against my lips. He kisses me quickly, just a peck on the corner of my mouth, before pulling away and shutting my door.

Once we're on the road headed toward his place, he reaches over and laces his fingers through mine. That's not something he would do if we were just casual, right? I mean, he didn't start being openly affectionate until a few months ago, after we slept together for the first time. I bite back a groan and stare out the window. I hate that I'm analyzing every step, every form of contact between us. My stupid heart had to go and fall in love with him, and won't let my mind shut off.

I want him to say we're more. That this is beyond the usual for him. I don't expect him to profess his love to me, but knowing it's above just being casual would be nice. Then again, despite what he says, if he's willing to continue down this path, regardless of how he wants to label us, I know I will follow along behind him. Even knowing the pain that will come when it does end. If that's the case, I'll still follow him. The pain of losing him is worth any amount of time spent with him.

He stays quiet as he pulls onto his street and then into his driveway. He releases his hold on my hand and climbs out of the truck. Taking a deep breath, I reach for the handle at the same time Mark pulls the door open. Hands on my hips, he lifts me from the truck. Holding me suspended in air, he kisses me softly before placing me on my feet. Tears prick my eyes. He's so damn sweet, and always tender and patient. A complete contrast to his outside appearance. Hand in hand, we enter his house. Still neither of us say a word.

The room is shadowed as day turns to night. The evening glow of the sun peeks through the blinds, creating a romantic feel. When Mark doesn't switch on the lights, I turn to look at him. He's standing next to me, watching and waiting for what, I'm not sure. I take off my coat and hang it on the hook by the door. He does the same, never taking his eyes off me. Reaching out, he cradles my face in his palm. His calloused fingers are familiar against my skin. Slowly he leans down. Closer and closer, inch by torturous slow inch, his lips descend on mine.

At the first touch, I melt into him. Nothing in this world compares to Mark's kisses. His touch is tender and his lips are soft. My hands grip his shirt, pulling him closer. I need him closer. I need there to be no space between us.

Dropping his hands, they settle on my hips, and I step into him. When his grip tightens and I'm lifted off my feet, I instinctively wrap my legs around his waist. A deep growl emits from somewhere deep in his chest, and I know there will be no talking. You would think with the growl that I'm in for it, but I know better than that. He's always so gentle with me, as if he's afraid he's going to hurt me.

Touching.

Caressing.

Feeling.

That's how this night is going to go.

# Chapter 2

## MARK

She wants to talk, and we will. I'm dreading it, but I've never been one to shy away from the hard stuff. I face life head-on and take each day as it comes. However, right now, all I want to do is cherish her. I have no idea what she wants to talk about, but from the sound of her voice and the hollowed look in her eyes when she asked me if we could talk, I'm almost certain I'm not going to like what she has to say.

I don't really know how we got here. How we got to the point where we spend all of our spare time together. I think about her when she's not with me, and I can't keep my hands off her when she is. Tonight is no exception.

Our kiss is soft and slow. Which is what she deserves. She's so damn tiny I'm always afraid I'm going to break her. My six-foot-four frame towers over her five-foot-four one. She's a full foot shorter than me and is like a pixie. *My pixie.*

Needing her closer, I grip her hips and lift her feet off the floor. My intention was to be able to deepen the kiss, but my pixie takes it a step further and wraps her legs around my waist. When she tilts her hips and rubs her pussy over my cock, fire burns deep inside me. Need like I've never felt thrashes through my veins, and suddenly I can't get close enough. My hands slide down to her ass and I grip her cheeks, one in each hand, as my tongue pushes past her lips. She moans, rocking her hips again, causing my cock to throb painfully behind my zipper.

Stroke after stroke, my tongue explores her mouth as I get lost in her taste. I'm in such a fog, lost in her, I don't realize what I'm doing until a whimper escapes her. Pulling back, I rest my forehead against hers. "I'm sorry," I pant as I fight to catch my breath. That's what she does to me.

"Stop." She gulps as she too works on catching her breath.

"I was rough with you." Rough doesn't really describe the death grip I had on her ass and the way I was grinding her against my cock. I'm always careful with her, never wanting to hurt her. I lost control and there is no excuse for that.

"Marcus," she whispers. Her lips find their way to my neck, driving me wild.

The sweet sound of my full name rolling off her lips twists me up inside. No one calls me that except for my mom, and dad when he's pissed. When Dawn does it, well, it lights me on fire. I can't explain it and I don't pretend to try.

"What, baby?" I ask, trying to maintain my composure.

She continues to kiss my neck, her lips finding their way to my ear. She nips at my lobe before whispering huskily, "Fuck me."

Her whispered plea is hot lava coursing through my veins. Keeping a tight grip on her ass with one hand, the other reaches back and turns the deadbolt on the front door. Then we're moving. She doesn't stop her assault on my neck as she licks and sucks, igniting a fire inside me I'm not sure I'll ever be able to tame.

Kicking open my bedroom door, I don't stop until we reach my king-size bed. "I need your lips," I say gruffly, and she complies, pulling her mouth from my neck and opening for me. Our kiss is urgent as my tongue battles with hers.

She tugs at my shirt. Pulling out of the kiss, I set her on the bed, allowing me to pull my shirt over my head. "Arms up." She smiles as she lifts her arms over her head, waiting for me to undress her.

Her shirt joins mine somewhere on the floor. I drink in the sight of her. Her long blonde hair cascades over her shoulders. Reaching out, I run my fingers over the silky strands. My index finger traces the strap of her bra, trailing to the mounds of her breasts. They're just the right size to fit nicely in the palm of my hands. Just the thought has my palms itching to feel their weight. Her bra, a green lacey number, has a clasp in the front, which is perfect. With deft fingers, I snap open the clasp and carefully, as if she were made of glass, remove each breast one by one, sucking her puckered nipples into my mouth.

"That. Definitely do more of that," she pants, tilting her head back, exposing her neck.

Giving my girl what she wants, I lavish her breasts, kneading them in the palms of my hands, tasting them with my tongue. I know this is what she likes. Her breasts are like an on switch to her sex drive. It's one I'd like to leave on all the time.

Tearing my mouth from her, I look up to find her watching me. "Stand up." I need her naked sooner rather than later. Offering her my hand, I help her stand. I step back, cataloguing every move she makes as she strips out of her jeans and panties, kicking them across the room.

"Mark." I pull my attention from her breasts to find her smiling softly. "You're overdressed."

I chuckle and make quick work of stripping what's left of my clothes. Reaching into the nightstand, I grab a condom and cover my cock. Dawn moves further up on the bed, and I climb over the top of her.

"Wait," she says, and I freeze. She turns over and braces her weight on her hands and knees.

I move in behind her, palming her ass, loving the way that it feels in my hands. She pushes back into me, causing my cock to be smashed against us. "Patience." I chuckle. Fisting my cock, I run it through her wet heat before pushing inside her. Her back arches and a low deep moan fills the room. Slowly, I pump in and out of her.

"Mark." She pushes back hard and I'm deep. So fucking deep. "More," she demands.

I pull out and then back in. My grip on her waist is firm, yet yielding as I try not to hurt her.

She again pushes back against me and grinds her hips. "Faster," she stresses. As if she needs to show me, she quickens her pace, sliding herself off and on my cock. My grip tightens as her walls grip me. The tight grasp has me clenching my jaw tightly, and I pull her back hard and fast.

"Ahh!" she screams and I still.

Leaning over her, I kiss her neck. "I'm sorry," I murmur. I'm being too rough. I trail kisses over her bare shoulder, trying to get my shit under control. I don't want to hurt her.

"No. No, no, no," she says, shaking her head. *Fuck.* I start to slide out of her, but she pushes back, stopping me. "Don't. I'm not made of glass. I want you, all of you. I want you to fuck me," she says again. Her voice is clear and firm, with zero hesitation.

"Dawn, I…" My voice trails off when she does that magical thing she does so well and squeezes my cock.

"Please," she begs.

Leaning back over her, I place my lips next to her ear. "I don't want to hurt you."

"You're hurting me by not giving me all of you. You're holding back, and I want it all. Give me everything."

There is something in her voice, something that tells me she's talking about more than just sex. Maybe we're on the same page after all. "You tell me to stop if it's too much. I need you to promise me you'll tell me to stop."

"I need you to promise me that you're going to give me all of you."

"Pixie," I warn.

"Fine, I promise. Now do the damn thing," she says, with laughter in her voice. I don't try to hold in the laugh that escapes me. I smack her ass playfully, and she moans. "Finally," she taunts.

My hands on her hips, I pull out then thrust back in. I repeat the motion over and over again, each time going deeper and harder. She's moaning, and the walls of her pussy are squeezing my cock like a vise. It's as if my body is on autopilot as I chase my release.

"There, Mark, there, please don't… don't stop," she gasps.

Before I can tell her that I have no plans on stopping, she screams out my name as her orgasm breaks free. The feel of her release is too much, and I follow along behind her. Careful of my weight, I lean over her body, kiss her bare shoulder, and then roll to my side, taking her with me. My cock is still buried deep inside her as I bury my face in her neck.

"That," she wheezes, "we need to do that again."

A breathless laugh breaks from my chest. "I need some recovery time after that one." Her pussy squeezes me. "Minx." I give her hip a gentle squeeze. Her soft laughter meets my ears.

"Thank you."

"Never thank me for that."

"I know you didn't want to."

"Oh, I wanted to. I was just afraid of hurting you."

"You would never hurt me."

Again, it feels as though her words have a double meaning. "Never," I say adamantly, kissing her shoulder. "I'll be right back." Reluctantly, I slide from her body and climb out of bed to handle the condom. I wash up and take her a washrag to clean her up as well. "Hey," I whisper, sitting on the edge of the bed. Her eyes flutter open. "Open for me." I tap her leg.

"You're always taking care of me," she mumbles.

"I'm good at it," I say, kissing her forehead. I make quick work of cleaning her up as well as I can. After tossing the wet cloth into the hamper, I slide in bed behind her. I pull her into me and bury my face in her neck. I've never been much of a cuddler, but with Dawn, it's like I can't control it. I want to be as close to her as possible all the time. It's not long before her even breaths lull me to sleep.

# Chapter 3

## Dawn

It's been a week since I asked Mark if we could talk. A week of me pretending like I didn't ask him. He's mentioned it a couple of times, and I keep blowing him off, telling him we'll talk this weekend. Part of me is fearful that what we have will end and I'll need some time to recover. No one wants to go to work the next day with eyes puffy from tears. At least I don't. It's an excuse and I know it, but it's all I've got. My phone vibrates across the bathroom counter. Glancing down, I see a new message alert with Mark's name.

> **Mark:** *I'm headed your way. I don't want to stay long. We need to have that talk you've been avoiding.*

He's persistent. I'm being a coward, and we both know it. Tonight, we'll talk, and if we end up parting ways, then it's for the best. I know that. I know I deserve to be with someone who wants the same future as I do. Someone who wants that future with me. I want that person to be Mark.

**Me:** *Sounds like a plan.*

**Mark:** *No more blowing me off?*

He's calling my bluff, and I need that. I need him to make me have this conversation. It's going to drive me insane until I know where he stands. Sure, we've only been intimate for a few months. However, we've been hanging out just the two of us a hell of a lot longer than that. Over a year. Sex just made me grow closer to him.

**Me:** *It's nothing bad. I'm just... hesitant I guess.*

**Mark:** *You can tell me anything.*

**Me:** *I know. I'll see you soon.*

Tossing my phone back on the counter, I finish applying a thin layer of mascara and call it good. I know what he's saying is true. Never has he made me feel as though I can't talk to him. The reluctance is all on me. I'm fearful of losing him. Confrontation leads to losing those you love, at least in my experience.

My high school boyfriend is the perfect example. We were both headed off to college. He was going to California while I stayed close to home. We needed to discuss how we were going to handle it. We'd been dating since sophomore year. I assumed we would stay together; he had other plans. He broke my heart. I've pretty much steered clear of serious relationships since then. Well, until Mark. We've not defined us as serious, but that's how I see us.

Then there's my little sister, Destiny, who offers a whole different level of hurt and anxiety. I knew something was off, had a feeling deep in my gut. I was a senior and she was a freshman. I heard the rumors and knew the crowd she was hanging with. I confronted her and she lied to me. Said she was fine. She continued to withdraw even further, and I did what I had to do and told my parents. We confronted her as a family. She denied using drugs and sleeping around. She blamed me. That was the first time she ran away. She was gone for two weeks. When she showed back up, she was a mess, filthy and strung out. She was begging for money for her next fix. My parents sent her to rehab. She made it six months that first time before she started using again. I've lost count of the number of times they've sent her. She has to want to help herself, and at this point, I'm not sure she ever will.

Turning the bathroom light off, I make my way toward the living room. Grabbing my purse, I make sure I have everything I need and tap my back pocket making sure my phone is there. I survey my apartment, and it's tidy, which is easy to do when you live alone. I scroll through social media for a few minutes until a knock sounds at the door. I know that knock.

*Mark.*

Giddy excitement washes over me, and that's crazy because he slept here last night. It's been a handful of hours since I've seen him, but that doesn't change my excitement at getting to see him. "Hey," I say, opening the door to greet him.

"Did you even check to see who it was?" he asks, a sour look on his face.

"Yes. Besides, it was your knock."

"My knock?" he asks, amused.

"Hush." I lightly push against his chest.

He captures my hands with his, holding them against him. He leans toward me, and I go up on my tiptoes to meet him with a kiss. "That's better," he says, releasing me. "You ready to go?"

"Yes."

"You have anything we need to take?"

"Nope. I did all of that last night at their place. Reagan's kitchen is bigger than my tiny galley."

"You could have cooked at my place."

He offered me his kitchen last night, but I was afraid he would push me to talk and I needed, more like wanted, just one more night for things to be… normal. For us to just be us before the possibility of tearing it all apart. I know I'm being irrational, but it's hard to not let past experiences shadow the future.

"I know, but it made sense to just make it there. Since that's where we're going to be today." We're headed to Tyler and Reagan's for Thanksgiving. It's a week early, but we all have family plans next week, so our Friendsgiving is today. I made two pumpkin pies and two apple pies. Reagan and the boys helped while Tyler and Mark played pool in the basement. By the time we made it back to my place, we were both worn out. We fell right asleep, which left no time for talking. This

15

morning, he had a job he was helping Ridge finish up so he was up and out of my apartment early.

"I guess," he grumbles. "I feel like I've hardly seen you this week. It's been a week since you asked if we could talk."

"I know. And we will. Tonight. I'm fine, I promise. Just something I want to run by you." I blow it off. It's so much more than that.

"Okay, Pixie," he says, kissing the corner of my mouth. "Grab your coat."

I do as he says, and we're out the door. Mark double-checks that my apartment door is locked before leading me out to his truck with his hand on the small of my back.

"Mom called me just before I got here. We're still good for dinner at their place next week, right?" he asks.

"Yeah, you sure they don't mind me crashing?"

"You know they don't mind. Wouldn't matter if they did. No way am I letting you spend Thanksgiving alone."

"Ridge and Kendall invited me," I remind him. My parents are going on a cruise next week. I'm happy they're going. They spend so much time, energy, and money on trying to get Destiny clean, they barely have the time or funds to do something just for them. Mom has asked me no less than what seems like a thousand times if I'm okay with them being gone for the holiday. I'm fine with it. I have close friends here, and Mark invited me to his family's. I won't be alone.

"You'll be with me." His tone of voice tells me that there's no sense in telling him otherwise. That's got to be a good sign, right?

"What can I do?" I ask Reagan. She's scurrying around the kitchen like a busy little bee.

"Umm…" She stops to look at me and starts laughing. "I don't really know. This is my first time hosting something big like this. I mean, this is more than just burgers on the grill."

"Let me help. What needs to be done?"

"Well, we need to get the rolls in the oven. We need serving spoons, the deviled eggs need to be set out, the potatoes are ready to be mashed, and we need to set out plates and silverware."

"Okay, you handle the rolls. I'll take care of the rest."

"What can I do?" Kendall asks a moment later, joining us and making Reagan and me laugh. "What?"

"Reagan is a little overwhelmed," I tell her. I then proceed to rattle off the list that Reagan just gave to me. Together, we get everything sorted. Once the turkey and ham are set on the table, Reagan expels a heavy sigh.

"You did it," I tell her, pulling her into a hug.

"Not without the two of you."

"That's how it should be. Just because you're hosting doesn't mean you do all the work," Kendall assures her.

"How did my mom do this all those years and make it look effortless?" She laughs.

"Right?" I agree with her. "They got their shit together before we were old enough not to remember. We'll get there," I say, and they laugh.

"Call in the troops," Kendall says.

The guys filter into the kitchen, each of them with a baby in their arms. Ridge has Everly, Seth has Knox, Mark has Ben—I know this because Reagan told me who was in blue and the other in red—while Tyler has Beck.

"We need another baby in the family," Kent announces.

"What?" Ridge asks.

"Another baby." He waves his hands around the room. "We need another baby."

"You know how that happens, right?" Mark goads.

"I do, but do you? You two need to get on that." He points at Mark and then to me.

"What's wrong with your d— equipment?" Mark asks, catching himself.

"Nothing, but you have the girl, so you're the obvious next choice."

Mark looks over at me and smirks. "Practicing is fun." He grins cheekily.

My face heats. It's not like we're a secret, so I'm not sure if it's the announcement that we're indeed having sex or the comment that we're practicing for a baby.

"Hurry the hell up," Kent grumbles.

"You need to be faster next time," Seth taunts him.

"Let's eat," Reagan says, shaking her head.

The guys insist that we fill our plates first. Reagan and Kendall try to make plates for the kids, but the guys insist they have it under control. So the three of us make our plates and head into the living room, letting the men and babies take the large dining table. The high chairs were already set up, so it's just easier this way.

The girls and I kick back and relax, enjoying the great food and the company. Raucous laughter flows in from the dining room, from the men and the babies. It's a great day with family and friends, and I'm grateful to be a part of it. My gut twists, wondering if things don't work out with Mark, how will Friendsgiving go next year. He's more of this family, been with them longer than I have. Will I be able to handle him being here like this with someone else? Will I be able to handle him talking about "practicing" for babies with someone else?

*Hell no.*

"Earth to Dawn." Kendall waves her hand in the air, pulling me out of my inner turmoil.

"Sorry, what?"

"You okay?" she asks.

"Yeah," I lie.

"You still haven't talked to him, have you?" Reagan inquires.

"What did I miss?" Kendall questions.

"She's worried that Mark's not feeling the same way she is," Reagan spills.

"What? That's crazy. Have you not seen the way he looks at you?" Kendall says.

"I know." I sigh. "I just worry that it's more serious for me."

"You never know until you ask him," Reagan states.

"I'm going to. Tonight. I just wanted some more time. You know, in case my talk scares him off."

Kendall shakes her head. She knows me better than anyone, and she's well aware of my hang-up on confronting those I care about. "This is different," she says softly.

"Babe!" Tyler calls out. "You've got to see this."

"We better go see what's up." I stand, ending our little chat. I'm nervous enough as it is. I don't need more false hope thrust at me. I just need to stop stalling and put it out there and see what he says.

"Oh my." Reagan laughs. "Looks like the boys like mashed potatoes."

I take in the twins who are covered in mashed potatoes. What's even cuter is Knox is now sitting on the table in front of both high chairs. Seth is holding onto him while he feeds them, which explains the mess. Reagan pulls her phone from her back pocket and snaps a few pictures.

"And you." Kendall sets her now empty plate on the table and pulls Everly from her high chair. "You did a great job of being messy all on your own." She smiles down at her daughter.

"We've got baby duty. You all get kitchen duty," Reagan announces.

I set my plate on the table, and scoop Beck out of his seat, while Reagan grabs Ben. Seth places Knox on his feet and he clasps Kendall's hand as we head down the hall to get them cleaned up.

"You ready to head home?" Mark asks.

Ridge and Kendall are packing up the kids, and the twins are already upstairs napping. "Yeah—" I stop talking when my phone vibrates in my back pocket. I assume it's my parents; they leave tomorrow for their cruise and Mom promised no less than five times she'd call me today. Pulling it out, I glance at the screen. It's not a number I recognize, but the area code is from my hometown. Swiping at the screen, I place the phone to my ear. "Hello."

"D-Dawn…" a female voice sobs.

"Destiny?" It sounds like her, but I'm not sure. It's hard to determine from the sobs that are coming through the line. "Is that you? What's wrong?" I fire off questions to my little sister.

"There was an accident." Her voice cracks.

My heart falls to the pit of my stomach. "What kind of accident?" I manage to ask. I feel Mark's arm slip around my waist, silently offering me comfort.

"I'm sorry," she cries.

"Destiny," I say, my voice stern. "Tell me what happened." It's been months since I've talked to her, and even then, she was so strung out I doubt that she remembers. She's twenty-two. I've lost track of the number of times she's been in rehab. It's almost impossible to help those who are not willing to help themselves.

"They're gone," she says, her voice breaking.

My chest tightens. "Who's gone?" I whisper the question when my gut tells me I already know.

This isn't happening.

"Mom and Dad. I'm so sorry," she says again, and the line goes dead. Nothing but silence greets me on the other end.

My hand falls to my side and I feel the phone slip from my grip, but I can't move to stop it. My parents are gone. My sister dropped the news and hung up on me. I have to know. Frantic, I drop to my knees for my phone, but Mark stops me.

"Hey," he says soothingly. "Tell me what's going on."

"I-I need my phone."

"Here," Kent says, appearing beside us. He bends to pick up my phone, offering it to me.

"Dawn." Mark frames my face with his large calloused hands. "Talk to me."

"I have to call the hospital."

"Okay, we can do that, but you have to tell me what's wrong."

"M-My parents," I choke out. "They're gone."

I feel a hand on my shoulder. I turn to look, causing Mark to drop his hands. I see Kendall. "That was Destiny," I tell her. "She said that… that Mom and Dad are gone."

"Oh, honey," she says and pulls me into a hug. "I'm so sorry."

"I-I don't know what that means. I mean, I think I do, but she just hung up on me. She fucking hung up on me," I say, louder this time. I smack my hand over my mouth as my eyes dart to the kids.

"It's fine," Kendall soothes. "What do you need?" Kendall asks. My best friend has always been there for me. She's been there for many of the drama-filled situations with my little sister.

"Breathe," Mark murmurs softly. His arm slides around my waist and he pulls me close, offering me comfort.

Doing as he says, I take a deep breath and slowly exhale. "I need to call the hospital. I need to know what's going on."

"Let me," Kendall says, pulling her phone from her back pocket.

It makes sense for her to call. We worked there together right out of nursing school. Maybe there will be an old connection she can reach out to and find out what's going on. I need to know what happened to my parents. I'm in no shape to call, but I need answers. With shaking hands, I hit the number that just called me, and it rings, and rings, and rings before going to voice mail. A generic message prompts me to leave a message, but I don't bother. It's hard to tell whose phone it is, and I can guarantee that Destiny's not going to call me back regardless.

"I've got you," Mark whispers in my ear. His hold on me is tight.

I hear Kendall talking, but I can't focus on what she's saying. I just keep hearing my sister's voice telling me she's sorry and that our parents are gone. Why is she sorry? What does that mean? What did she do this time?

# Chapter 4

## MARK

She's shaking. I hold her close to my chest as her body trembles from the bomb that her sister just dropped on her. They're not close, and from what she's told me, it's been that way since high school. I've never met her. I've never talked to her, but right now, I wish I had her number so I could call her and give her a piece of my mind. Who calls and delivers that kind of information and just hangs up?

"I'm right here," I comfort her. I don't know what she needs. Hell, I have no experience with this. I've never cared this much, never had a woman in my life longer than a few weeks. All I can do is hold her and be here for whatever she needs.

"Okay," Kendall says, ending the call. "They didn't tell me much. Just that there was an accident. Destiny was in the car with them, but she's okay. They just released her."

"M-My parents?" Dawn asks, and you can hear the pain in her voice.

Kendall grimaces. "I'm so sorry." She steps forward and wraps her arms around both of us. No way am I letting her go right now.

"I have to go," Dawn says through her tears.

Kendall steps back, and her eyes find mine. "I've got her."

"I'll drive," Seth offers.

I'm ready to tell him that's not necessary but the way Dawn's clinging to me, it's probably a good idea. I don't want to let her go. Not right now. Not when she needs me most. "Thanks, man."

"I'll come too," Kendall offers, looking at Ridge. He nods.

"You don't have to," Dawn says, but even I can hear that she wants her there.

"I want to."

"Be safe. Call me when you get there." Ridge leans in and kisses Kendall on the cheek.

"Leave the kids with us," Tyler says. "Go with them."

"No, that's okay," Kendall says. "I'd rather them be in their own beds. It's only an hour and a half drive. We'll be home tonight."

"Okay, sweet girl, you call me if you need me," he tells her.

"I'll help Ridge with the littles," Kent offers.

"Let's go," I whisper softly. Clinging to me, Dawn allows me to help her into her coat, and lead her out to Kendall's SUV. Seth tells Kendall that he'll drive, and she doesn't argue, climbing into the passenger seat. Once we're on the road, she turns to look at us in the back seat. Dawn is curled into my chest, and from the damp feel of my shirt, I know she's still crying. Kendall gives me a sad smile, then turns back around.

By the time we make it to the hospital, my arm is stiff from holding her so tightly and my shirt is soaked, but my pixie has calmed down. Her last sniffle was almost ten minutes ago. I wish there was something that I could do to take her pain away. I can't imagine losing one of my parents, let alone both of them. On top of that, I can't imagine my sister and her family—her husband and their twins—not being in my life.

"Dawn, we're here," I say softly. I'm not sure if she's sleeping. I know her breathing has evened out and her whimpers have stopped.

She sits up and blinks. "Okay," she says, reaching for the door handle. I move across the seat and follow her out. I'm going to be stuck to her like glue.

"Mary told me for us to go to the Emergency Room," Kendall says, appearing beside us. Seth walks along beside her; he too is giving her silent support.

"Okay." Dawn's broken reply comes out as barely a whisper.

One word. *Okay.* Softly spoken when we all know that she's anything but okay. I keep my arm around her, letting her lean on me as we make our way to the ER. Kendall stops at the desk and lets them know that we're here representing the Miller family. From the grim expression on the receptionist's face, I know that the phone call is real. Somewhere in the back of my mind, I was hoping that maybe this was just a stunt from her sister. Maybe a ploy to bring her home. A shitty one, but from what I know of her sister, that's to be expected.

"This way. I'll let the doctor know you're here." Seth and Kendall lead the way, following along behind the receptionist. "Have a seat. The doctor will be right in."

"You want to sit?" I whisper to Dawn.

She doesn't say anything as she clings to me. I decide we'll stand like this and I can give her my strength. The strength to hold her up and hopefully the strength to get through this.

"Hello," a short dark-haired man, who looks barely old enough to drive let alone be practicing medicine, says, entering the room. He quietly closes the door behind him. "I'm Doctor Travis. I was the one who worked on Tina and Don Miller. Are you family?" he asks.

"Yes," Kendall replies.

Dr. Travis looks at each of us, stopping when he gets to Dawn. "Mr. and Mrs. Miller were involved in an auto accident. From what we were able to gather from witnesses, the car started swerving and the driver, Mr. Miller, lost control. We later learned that their daughter, who was in the car with them, was trying to exit the car while moving. It's the assumption that's when Mr. Miller lost control of the vehicle. Apparently, there was some sort of disagreement. We couldn't get much from her, just that she didn't want to go and was trying to get out of the car. When the police arrived to speak with her, she was gone."

"Destiny?" I ask, speaking for the first time.

Dr. Travis nods. "She said she had a sister, but no one else."

"Dawn," I say, my voice cracking. "This is her sister." I motion to Dawn, who is huddled against my chest. Her tears have reappeared and her soft sobs are ripping my heart to shreds. "Was her sister, was Destiny hurt?"

"No. A few scrapes and bruises, but nothing threatening. She was under the influence, of what we're not sure. We couldn't get her to settle down long enough to draw labs. She kept muttering that she was sorry and she didn't want to go. That's all we know at this point."

"Can I see them?" Dawn's small voice surprises us all.

I want to tell her no, that she can't see them. I don't want her to go through that pain and remember them that way. I want to shield her from all of this. However, I know that I can't do that. I can't take away this final goodbye, her closure. No matter how bad I want to protect her, I just can't with this. Instead, I'm going to be her shoulder, stand tall, and be here for the fall.

"Dawn, I'm not sure that's a good idea," Kendall says gently. "We're nurses. We know the outcome," she adds. "We know what that looks like."

"I have to agree," Dr. Travis says. "I highly advise against it, but of course it's your decision."

"Is this how you want to remember them?" Kendall asks.

"I just… need something." Her hazel eyes look up at me, pleading for answers that I don't have.

"Dr. Travis, is it possible to keep the bodies covered? Maybe let her hold their hands, give her the closure she needs without seeing them fully?" Kendall questions.

"We can do that. Give me a little time to have the nursing staff do what they need to do. You all are welcome to stay here in this room until they come and get you," he tells us before focusing his attention on Dawn. "I'm so sorry for your loss," he says kindly, before leaving the room.

"Tell me what you need, baby." I hold her close.

"We're here," Kendall says, reaching out and taking her hand.

"Name it," Seth says and steps closer.

Her bloodshot eyes and tearstained cheeks are ripping apart my soul. She looks up at me, and I would give anything to take her pain away. "Will you come with me?"

"Of course," I say, with more confidence than I feel. This entire situation is fucked.

"We'll all be there," Seth assures her.

I give him a nod, letting him know I appreciate it. Hell, I'm not sure I can handle seeing them, being there with them like that. The more support I have, the more I can support her. At least I hope that's how it turns out.

"Are you sure about this, Dawn?" Kendall asks.

"No."

"We don't have to go in," I tell her.

"I know, but I feel like I need to see them. I need to know that this isn't just a bad dream."

"At any point, if you change your mind, you tell me. I'll get you out of there," I say, hugging her a little tighter.

"Thank you. Thank you, guys, for being here and bringing me. I couldn't do this alone."

"Of course," Seth and Kendall say at the same time. I don't speak. Instead, I place a kiss on the top of her head just as a nurse enters the room.

"Ms. Miller, if you'll come with me," she says, motioning for Dawn to follow her.

"We're coming with her," I state. My voice leaves no room for negotiation. She hesitates slightly but then nods her agreement. I'm glad she's seeing things my way. No way would I let my girl do this alone.

We follow her out of the room and down the long hallway to the last door on the right. Behind that door, what we're about to see, what she's about to see is going to alter her life forever.

"Stop," Kendall says as the nurse pushes open the door. "Dawn, let me go in first. Let me just… make sure it's all… just let me go in first," she says again.

"You shouldn't have to do that," Dawn tells her.

"I'll go with her." Seth steps up. "Kendall and I will go in, and then if she thinks it's okay, we'll come back to get you."

"I need to see them," Dawn says meekly.

"I know you do, but I don't want your last memory of them to be like this. We don't know the details of their injuries," she replies.

I'm kicking myself for not asking that, but then again, does it really matter? They're gone, and like Kendall said, she doesn't need to have that on her mind as her final memory of them.

"Okay." Again, her one-word reply is all we're getting.

Seth and Kendall disappear behind the door, leaving us out in the hallway on our own. I wrap my other arm around her waist and just hold her. "I'm so sorry, baby," I whisper softly.

"I can't believe this is real. I keep hoping that it's a bad dream or something."

I don't know what to say. I'm not good at this shit. I don't know what to tell her to make it better. I don't know what to do to take her pain away. I don't even try. I just hold her tightly against me, being her strength. I know I can at least give her that.

When the door opens, Kendall is standing there with tears flowing down her cheeks. "You sure about this?" she asks.

"I need to" is Dawn's answer.

Kendall nods and holds out her hand. Dawn steps away from me, and I want to protest and tell her she can't do that. She can't go into that room without my arms around her so she knows I'm here for her. However, I don't. I keep my mouth shut and follow in behind her.

The room has that antiseptic smell, the one that all hospitals seem to have. It's dimly lit, and in the center are two beds, both draped with white sheets, outlining bodies. I swallow hard, fighting against the lump in the back of my throat.

"I pulled their hands out for you," Kendall says, wiping her tears. Not that it does any good, more fall and coat her cheeks instantly.

My eyes follow Dawn as she goes to the right side of the first bed and peers down at the hand. "He got her these last year for their anniversary," she mumbles. The room is eerily quiet, so we hear her loud and clear. "She was so excited. Her original was so small, barely a chip of a diamond." Her voice cracks. "Dad said that after thirty years with him, she'd earned it." A sob racks from her chest, and I rush to her.

When I reach her, I place my hand on the small of her back and she leans into me. "I'm right here," I whisper.

"Their anniversary is next month," she says solemnly.

I watch as her index finger reaches out and trails down the back of her mother's hand until she reaches the rings. She wobbles a little on her feet, but I'm here to catch her, wrapping my arm around her.

"You can take them," the nurse tells her.

Her hand shakes as she picks up her mother's. A sob racks from her chest and I have to fight my own tears. This shit is heavy, but watching my pixie go through this is killing me.

"I can do it." Kendall steps up next to us. Gently, she takes Dawn's mother's hand and slides her rings from her fingers. "I'll keep them with me," she tells Dawn.

My girl nods, turning her head into my chest. She grips my shirt and I wrap my arms around her. I hold her tightly and kiss the top of her head. I don't have words. I can't tell her this is going to be okay. I can't tell her that it will get better in time. Sure, those things are true, but right now she's too raw. This moment is too painful.

Steeling her resolve, she lifts her head from my chest and wipes her eyes with her sleeve. She takes a step away from me, and my instinct is to follow her, so I do. Step for step, I'm behind her as she makes her way between the two beds and stares down at her father's hand. "He cut his hand building Destiny and me a treehouse." Her hand runs over a jagged scar on the back of his hand. "I can't remember how he did it. I remember him coming into the house with his T-shirt wrapped around it and Mom telling us to leave the room."

She looks up at me and smiles through her tears. It's a sad smile, but it's there all the same. "He was that kind of dad, you know? We were definitely daddy's girls."

"He loved you." The words are out of my mouth before I can think about what I'm saying.

She nods. "He did. They both did. They wanted us to have the best in life. They encouraged us to follow our dreams." Her hands clasp together as she brings them to her mouth as if she's praying. "He used to say he was loving Mom by example. He wanted us to find a man who cherished us like he cherished her."

My heart hammers in my chest. I want to tell her she's found that man. That I'm standing right here and I'm not going anywhere. However, we never got to have that conversation, and now is not the time. So I remain quiet, stewing inside that we haven't talked about what we are officially before now.

"Can you—" She turns her head and looks at Kendall. Tears stream down her cheeks. "Can you get his ring too?"

"Are there any other personal items?" Kendall asks the nurse.

She winces. "Yes, but your sister, she left with them."

"Of course she did." Dawn shakes her head. I watch as she slides her hand under her father's. "I-I love you, Dad." She sobs. I want to pull her into my arms and drag her from this room, end this, but I know I can't. She walks back around the table and does the same to her mother. "I love you, Mom," she whispers, her voice broken. She stares at the two tables, tears pouring from her eyes. And watching her heart break is breaking mine. "Mark?"

"Yeah, baby?" I step up behind her and place my arm around her shoulders.

Her answer is to turn in my arms and slide her arms around my waist. My hand settles on the back of her head, holding her to me as she falls apart. Her sobs echo through the room. I can not only hear but feel her heart breaking. I feel it deep in my soul, and there isn't a damn thing I can do to make it better.

"Can we—" She looks up at me. "Can we go to their place?"

"Anything you want," I say, tucking her hair behind her ears. My hands cradle her cheeks and I wipe her tears with my thumbs. "I don't know what to do. I don't know how to help you, so you have to tell me. Whatever you need, it's yours. You just have to tell me."

She nods and turns to look at Kendall and Seth. I don't loosen my hold on her. I need her close to me. "We're going to stay at my parents' tonight. You guys can go."

Seth looks at Kendall, and they seem to have a silent conversation. "We're good," Kendall tells her.

"You have the kids, and Ridge," Dawn says meekly.

"And I have you. My best friend who needs me. My husband and kids are safely tucked away in bed. I'm where I need to be."

"I'm all yours," Seth says, holding his arms open.

She pulls away from me, and I want to protest, but hold my tongue. She walks into his arms and he engulfs her in a hug. "Let him help you." I hear my best friend whisper. My heart stutters in my chest.

"Hey." Kendall opens her arms. "Best friend over here," she says, and Dawn rushes toward her and they hold onto each other as if they need the embrace to breathe. "Let's go," Kendall whispers and leads Dawn from the room.

"What's next?" I ask the nurse. I've never been in this situation and neither has Dawn. I need to know what's ahead of us.

"We'll release the bodies to the funeral home of your choosing."

I nod. "Okay. Give me until tomorrow to see what she wants to do. We'll be in touch." I don't wait for her reply. I walk toward the door with Seth on my heels.

"Thank you," I tell him.

"That's what brothers do. Let's go take care of your girl." With his hand on my shoulder, we head down the hall where Dawn and Kendall are still embracing several paces in front of us, headed for the exit.

# Chapter 5

## Dawn

Kendall climbs into the back of the car with me. Her hand grips mine tightly as she gives Seth direction to my parents' house. I still can't believe this is real. It's as if I'm on the set of a movie, watching the drama unfold. Closing my eyes, I rest my head on Kendall's shoulder, reliving the events of tonight. My sister should be here. We should be leaning on one another, but she left. I guess at least she had the decency to call me. We've tried to help her so many times, and now... now I'm not sure where to go from here. I love her, she's my sister, but I hate her too.

"We're here," Kendall says.

My eyes pop open, and sure enough, we're parked in the driveway of my childhood home. A three-bedroom ranch-style house, in a small subdivision on the edge of town. So many memories were made here.

"I-I don't know if I can." The whispered confession bounces off the windows of the car as if I yelled the words.

Kendall starts to speak, but Mark turns in the seat and reaches for my hand. "Pixie, we can sit here all damn night, we can go to a hotel, we can go home, we can do whatever you need us to do." His voice is firm.

My rock.

I love him. I've never told him. We were supposed to talk tonight, but here we are again, life getting in the way. I should tell him, but I don't want this to be the way we remember it. Not to mention, I couldn't handle losing him after losing my family. I lost my sister years ago, and with my parents gone… I swallow back the sob that wants to escape me. I can't speak for fear of what I might say, so I nod instead.

"We've got company," Seth says, looking in the rearview mirror.

Whipping my head around to look out the back window of the SUV, I watch as my sister stumbles from the car. Smoke rolls out, following her like a shadow. "What the fuck?" I mutter, throwing open my door and rushing toward her. "What the fuck are you doing?" I seethe, stopping and crossing my arms over my chest. I don't have to pretend to glare at her. My anger is real.

"D-Dawn, what are you doing here?"

"Are you fucking kidding me right now?" I feel strong hands grip my shoulders, and I don't have to look to know it's Mark. I would know his touch anywhere. "Where have you been?"

"You're not my mother," she slurs.

"No, she's dead!" I scream. Mark moves in closer and wraps his arms around my waist from behind.

"W-What?" Destiny stumbles some more.

"You called me," I tell her. "You're the one who told me."

"No, that was a dream," she says, and I can tell that's what she thinks. "This"—she pulls a bag of white powder from her pocket—"makes it feel real, but it's not real."

"Oh my God." I sway on my feet, but Mark is there holding strong. "They're dead, Destiny." I think back to her phone call, and then it hits me. She said she was sorry and that she didn't want to go. "What did you do?" Anger rides my words.

"Nothing," she scoffs.

"You said you were sorry and that you didn't want to go. Where were you going, Destiny?"

"It was a dream," she says, this time not so sure of herself.

"It's fucking real life!" I yell. "Our life. They're dead. Tell me what you did?" She turns to the car she just climbed out of, but the door slams and the car speeds off before she can escape.

Slowly she turns to face us. Mark is wrapped around me, and Kendall and Seth stand on either side of us. "Who are they?" she asks.

"We're her family," Mark says from behind me. I relax into him at his words.

"Why don't we go inside?" Kendall suggests.

"No." I don't want her here. "Tell me, Destiny."

"I was here earlier," she says, closing her eyes. "I needed money, just enough to get me by."

"You mean enough for your next fix?" I state the obvious.

She doesn't even flinch. "They were talking about this new facility. They wanted me to go to get clean. Dad suggested we go for a drive." She opens her eyes and looks at me. "I saw the sign for the facility and freaked out. I opened the door to get out when he refused to turn around." She drops to her knees and begins to sob.

I know I should go to her, that I should try to comfort her, but she killed our parents.

"Keep talking," this from Seth. His arms are crossed over his chest too, and he looks intimidating as hell.

"It was a dream, right, Dawn? Tell me it was a dream."

"What happened next?" I ask, calmer than I feel.

"The car swerved. There was yelling, and then we were flipping." She covers her mouth with her hand. "Oh, God."

"You killed them."

Tears are now streaming down her face. "I didn't mean to, but I didn't want to go. I don't need to go. I just wanted out of the car. I didn't kill them," she says quietly. "I just wanted out. I didn't want to go. I didn't know they would try to stop me. I didn't know we would wreck."

"Do you hear yourself, Destiny? You caused an accident that killed our parents because all you wanted was your next fix. Then you skipped from the hospital. The police need to talk to you, question you. You might not have killed them, but your actions…" I let my voice trail off. We all know what I mean.

"Please," she pleads. "I didn't mean to do it. I'm so sorry. It was just a dream." She stands up and rushes to the house. I don't move as I watch her pound on the front door, screaming for our parents to open up. When the door doesn't open, she comes back to where we're still standing, watching her unravel.

"You have two choices." My voice is calm as I stare at my little sister. We have the same hazel eyes and blonde hair. She's taller like my dad, where I'm short like my mom. She just stares at me, her body void of all emotion. "You can check yourself into rehab, and complete the program, or you can leave. If I were you, I'd be looking over my shoulder. They want to talk to you, so they're going to be looking."

"You don't get to make the decision for me," she bites back.

"I know that. That's why you get to choose. If you leave, don't come back." My chest feels like it's cracking wide open as I say the words, but it's time for some tough love. She killed our parents. I can't help her if she's not willing to help herself.

"You're such a bitch. You were always the favorite. Going to college, never getting into trouble. You were a suck-up."

"It's called being responsible. You should try it sometime."

"I don't need this, and I don't need you." She stumbles down the driveway and disappears down the street.

I turn in Mark's arms. "Can I use your phone?"

He reaches into his pocket and hands it to me. I swipe the screen and, my hands are shaking as I dial the local police station. A number I know by heart having called one too many times looking for my sister. Hoping she got picked up somewhere and was there, safe. My efforts were fruitless; she was never there, but I still called every few days until I realized she was never going to be there. Not long after that, Kendall and I moved to Jackson. I needed a change. "Hi, my name is Dawn Miller." I rattle off my address. "My sister." I swallow hard. "Destiny Miller. She's an addict and walking the street." I give them my parents' address and listen to the officer tell me that they'll dispatch someone. "Thank you," I say, ending the call. I bury my face in his chest and cry. I cry for my parents, for my sister, and for me. I allow myself the time to expel it all in the safety of his arms.

"Dawn." His voice cracks. Pulling away, I look up to see tears swimming in his eyes. "What can I do?" he asks tenderly, holding me close.

"I'm sorry." I try to step away, but his grip is firm. "I'm trying not to fall apart."

"Stop." He rests his forehead against mine. "Feel, baby. Let it all out, and when you fall, I'll be here to catch you."

My breath shudders in my chest as I grip his shirt. "I-I don't know if I can go in there."

"You don't have to," he tells me. "But if you do, I'll be right there with you."

"We all will," Kendall adds.

"Do you have a key?" Seth asks.

"Not with me, but there's one under the rock. That's what Destiny was trying to get, but she was too messed up to make it happen."

Seth makes his way to the front porch and easily snags the key from under the rock. "You tell me when, D." He holds the key up for me to see.

"I don't know what to do. I don't know where to start." The pressure on my shoulders is the weight of an elephant. I'm overwhelmed, my heart is broken, and I'm at a loss for how to handle any of it.

"We need to choose a funeral home," Mark says woefully. "That's what the hospital told me."

"Okay. There's one here in town. That's where we—" I swallow the lump in my throat. "My grandparents," I finally say. "That's where—" I stop because my tears are thick.

"I'll take care of it," Mark assures me.

I nod, knowing if he says he'll take care of it, that he's going to do it. I feel bad to be leaning on him, on all of them so much, but right now, I need them. I need him. I'm at a loss as to what needs to be done, or how to handle it.

My parents are dead, and my sister, well, she might as well be.

# Chapter 6

## MARK

The last five days have been challenging and emotional. We've all rallied around Dawn, trying to help her and give her our support. Try is the keyword. We don't know what she needs, and honestly, neither does she.

After that first night, the four of us drove home. Dawn and I grabbed some clothes and headed back to her parents' place. Kendall and Seth stayed behind. They offered to come back with us, but Dawn declined. As for me, I didn't give her the option to decline. I wasn't leaving her side. I haven't since that night.

On our way back that first day, Dawn got a phone call from the local police. They picked her sister up the night before, thanks to her anonymous tip. They were holding her for a few days until a bed opened up at a rehab facility. They were mandating a thirty-day stay, which Dawn says she's done multiple times. They can't charge her for the accident, even though we all know she caused it. Her actions caused the reactions in the car that night, leading to the death of their parents. However, she wasn't found directly responsible.

Together, we visited the funeral home to make the final arrangements and went through mountains of paperwork, trying to work out finances. Luckily for us, her parents were very organized and prepared for this type of event. Life insurance policies were in place, burials paid for, and even the headstones and the burial plots had been picked out. Those plans were accompanied with a letter, addressed to Dawn.

The gist of the letter was that her parents didn't want to burden her with the details knowing that it would all fall on her shoulders. Sentiments of love, and we're sorry you're reading this. It was a tearful evening that night, but something about finding that letter lifted some of the weight she's been carrying on her shoulders. Almost as if it gave her closure.

The following two days we went through photo albums as Dawn walked me down memory lane. There was laughter and lots of tears. Each night I've held her in my arms, hoping that my love for her will be enough. I knew I cared about her, but all of this, it's made me realize what she truly means to me. I don't want to think about my life without her in it. I haven't told her, though. Now's not the time, but I will.

Just not today.

Today we lay her parents to rest. As I stand here beside two closed caskets, my hand alternates from resting on the small of her back to resting on her shoulder. I don't know what else to do but to offer her my silent support. It's just the two of us standing up here. The realization hits me that Destiny is really all she has left. Both sets of grandparents have passed, and her mom was an only child. Her dad had an older brother who was never married and passed away four years ago from a massive heart attack.

I'm all she has.

Well, and the guys and their wives, and the kids, and our families, but if we're talking someone who's just hers, other than her sister, who's too far gone to be counted, it's just me. I'm hers.

"You doing okay?" I whisper in her ear. The line of people who are here to pay their respects is long and winding, and I don't see an end in sight anytime soon.

"What time is it?" she asks softly before addressing the next guest. A man with graying hair who says he worked with her father. He tells her how great of a man he was and how much he'll be missed.

"Ten thirty."

"Okay." She exhales slowly. "Thirty more minutes." She opted to have the visitation and the funeral on the same day. She knew it was going to be rough so she just wanted to get it over with.

I've been to funerals before, but never really thought much about them until now. I get it, you want to pay your respects, but do you think she doesn't know the kind of man he was? That he'll be missed? I get it, no one ever knows what to say in these situations, but leaving it at "I'm sorry for your loss" is sufficient.

"It's a shame your sister isn't here," a lady, probably in her late fifties if I would have to guess, says as she reaches us. "Those drugs she's on, I tell you, your mother would be turning over in her grave."

Dawn stiffens next to me, and I've had about all I can handle. "Enough." My voice is quiet yet stern and the look I'm giving the woman could melt ice. "We're here to pay respects to Mr. and Mrs. Miller. If you have nothing nice to say, I advise you to keep it to yourself and move on." I wrap my arm around Dawn's waist.

"Why, I never," she huffs and walks off.

Before the next person can step up, Dawn turns and looks up at me. "I don't know what I did to deserve you, Marcus Adams, but I'm so glad you're here," she whispers as her eyes well with tears.

"Just being you," I say, leaning down and pressing my lips against her temple. I want to tell her that she has it all wrong, that I'm the lucky one. Now's not the time.

Turning her attention back to the many people who are here to say goodbye, she accepts more hugs, shakes more hands, and nods more times than I can count. I'm introduced to all of them as her boyfriend, and that title doesn't seem significant enough. Husband sounds better. I'm going to have to work on that.

A few minutes before eleven, our crew steps in front of us. Reagan and Tyler give us both hugs. "Is there anything that we can do?" Reagan asks.

"No, but thank you," Dawn says politely.

"Actually, there is," I tell her. Dawn glances at me curiously. "There are about a month's worth of casseroles and desserts, and I don't even know what else back at the house. Can you maybe go and get it all set up for after?" I ask.

41

"Of course," Reagan agrees.

"I'll help," Kendall says, stepping up and wrapping Dawn in a hug.

"We're going to go find a seat," Tyler says, gripping me on the shoulder and walking to the back of the room.

"I love you." I hear Kendall whisper, and that's all it takes for Dawn's shoulders to shake and a sob filled with pain and sorrow to escape her lips.

I want to pull her from Kendall's embrace and into mine, but I know I can't do that. Kendall knew her parents, knows her sister. She's closer to her in that aspect than any of us. When they finally pull apart, Dawn wipes her eyes and looks over at Ridge. "Thank you both for coming."

He engulfs her in a hug. "We're here for you."

My brothers, maybe not by blood, but by choice, they're rallying around my girl, and I have to swallow the lump in my throat. She's hurting, but I know that we're all going to be here to help her pick up the pieces. I meant it when I told her I will be here to catch her. This fall might not have been expected, but my arms are open and waiting all the same.

Seth and Kent step up as Kendall and Ridge walk away. I watch as they both hug her tightly and tell her they're sorry for her loss, before turning to me.

"What do you need, Mark?" Seth asks.

"We're good, man. Thanks for being here."

"We've got you, brother," Kent says.

I nod and they walk off to sit with the others.

"Honey, I'm so sorry." I hear a familiar female voice.

Turning my attention from the guys, I see my parents standing in front of us. Mom has Dawn wrapped in her arms, and Dad has one hand on Dawn's back and the other on Mom's. My throat swells.

"Meghan sends her condolences," Mom says when she finally steps back. "Paul's out of town, and she has the twins. It was her or us, and we won," Mom says with a soft chuckle.

"Thank you for being here," Dawn replies.

"Of course," Dad chimes in. "You're family."

He says it so simply, as if her being a permanent part of my life, of our lives is a forgone conclusion. I like it. I like it a lot. After we each hug my parents one more time, they take their seats.

"Dawn," the funeral director greets us. "If you'll take your seats, we'll get started."

"Thank you," she tells him.

Taking her hand in mine, I lead us to the front row, where two open seats remain. We settle on the pew and I wrap my arm around her shoulders, holding her. The service is nice, not too long, not too short. Dawn declines getting up to speak. The pastor does a wonderful job. A few ladies from the church sing "Amazing Grace," and even though I don't look around the room for confirmation, I know there's not a dry eye in the house.

After a small graveside service, we gather at her parents' place. More people I've never met, and many Dawn has never met either, filter in and out throughout the afternoon. Kendall and Reagan keep things rolling in the kitchen, playing hostess. The guys help out where they can, and I even catch a glimpse of Kent with his sleeves rolled up doing dishes.

"Everyone's gone," Ridge says, closing the front door.

"Finally." Dawn takes a seat on the couch. "Please don't take this the wrong way, I'm grateful they were here, but I thought they would never leave. Present company excluded." She closes her eyes and takes a deep breath. When she opens them, she makes a point to look at each of us. "I can't tell you what it means to me to have all of you here. To know that I have you in my corner," she says, swallowing hard.

The women rally around her before I have a chance to. "You want to get some air?" Seth asks.

"Yeah," I quickly agree. In a few long strides, I'm standing behind Dawn, where she sits on the couch. "We're going out on the porch," I tell her, massaging her shoulders gently.

"Okay." She looks up at me upside down. Not able to resist, I lean over her and place a soft kiss to her lips. It's not our normal, being overly affectionate in front of anyone really. However, these past few days have changed things. Not just between us, but it's changed us. As for me, it's a reminder that life is short and you never know how long you have on this earth. It's a reminder to love those you love hard and never hold back.

"How's she holding up?" Seth asks once we're outside on the porch.

The cold air burns my lungs as I suck in a deep breath. "She's doing okay."

"How about you?" Ridge asks.

"I just wish I knew how to help her," I confess. "And Destiny, what a clusterfuck. I know that's messing with her as well. That she had her picked up and couldn't be here today."

"Who knows if she even would have shown up," Kent comments.

"Doubtful," I scoff. My anger toward Destiny and the hand she played in all of this is beyond measure. I understand she has an addiction, but she picked that shit up the first time. She was completely sober when she tried it the first time. She knew what she was doing then.

"Is she coming back with you?" Tyler asks.

My head snaps up to look at him. "What?" I ask, barely able to form the word.

He shrugs. "I just thought maybe she'd want to be here, in their house, to feel closer to them. Women do that shit, right?" he asks.

I never considered that she wouldn't be coming back home with me. I mean, we've been packing up the house, donating clothes, so I just assumed. *Fuck me. She has to come home.* A loud crash from inside startles us, and we're all rushing through the door to see what happened. The five of us stop in our tracks and take in the scene before us.

Dawn, Kendall, and Reagan are standing in the living room. Kendall and Reagan have sympathetic looks on their face as they watch Dawn. My eyes take her in as she lifts a vase of flowers from the funeral and tosses them into the fireplace. Glass shatters and the sound echoes throughout the room.

"Why!" Dawn screams through her tears. She reaches for another vase of flowers, and neither Kendall nor Reagan make a move to stop her. I step forward, but a strong hand on each of my shoulders stops me. "It's not fair," she sobs as she tosses another vase.

I watch as her knees buckle and she stumbles. Reagan and Kendall catch her. Nothing could keep me from her at this point. I shrug the guys from holding me back and rush to her. Kendall and Reagan give me a sad smile as I approach. "Dawn," I whisper, my voice gruff.

Lifting her head, she looks at me. Her hazel eyes are filled with so much sorrow that I feel it deep in my gut. There are tear stains tracking down her face. I feel her sadness in my soul. I open my arms for her and she stumbles into my embrace. Her hands grip my shirt as sobs rack her body. When I lift her, the girls step back, allowing me to make my way to the couch. I sit down with her on my lap and hold her.

I kiss the top of her head. "I've got you, Pixie. I'm right here." My eyes seek out our friends, our family, and I know the look I'm giving them is pleading. *Help me help her.* From the looks on their faces, they hear my silent plea. Kendall snuggles into Ridge, and Reagan does the same with Tyler. Seth and Kent bury their hands in their pockets, a look of worry mixed with sadness on their faces.

"We're going to give you some time," Kendall whispers, wiping under her eyes.

I nod and watch as they disappear into the kitchen. "I'm so sorry," I say, burying my face in her hair. My whispered apology only seems to cause her to cry harder. I tighten my hold, hugging her close to my chest, not leaving an ounce of space between us. I continue to hold her as if my life depends on it, and place soft kisses to her head. I whisper that I'm here and not going anywhere, telling her I've got her. Minutes, hours, hell, I'm not sure how much time passes but eventually, her sobs quiet to just sniffles.

Slowly, she lifts her head and her hazel eyes lock on mine. "I'm sorry," she mumbles.

Cupping her face in my hands, I wipe under her eyes with my thumbs. "Baby," I say softly. "You have nothing to be sorry for. It's okay to cry, to scream, and throw things. You're grieving. All of that is okay, but you have to promise me something."

"Okay," she agrees quickly, not even knowing what I'm going to ask of her.

"You have to stay with me," I tell her. "You have to let me be here like this with you. Don't hide your pain from me. Share it with me, Pixie. Let me help you through this."

"You didn't sign on for this." She pulls back, causing me to drop my hands from her face. She runs her palms over her eyes before she speaks again. "I don't know how to get past this, Mark. How do I deal with the fact that my parents are dead? How do I deal with the fact that my drug-addicted sister caused their accident?"

"With me by your side. And you take it one day at a time."

"That's more than just a hook-up bargained for," she remarks, averting her gaze.

I have to remind myself she's grieving and the talk we've been putting off has never happened. "Dawn." I wait, but she doesn't look at me. "Can you look at me?" I ask. She hesitates but turns her once-again tear-filled eyes to face me. "Is that what you think this is? That you and I are just... hooking up?"

"Isn't it?" she counters.

"No."

"Look, I know I'm a mess right now, but honesty is important."

"I'm telling you the truth." I capture her hands with mine and place them over my chest. Over my heart. "We're more." I whisper the words as her bottom lip trembles. "Let me be here for you."

She nods as more tears escape. She stands from my lap and wipes at her face. "Take me home." She must read the confused expression on my face. "Not here, my home. I need... I need to get out of here. At least for a few days."

"Okay." I stand to go tell the others when they enter the room.

"You go on ahead. I'm going to wrap up this food, take some with us, and toss the rest. We'll lock up," Kendall says.

"I can do it," Dawn says.

"I know, but how often does Mark offer to take care of you?" Kendall smiles softly. "Take advantage while you can."

"Right?" Reagan chimes in. "You're in need of a massage, right?" She winks.

Dawn looks up at me and smiles. "He always takes care of me."

"Well, regardless, take what he's offering. We'll be right behind you," Kendall insists.

"Thank you." Dawn throws her arms around Kendall and hugs her tightly. I watch as she hugs everyone else just the same, before coming back to me.

"We'll see you guys later." I wave and lead Dawn out to my truck. She snuggles into the passenger seat with the heater on high. She's sound asleep before we hit the highway.

# Chapter 7

## Dawn

These last few weeks have been hard. We buried my parents two days before Thanksgiving. When that should have been a happy time, celebrating what we're most thankful for in life, I was grieving the loss of the people who gave me life. I was mourning my sister, who was in court-mandated rehab because I called the cops on her. She missed our parents' funeral. She didn't get to say goodbye. She caused the accident by her own admission, so I shouldn't feel sorry for her. Yet, I do. The guilt eats at me. I know that the chances of her actually showing up at the services was slim to none and even if she did show she more than likely would have been high out of her mind, but still, I took that choice.

Kendall assures me that Destiny took that choice all on her own when she started using. She made the choice to use, and the consequences of her actions alone are what prevented her from being at the funeral. I know she's right, and my head knows that she's right, but my heart, the one that still aches for my baby sister, can't seem to understand.

Destiny was released from rehab two weeks ago, and I have no idea where she is. I don't know where she's living or if she's okay. I left a note for her for the day she was released to call me. That call never came. I have a real estate agent who has shown the house almost daily since we listed it and she has assured me no one is staying in the house. Mom and Dad left it all to me, knowing I would do the right thing. In other words, not let Destiny sell it or their belongings for her next fix. If only she would get clean and stay that way. I wish there was some way I could help her. Some way I could get through to her.

I'm learning to live in a world without them, which makes today so much harder. It's Christmas Day. Last night we celebrated with our friends and their kids. Knox, Everly, Ben, and Beck had a blast opening their gifts. They seemed to prefer the boxes and the paper over the actual toys, though, but regardless, they were adorable, and it was a good day. I smiled a lot, and that's been a rarity for me over the past few weeks.

Today, however, is altogether different. Mark and I are going to his parents.' I tried every excuse under the sun to get out of going, but he wouldn't hear of it. Marcus Adams has been my saving grace since the day my world was ripped apart. He has the patience of a saint, and no matter how sad, or angry, or distant I seem to be, he keeps coming around.

"Dawn." He gives my thigh a gentle squeeze, pulling me out of my thoughts. Blinking twice, I turn from where I've been staring out the window of his truck to look at him. "We're here. You okay?"

"Not really," I admit. "But I will be."

"I'm sorry," he says, rubbing his hands over his face. "I shouldn't have forced you to be here. I just… the thought of you being at your place on Christmas without me killed me. I need you here."

"It's okay." I reach out and place my hand on his cheek. "I need you to push me, Mark."

"You're still grieving."

"I am," I agree. "But I'm also living. Well, I'm alive. I need to live my life. If not for me, then for them."

"That's—"

I smile. "A change?" I finish for him. "Yeah, it is. I've been thinking a lot about them, and they would never want me to stop living life.

Losing them—" I swallow hard. "Losing them splintered my heart, but they gave me life, and I need to live it for them."

"There's my pixie," he says affectionately. "I know today is going to be hard on you, and well—" He stops as if trying to organize his thoughts. "I wanted to share my family with you," he says softly. "You're important to me, and so are they, and I just thought… I want you here," he finishes.

"You're an amazing man, Marcus Adams."

He leans in and lightly presses his lips to mine. "You make me a better man," he says before pulling back. "Now, are you ready for the Adams family madness?"

I throw my head back and laugh. "It's a good thing I've met your family or that would have me running in the opposite direction."

His blue eyes twinkle with laughter as he winks. He pushes open his door and collects the two bags of gifts from the back of the truck. I do the same, picking up the red velvet cake I made. It was my grandmother's recipe, and my mom made it every year for Christmas. It's my turn to keep those traditions alive.

Before I can get the door open, his sister, Meghan, is there to greet us. Her smile is bright as she holds her son, Isaac, on her hip. "Look who's here, buddy," she tells him.

"Is that my son?" His mom, Theresa, appears, holding Imogen in her arms.

Isaac and Imogen are twins and were born not long after Knox was. They're adorable, with dark hair like their daddy, and big blue eyes that mirror their Uncle Mark, as well as their mom.

"Get in here, you two," Theresa says, stepping back and ushering us in. Imogen reaches for Mark.

"Let me put this down, baby girl, and then I'll get you," he tells her. I follow him into the living room where he places the two bags of gifts by the tree and then takes the cake from me. He kisses my nose and takes off for the kitchen.

I've been here a handful of times over the last couple of years, but he's never shown me any kind of affection in front of his family, so the fact that he just did kind of stuns me. We don't hide that we're… whatever we are from our friends, but his family and mine, we were always just friends in their eyes. Sadness washes over me when I think about my parents not being there when I get married or for one day when I have kids of my own.

"You okay, baby?" Mark comes up behind me, his hands landing on my hips.

Turning to face him, I force a smile and nod. "Yeah, just… taking it all in," I tell him honestly.

He laces his fingers through mine and leads us into the family room. Keeping his promise, he releases my hand and heads to where his mom is standing and takes Imogen from her arms. She giggles when he kisses her cheek, and she lays a sloppy kiss right on his lips.

"What can I do to help?" I ask Theresa.

"Not a thing. We're ready to eat. I just have to put the rolls in the oven."

"Are you sure?"

"Positive. Go have a seat. It'll be ready in a few." With that, she walks past me to the kitchen.

"Hey," Meghan says, coming to stand next to me. Isaac reaches out for me to take him, and I do easily. "He doesn't know a stranger that one." She laughs.

"Hey, buddy," I say, and he gets shy and rests his head on my shoulder.

"Hold up," Mark says, joining us with Imogen still in his arms. "You're going to have to find your own girl, little man. This one's already taken," he tells Isaac, tickling his side. Isaac just giggles and snuggles further into me. In turn, I wrap my arms around him, soaking up all of the snuggles he's willing to offer. "Of course." Mark laughs. "They always leave you for the younger ones." He grins.

"Jealous, baby brother?" Meghan teases.

His eyes find mine. "Absolutely."

"He's a toddler," Paul, Meghan's husband, says, joining us and the conversation.

"That's my girl," Mark counters.

I feel an arm around my opposite shoulder of where Isaac is laying. Turning my head, I see Keith, Mark's dad, standing there grinning. "Not

50

just the younger ones, son," he says, pulling me and Isaac into him. "Good to see you," he says, low just for me.

"Thank you for having me," I tell him.

"Dad," Mark says with a mock glare.

"Hey, the old man's still got it." Keith chuckles, before releasing me and walking off toward the kitchen.

"Come and get it," his mom calls out.

Meghan and Paul take the kids to get them set up in their high chairs, leaving Mark and me alone. He wraps his arms around my waist and pulls me into him. "I can't take you anywhere." He grins. "Can't even trust my family with my girl."

He's been doing that a lot lately, referring to me as his. We still haven't had that talk, so he doesn't know that I'm madly in love with him. However, over the last few weeks, I'm not as worried that he doesn't feel the same. His actions have proven he's where he wants to be. Unless he feels sorry for me? I immediately dismiss that idea. Mark's not the kind of guy who says or does things he doesn't mean. He's the real deal. A "what you see is what you get" kind of guy.

The kitchen island is covered in food, set up buffet style. Mark and I are at the back of the line, the last two to grab a plate and start filling it. I haven't had much of an appetite the last few weeks, but everything looks and smells amazing. Suddenly, I'm starving. Mark snags us both a bottle of water from the fridge, and I follow him to the large dining room. His dad sits at the head of the table, Theresa sits to his left, with Imogen in her high chair, then Meghan has Isaac beside her, and Paul's at the opposite end of Kevin. Mark stops, and I almost crash into him as I take in the table. I get to the right side that's empty and my breath falters in my chest. There are four open seats, the two closest to Kevin are open, while the remaining two sit empty with small battery-operated white candles sitting in front of them.

Mark quickly sets his plate and our waters on the table, and his dad, with his hand on the small of my back, takes mine. I didn't even realize he'd stood. My eyes blur as I take in the two empty seats.

"Dawn," Theresa says softly and her hand lands on my arm. Forcing myself, I turn to look at her. "We wanted them to be here with you, with us for the holiday. I'm sorry if it's too much," she says, with sympathy in her gaze.

"Mom," Mark growls. "You should have talked to me about this." He steps next to me and slides his arm around my waist, pulling me into him and dropping a kiss to my temple. "I'm sorry," he whispers.

I look up at him and see the worry in his eyes. He's afraid I'm going to lose it right here in the middle of his parents' dining room. "I'm okay," I tell him. "It just kind of took me off guard." I turn to his mom. "Theresa," I swallow hard. "Thank you for thinking of me, for thinking of them."

"Oh, honey." She pulls me from Mark's arms into hers. Her arms wrap around me in an embrace only a mother can give. Hot tears prick my eyes. She pulls back, and I'm immediately engulfed in Kevin's arms much the same, giving me the hug of a father. I lose the battle with my tears as they slide over my cheeks.

"I'm sorry," I say, stepping back. Mark is there, immediately enfolding his arms around my waist from behind. He presses a kiss to the top of my head. Turning, I look up at him. He's a foot taller than me, and I have to crane my neck, but the look on his face is the same no matter the height difference. Sadness. Worry. And something else I can't quite name.

"I just didn't… expect that," I say, wiping my eyes.

"I'll move them." Mark releases me from his hold.

"No." I reach out and grab his arm. "Please, leave them there. I-I like the thought of them being here with us." I know it's just a placeholder, a memorial, but the thought touches me deep in my chest, like a vise gripping my heart.

"You sure?" He cups my face in his hands and wipes my tears with his thumbs. An act he's gotten lots of practice with over the last few weeks.

"Yes, I'm sure."

Dropping his hands from my face, he crushes me to his side.

"Thank you," I tell Theresa. "It was very thoughtful. I'm sorry I ruined dinner."

"You haven't ruined anything," Kevin promises.

"Besides, that gave us time to get these little monsters fed, so we can eat with everyone else." Meghan offers me a kind smile.

With his hand on the small of my back, Mark leads me to my seat.

The one next to the two empty places with the lit candles. One for each of my parents. As I take my seat, I see a Christmas ornament around each candle. *In Loving Memory.* One for each of them. My heart flips over in my chest as my eyes find Theresa's. "Thank you," I say, wiping yet another tear that falls across my cheek. She nods, picks up her fork, and begins to eat.

Glancing over at the empty place settings, I send up a silent *I love you* to my parents. Then, I do what they would want me to do. I pick up my fork and begin to eat. I laugh as Imogen covers her tiny little face with mashed potatoes, and when Isaac belly laughs at his sister, I can't help but join everyone and laugh with him as well. My smiles aren't forced. They aren't fake. My heart is empty, yet sitting here with this family, it's full at the same time.

*Merry Christmas, Mom and Dad.*

# Chapter 8

## MARK

Christmas Day could have been bad, so terribly bad, but it wasn't. I had no idea that my mom was including a place for her parents at the table. I'm kicking myself in the ass for not thinking of doing something like that. Then again, I've been walking on eggshells around Dawn. I don't know what to say or what to do to make it better. I'm not good at that shit, so instead, I leave her be. We still go out to dinner, hang out all the time, so nothing has changed. Nothing but the distance I'm starting to feel between us.

I've tried to keep her occupied with my house hunting. I've decided it's time for a bigger place. I'm thinking about the future, our future, and it's time. I had been looking prior to the accident, and the week we came home my realtor called with what she described as my perfect house. Turns out she was right. I loved it, Dawn loved it, so I bought it. For us, she just doesn't know that part yet.

Still, there is distance between us. Her pain is like an invisible third wheel. I hate it. I hate that I feel like I'm losing her to her pain. So tonight, I'm pulling out all the stops. I'm making damn sure my girl has a great time. It's New Year's Eve. A new year is upon us, and hers is going to be fan-fucking-tastic if I have anything to say about it.

"You're amping up your game," Seth says from his seat beside me.

"She's been through hell," I tell him. He knows this.

"Yeah." He nods. "I get that, but, man, you're... getting all domesticated on me."

I scowl at him. "What the fuck are you yapping about?"

"This." He waves his hand around the room. "Since when do you care about decorations and shit?"

I take a look around at our handiwork, pleased with the outcome. "New year, new start."

"Well, if anyone can make your intense broody ass turn a new leaf, it's Dawn."

"What's that supposed to mean?"

"Come on, Mark. You've been seeing her for how long now? You just told us about it a few months ago."

"You knew we were hanging out," I defend.

"Right." He nods. "Hanging out. Not getting your dick wet."

"Watch it," I warn.

"I like her for you." He shrugs. "I'm just glad you're finally seeing it."

I've seen it... hell, I've known it all along. I just wasn't sure where she was at with it all. Not to mention, Dawn isn't just some random you pick up at a bar. No, she's the girl you take home to your mother. I knew that the moment I met her. I wasn't ready to get involved with her until I knew she was the one that I wanted to take home to Mom. I know what Seth's saying, though. I kept my feelings for her close to my chest, not even really sharing them with her, until recently, and I've not really done that either. She knows I'm in this, that she's the only one I'm interested in, but I've yet to tell her that I'm in love with her. When I thought I would, something would happen, and then her parents, and it just hasn't felt like the right time to tell her. Instead, I plan to show her. I've gone out of my way to make this night fun for her.

"You plan on buying any furniture?" he asks as he glances around my new house.

"I haven't even had the keys for twenty-four hours," I remind him.

"What are you going to do with all this space anyway?"

"What do most people do with big houses?" I ask.

"Something you're not telling me?"

"No, but I'm not opposed to the idea." In fact, that's why I bought this place. I'm ready to settle down. I want to do the whole wife and kids thing. Ridge and Ty make it look easy, and I envy them.

"She know that?" Seth asks.

"Nope."

He throws his head back and laughs. "You think that you ought to clue her in?"

"There's no rush. She's been through a lot. One small step at a time. She's healing."

He nods. "She's lucky to have you," he says, going all serious on me.

"She's lucky to have all of us. You were there," I remind him.

"You're family. So is she," he adds. "So, you selling your old place?"

"Nah, I'm going to rent it." I bought it cheap and did all the renovations myself. Well, the guys helped as well.

"Good source of income," he agrees.

"That it is," I say, tossing some noisemakers from their package onto the long table in the living room.

"I'm out. Heading home to change."

"Thanks for your help."

"Anytime, brother." He waves over his shoulder and walks out the door.

Taking a look around, I see the end result of a couple hundred dollars' worth of cheap decorations, and I'm pleased with myself. Kendall, Reagan, and Dawn are making some dips, Kent is in charge of chips and cookies of all things. His idea, not mine. I didn't remind him that the kids are going to be here. I know he has a sweet tooth.

Balloons, streamers, and about a dozen other items declaring it the New Year adorn the room. I've yet to move any furniture, except for my bed, so it's basically all open. I bought some paper plates, and forks, spoons, napkins, and cups. I plan on staying here tonight, and I've advised the guys that they are too. This place has five bedrooms, plus with a fully finished basement, there won't be a need for anyone to worry about how they're getting home. Although, they do need their own bedding. I better remind them while I'm thinking of it.

**Group text:** *Bring blankets and pillows.*

**Group text:** *Air mattress if you have it. Only moved my bed.*

**Ridge:** *Kendall and I are at the store. Anyone need us to pick up anything?*

It's followed by a picture of an air mattress in their cart.

**Seth:** *Get me one.*

**Kent:** *Me too.*

**Tyler:** *We'll bring ours.*

**Seth:** *You have an air mattress?*

**Tyler:** *Yeah, we "camp out" with the boys in the living room. They love it.*

I smile because the boys, his twins, are not even a year old yet. I'm not sure they really understand the concept of camping. However, after the year they've had, I'm sure having his wife and babies snuggled up with him at night is exactly what he wants. I know Reagan is big on a schedule for them, as is Kendall with Knox and Everly. My sister is as well with her two kids. Routine is key, she once told me. I never questioned her because what the fuck do I know about raising kids? I know my buddies fell into it seamlessly and they make that shit look easy.

**Ridge:** *Kendall and I are stealing that idea.*

**Tyler:** *You're welcome.*

**Ridge:** *Kendall wants to know if you have champagne?*

**Me:** *Yes.*

**Ridge:** *Glasses?*

I add a picture of the plastic champagne glasses that are sitting on the kitchen counter with the rest of the party items I bought yesterday.

**Ridge:** *She's impressed.*

**Kent:** *Suck up.*

**Seth:** *Making us look bad.*

**Tyler:** *Good job, bro.*

With a chuckle, I slide my phone back in my pocket and get back to work. I have to run to my parents' to pick up a couple of tables and some chairs and then get back here to fire up the grill. It's freezing-ass cold outside, but there is nothing better than grilled steak. I picked up some chicken for the ladies, well, Dawn mostly, she's not much of a steak fan. Grabbing my keys, I lock up and head out.

✻✻✻

I'm pulling into the driveway of the new house when my phone rings. Glancing at the screen, I see Dawn's smiling face. "Hey," I greet her.

"Hey, yourself. Just checking in to see if there's anything I need to pick up on my way over?"

"I don't think so. Honestly, I'm not sure. I've never been the host before." I chuckle.

"Tell me what we've got so far."

We. I rattle off what I know as far as food and drinks. "Oh, pack a bag. My bed is all moved so we're staying here tonight."

"You sure?"

She's been doing that a lot lately. Asking if I'm sure I want to spend time with her. "Positive."

"I haven't exactly been fun to be around," she muses.

"Pixie." I pause, not really knowing what to say. "As long as we're together, it's all going to be okay." That I can promise her. Because as long as I'm breathing, she has a place in my arms. No matter how far she falls, I'm going to be there.

"I don't know what I would have done without you since… that night."

59

"You don't have to find out."

"Mark, I— Thank you for all that you do for me."

"Pix?"

"Yeah?"

"Get your ass over here. It's been two days since I've laid eyes on you."

"You saw me yesterday morning."

I glance at the clock on the dash. "It's after three."

"That's hardly two days," she counters, but I can hear the smile in her voice, which is what I wanted.

"It's too damn long, woman. Pack a bag."

"Okay. As soon as I get that done and load up the car, I'll be over."

"Be safe." It's on the tip of my tongue to tell her that I love her, but I bite down to prevent the words from spilling over. I'm not telling her over the phone. No, I want her in front of me so I can see those hazel eyes as I tell her. I want her in my arms, feeling her next to me when I confess that she's stolen my heart. Who knows, maybe tonight will be the night.

"Always," she says before the line goes dead.

Climbing out of the truck, I slide my phone in my pocket and get busy carrying in the tables and chairs. Once I have them all set up in the living room, I remember that I don't have clothes here either. It's just before five. Everyone is supposed to be here around seven, so I still have time. Locking up, I dash back out into the cold December weather and head toward home, my old home. I hope to get everything moved this coming week and put it on the market for rent.

"Shit," I mumble when I realize Dawn should be at the new place any minute. Digging my phone out of my pocket, I hit her contact, and the call connects through the truck's speakers.

"You forget something?" she asks in greeting.

"I did actually. Clothes. I'm on my way to my place… my old place to pack a bag."

"I'm actually not far from there. You want me to stop and help?"

"No, you can go on over to the new place."

"Okay, I'll just wait for you."

"No, go on in."

"Did you not lock the door?"

"No, I did. Check your key ring," I say, smiling like a fool. I'm glad there's no one in the truck with me to witness this. Then again, who am I kidding? I don't give a fuck who knows or sees me.

"Is that…? How did you…?" she splutters.

"That, Pixie, is a key to my new place. I stopped by your office yesterday, and Kendall said you were slammed. Something about triplets or something. So I asked her to grab your keys for me. I slipped the key on and left."

"You didn't tell me."

"Things have been so crazy with getting ready for tonight it slipped my mind when we talked last night." She had to work late and I was exhausted from working all day, and then with moving my bed and dressers. Seth, Kent, and I went to grab a couple of beers and some dinner. She was drained, so we stayed at our own places. I hated it, not wanting her to be alone. I never want her to feel as if she's all alone. Which is why as soon as I got the keys, I had one made and dropped it off to her at work. I want her to always know that she has a place in this world. With me.

"I-I don't really know what to say to that," she says softly.

"Say, 'thank you, Mark. I'll be at your place when you get there.'"

She laughs. A sound that I've not heard often enough from her lately. "Thank you, Mark. I'll be at your place when you get there."

"Ah, just what I was hoping for."

Another laugh escapes her. "What do you need me to do when I get there?"

"First thing is to take your bag to my room and settle in. Then just hang out. I think I have it all set up."

"I have a couple of dips, but they need to be put into the oven to be warmed up. I don't want to do that until it's almost time to eat."

"Sounds good. Really, just relax. Take a look at the place. I was hoping you would go with me to look at some furniture and decorations and all that stuff. Stroll through and get some ideas. Other than a big-ass TV for the living room and basement, oh, and a pool table, I've got nothing."

"What is it with you guys and your big TVs?" She chuckles.

"If we can't be there, we want to feel like we're there," I explain. "The bigger, the better."

"Oh, really? So you're telling me that size really does matter?"

"Pixie," I say huskily. "Do I need to show you my… size?"

"Hmmm." She pretends to think it over. "Maybe, if you're lucky."

Once again, it's on the tip of my tongue to tell her that I love her. "Okay, babe. I'll see you soon," I say instead. After ending the call, I toss my phone in the cupholder and press just a little harder on the accelerator, anything that gets me to her faster.

At my place, I grab an old suitcase and throw in some jeans, a couple of hoodies, T-shirts, underwear, and then I grab some sweats. I toss in a few extra T-shirts because I know my pixie likes to sleep in them. Grabbing some toiletries, I put them in a trash bag, not willing to risk them leaking all over my clothes. On my way out the door, I spy the soft throw that Dawn loves. I bought it for her because she always likes to snuggle and seems to be cold. Grabbing the blanket, I toss it over my shoulder and head back out the door.

# Chapter 9

## Dawn

My hand shakes as I put the key into the door. Why, I have no idea. I'm not breaking the law. However, this feels like *something*. Something I'm trying really hard to not name. Pushing open the door, I take in the foyer that leads into the living room. Deep mahogany hardwood floors greet me and run throughout the house. This place is beautiful. I downplayed it when he asked me if I liked it. I wanted to scream that I loved it, and beg him to let me live here with him. Instead, I told him I really liked it, and that I could see him living here. All true. Just not as outspoken as I could have been.

Tossing my keys on the kitchen counter, I also set down the bag that contains the two dips I made, as well as a bag full of a variety of chips for tonight. Heading back outside, I grab my bag, lock my car, and rush back inside. The chill of the December air seems to be cutting through me, even with my down jacket.

After kicking off my shoes, I take off my coat and eye the closet. I wonder if there are any hangers. With the door open, I see a new single pack of white plastic hangers in the bundle they were packaged in. A laugh escapes me. I'm surprised he thought of hangers. I can picture him hanging them up and being proud of himself for remembering. Shaking my head, I unwrap the bundle, grab one for my coat, then take the trash to the kitchen.

My sock-covered feet pad down the hall to the master bedroom. The house is split up with the master bedroom, an office, and the laundry room on one side, the other bedrooms are on the opposite end of the house. Pushing open the bedroom door, I take in his huge sleigh bed. It's the same dark mahogany as the floor. It's a perfect fit. The bedding is folded, sitting on the bare mattress in a clothes basket.

Setting my bag on the floor, I get to work making the bed. His sheets smell like him, and I can't help but bring them close to my face and inhale. Mark's scent is uniquely him, manly and woodsy. It's a scent that's become a comfort to me over the last few months.

After the sheets are on, I slide the pillows into their cases and then toss his comforter over the bed. It's not perfect, but we'll be right back here in a few hours. At least when we're exhausted, we won't have to deal with making the bed before we crash for the night. Glancing at the nightstand to see the time, a picture in a dark mahogany frame catches my eye. Lifting the picture, I can't help but smile. It's Mark and me at Ridge and Kendall's Memorial Day weekend. Flashbacks of the day flash through my mind. The good and the bad. We all thought we were losing Ben. That little boy has been through so much.

The picture is Mark standing behind me, his hands on my shoulders and he's smiling wide. My head is tilted back, looking up at him upside down. He's over a head taller than me, but despite the height difference, we look good together. Then again, maybe that's my heart talking.

"I love that one." His deep husky voice comes from behind me.

Slowly, I turn to face him, gripping the frame to my chest. "I didn't hear you come in."

"You were lost in thought." His eyes flash toward the bed. "Thanks for that." He nods at the freshly made bed.

"Figured we wouldn't feel like it later."

He grins. "You plan on tying one on tonight, Pixie?"

His grin is infectious. "I don't know just yet. The night is still young," I counter.

"You're still packed," he says, noticing my bag on the floor.

"Yeah, I made the bed, then this—" I hold up the frame before placing it back on the nightstand. "—distracted me."

He moves into the room. One step then another carries him closer to me. When he reaches me, he grips my hips and lifts me in the air, tossing me gently on the bed.

"W-What are you doing?" I laugh.

"That." He points at me, his blue eyes shining with mischief. "I wanted you to do that," he says, leaning over the bed. He braces his arms on either side of me and brings his lips to mine. He takes his time, traces my lips with his tongue, nipping at my bottom lip. "Love that sound, Pixie," he mumbles, before taking the kiss deeper, his tongue exploring my mouth in a way that only Mark can.

He's pulling back too soon for my liking. I loop my arms around his neck, trying to keep him there, but he breaks free. Sitting up, I watch him as he picks up my bag from the floor and sets it next to me on the bed. I don't say a word as I watch him unzip the tote and start laying my clothes out on the bed. My eyes follow him as he opens up one of the dresser drawers and places all of my clothes inside.

"Mark?"

He ignores me and comes back to my bag. He pulls out my toiletry bag, my hairdryer, and my flat iron, and turns, disappearing into the attached bathroom. When he returns a few moments later, he does the same to his bag that I just now noticed. When he's satisfied, he tosses our bags through the door of one of the walk-in closets. "You can pick which one is yours later," he says, climbing on the bed and stretching out next to me.

"Uh, they're your closets," I remind him. My heart is hammering in my chest. It's so loud I know he has to be able to hear it.

He shrugs. "I'm giving one of them to you."

"I have a closet at my place."

He opens his mouth, then closes it. Leaning down, he kisses the tip of my nose. "Well, now you have one here too." He props himself up on his elbow to stare down at me. He stares at me intently, waiting for what I'm not sure. For me to freak out maybe? I've been overemotional these past few months, but he's been there right beside me through it all.

I shiver when his large calloused hand slides under my sweater. "Cold?" he asks huskily.

"Never been warmer," I murmur, my eyes locked on his.

Slowly, his hand slides up until he's running the pad of his thumb over my silk-covered nipple. "I don't know," he muses. "This tells me you might be a little cold," he says as he continues to caress my nipple through my bra.

"That's all you," I confess.

"Yeah?" His smirk tells me he knows damn well what he's doing to me. "I'm thinking maybe I should help warm you up, you know, just in case."

My breath hitches in my chest when he slides my sweater up, and his wet hot mouth latches on through the silky material of my bra. "Mark," I say breathily, my hands gripping the sheets.

With skillful precision, he has the cup of my bra pulled down and is sucking my pebbled bud into his mouth. I squirm under him, wanting more. I'm just about to beg for it when the doorbell chimes, echoing through the mostly empty house. I groan, which causes Mark to chuckle as he slides my bra back into place and pulls my sweater back down.

"Sorry, babe. We'll pick this up later." He winks, then climbs off the bed. I watch as he adjusts himself as the doorbell sounds a second time, and disappears to go greet his guests.

I take a minute to get myself under control. He's a damn tease, but that's okay. Payback's are a bitch. I hear deep voices but can't make out what they're saying. Forcing myself from his bed, I stop in the bathroom and make sure I'm decent. I adjust my bra and put my hair that is somehow out of place back in order. My cheeks are flushed, but there is nothing I can do about that. Maybe I can blame it on the cold. I smile to myself and follow the voices to the living room.

"There she is." Kent opens his arms, and I don't hesitate to walk into them. He wraps me in a tight hug.

"Kenton," Mark says, his voice low, making Kent laugh.

"Don't leave me hanging." Seth grins cheekily. Kent releases me and I walk to Seth, repeating the process over again.

"I thought the two of you were going to finish setting up the tables?" Mark grumbles. They laugh, and Seth releases his hold on me and they get to work.

"What time are the others getting here?" I ask Mark, following him into the kitchen. He turns to face me, but instead of answering, he lifts me from my feet, yet again. Only this time, he places me on the center island that separates the kitchen from the living area.

He steps between my legs, bracing his hands on the counter on either side of me. "My buddies can't seem to keep their paws off you," he says, bending and kissing my neck.

"They were saying hello," I point out. I've not seen this side of Mark, not really. We've been easygoing in our entire relationship, if that's what you want to call it. So this is new. This… territorial thing he has going on.

"They can say hello without touching you." His blue eyes bore into mine.

"Why does that bother you?" I ask.

"Pixie," he says just as Ridge and Kendall walk into the house.

"Hey, guys. Sorry we're late. Everly did not want us to leave," Kendall says.

"Aww, you should have brought her," I reply.

Mark kisses the corner of my mouth then turns to face them, remaining between my legs where I'm perched up on the counter. "You know the kids are welcome," he tells them.

"Momma needs a night out," Kendall says. "Don't get me wrong, I love our children with everything in me, but it's nice to get a small break once in a while."

"Of course it is," I assure her.

"Where do you want this?" Ridge motions to the crockpot in his hands.

"Oh, just park it over there on the counter. There's an outlet for you to plug it in."

"Cheeseball?" Kendall makes a goofy face as she pulls a container out of the bag she's carrying.

"Fridge for now, at least until we're ready to heat everything up."

"This place is great," Ridge says, coming to stand beside us. "Nice work, Adams." Ridge holds his fist out for Mark and they bump.

"Amelia's on her way," Seth says.

"I'm glad to see she's still in town," Kent comments. "I wasn't sure when she left for college if she would ever come home."

"Did any of you, you know, date her?" I ask.

All five of them shake their heads.

"We were all just really close growing up. She's like a little sister to all of us. She went away to college for some kind of math degree or some shit. She's smart as hell," Mark explains.

"It'll be nice to have another female around to balance out all this testosterone," Kendall says with a laugh.

"Right? Then y'all keep having boys. Ben, Beck, and Knox. We need someone to start making some baby girls," I tease. "Poor Everly is never going to be able to date when she gets older."

"Damn straight," the four guys say in unison.

"You get right on that." Seth smirks.

"Who says we're not?" Mark counters.

"Who's not doing what?" Tyler asks, coming through the front door. He stops and holds it open for Reagan.

"Nothing." I'm quick to shut down the conversation. I don't know what he's thinking, but making babies is not something that we've talked about. Not that I'd be opposed to it. I just think it's best if we table that discussion for just the two of us for the first time. "How are the boys?" I ask Reagan.

"Perfect." She smiles. It's a smile that lightens her features, one we didn't see for a few months. I'm thrilled to know all is well with Ben, and Beck too.

"Just put it anywhere," Mark tells Tyler when he holds up the pan he's carrying.

"We have enough food for an army," I say, looking at the littered countertop.

"We'll eat," the guys say, making the women in the room laugh.

"What about you?" I ask Kent. "No date tonight?"

"Nah, just wanted to be with family."

"Hey, I'm dateless," Seth reminds me. "You not worried about me?" He gives me puppy-dog eyes.

"I just assumed, Amelia…" I let the words hang between us.

"Nope." He checks his phone. "She'll be here in ten." I don't comment further. He says they're just friends, I trust him.

"All right, well, I'll put my dips in the oven to warm them up and then we can eat." I tap on Mark's shoulder for him to move, but he doesn't budge. Leaning around him, I smile goofily. "Hey, tall man up front. The short girl has food to make," I say, making him chuckle.

"Fine," he concedes. He turns and grips my hips, lifting me into the air. As he slowly brings me down his body, he stops to steal a quick kiss before placing me on my feet.

"That's new," Seth announces.

"Not so new," Mark rebuffs.

"It's pretty new," Kent agrees.

"What? We've… been together for months now," Mark argues.

"That's not what's new," Tyler chimes in.

"What you just did there." Ridge points his finger and makes a circular motion toward the two of us. "That's new."

My cheeks growing hot, I move to step around Mark, and he lets me go.

"What? Kissing my girl's a crime?" he asks his friends.

"Nope," Ridge quips, and even though I'm not looking at them, I can hear the grin in his voice.

"So," Reagan whispers, "did you two finally have the talk?"

"No," I hiss.

"What talk?" Tyler asks.

"Nosey." Reagan sticks her tongue out at him.

He smacks her on the ass, wearing a shit-eating grin before taking a seat at the island. "Really, what talk?" he asks again.

"Nothing," I say quickly.

"It's something," Kent says.

"I wanted her to ask Mark if they could watch the boys for us," Reagan tells them.

"What's the big secret about that?" Seth asks.

"Nothing. I just didn't know if Mark would be up for it, that's all." Reagan's lies fall from her lips, and she's rather convincing.

"You tell me when and it's done," Mark says, nodding. "I need more time with my nephews."

It takes extreme effort to not let my shoulders drop with relief. That's all I need is our entire group to be involved in the "are we more or aren't we" conversation. Maybe I don't need the conversation after all. I mean, he called me his girl. Shaking out of my thoughts, I get busy heating up the dips that I made. I'm excited to spend a night with our friends and am determined to have a good time. To start living again.

# Chapter 10

## MARK

I'm buzzed, well on my way to drunk. Midnight passed us about an hour ago, and my kiss at the stroke of midnight was one for the record books. Dawn has been so carefree tonight, laughing and joking with the girls. They turned the dining room into their dance floor. I'm sure it was a sight—the four of them out there dancing as if this was their last chance, and the five us standing in the doorway watching their every move. Well, I only had eyes for my pixie. She's beautiful, and I don't think I tell her that enough. I need to do better.

"Do better at what?" Kent asks.

"Shit." I chuckle. "Did I say that out loud?"

"Yep. So don't leave me hanging."

I raise my hand that's holding my red solo cup full of some type of concoction that Seth created. I don't know what it is, but it's damn good. And it's damn potent. Pointing to Dawn, I say, "I need to tell her she's beautiful. I don't do that enough," I confess.

"That she is," he agrees. "You going to tie that down?"

I turn to look at him. His eyes are on the ladies as they dance like no one's watching. "I thought I already had."

"She know that?"

"She's with me, isn't she?"

"She is. She's been through a lot."

"You think I don't know that?" I ask incredulously.

He finally turns to look at me. "I know you do, better than any of us. She's all alone," he says sadly. "I just think you should make it known she has a place with you."

"I gave her a key." My buzzed brain seems to think that's enough.

He nods. "Good."

Before we can take this riveting conversation any further, the girls descend upon us. Kendall and Reagan drag Ty and Ridge to the middle of the floor. I watch with amusement as Amelia drags both Seth and Kent, and they sandwich her between them.

"You going to leave me hanging?" her slightly slurred voice greets me.

I look down at her. Her hair is crazy wild, almost like it is after I've made love to her. Reaching out, I smooth it back out of her face. "Never," I say, and her hazel eyes, although a little glassy, soften at my confession.

"Dance with me, Adams." She laces her fingers through mine and pulls me to the middle of the dining room floor, joining our friends.

I make a big deal about it, like she's forcing me to go. We both know better. I'd follow her anywhere. Her knowing grin when I tug her impossibly close tells me exactly that.

I don't know how much time passes. Could be minutes, could be hours. All I know is that her tight little body is pressed against mine, my hands are resting on the curve of her ass, and her head is on my chest, over my heart.

"We're going to call it a night," Tyler says. Glancing over, I catch Reagan covering a yawn.

"The boys were up at six this morning," she says in explanation.

"My house is your house," I tell them.

"Us too," Ridge says, and Kendall looks about as tired as Reagan.

"Can that be me three?" Amelia asks, raising her hand. "I feel old." She laughs.

"Right? Run after twin boys who are getting into everything," Reagan tells her.

"Mom life." Kendall holds her hand out for Dawn and they high-five.

"Everyone's staying, right?" I ask.

"Which one of you is letting me share your mattress?" Amelia asks.

"Take your pick," Kent says.

"Whose is closer?" she asks.

"Mine. First door on the left," Seth tells her.

"Thanks." She stands on tiptoes and kisses his cheek.

"She kicks," Kent taunts Seth.

"Hey." Amelia places her hand on her hip. "That tent was the size of a toddler bed and the seven of us were sleeping in it."

"Oh my God, it was so damn tiny," Kendall chimes in.

"We were kids," Seth counters.

"Y'all were what, twelve and thirteen? You were huge even then," Amelia says. Then she points to me. "You were like six-foot tall."

"Not quite." I chuckle.

"Whatever, I don't kick." She sticks her tongue out at us and heads down the hall, a little unsteady on her feet.

"What about you, baby? You ready for bed?"

She peers up at me. "Yes. That bed is calling my name."

"Make yourselves at home," I tell our friends, and with my hand on the small of her back, I lead Dawn to the opposite side of the house to my room. She grabs one of my T-shirts to sleep in and disappears behind the bathroom door. I empty out my pockets on the nightstand, and lie back on the bed.

"Tired?" Her soft voice greets me.

Peeling open my eyes, I see her standing by the bed. Her hair is pulled up in a knot on top of her head, and her face is scrubbed free of makeup. "You're beautiful."

A blush coats her cheeks. "You're drunk."

"I'm buzzed," I counter.

"You ready for bed?" she asks, shaking her head.

"Yeah, I gotta piss." I hold out my hand and she takes it, helping me off the bed. I place a kiss on her temple and head to the bathroom to take care of business. I strip out of my clothes and toss them in the hamper, staying in just my boxer briefs. If we didn't have guests, I'd go for bare. My cock hardens at the thought of her skin against mine and nothing between us. Fuck, being the host sucks sometimes. However, I'm glad to know everyone is here safe and sound. Turning off the light, I walk out of the bathroom.

Dawn is standing with her back to me, but her shoulders are shaking. I've seen the sight of that more times than I care to admit over the past couple of months. My feet carry me to her. Gently, I rest a hand on her shoulder. "Dawn."

Wet eyes peer up at me. "I was plugging in your phone," she says, holding it up.

"Okay?" I say cautiously. I don't know what about her plugging in my phone would upset her. There is no one but her in my life.

"The screen lit up," she explains.

Fuck, did some chick text me? Surely not. It's been just her for far longer than we've been admitting there was something between us.

"I wasn't looking. I mean, I wasn't snooping." She hands me my phone.

"Dawn." I cup her face with one hand while the other holds my phone, afraid to look. Softly, I wipe under her eyes with my thumb.

"I'm sorry," she says, her voice breaking.

Pressing the home screen button on my phone, I see a text message from my mom.

**Mom:** *Happy New Year from Dad and me. We love you.*

*Fuck.* At this point, I'm wishing it would have been some random drunk text from a girl from my past. Tossing my phone on the bed, I wrap my arms around her. I don't know what else to do or what to say in this moment. She misses them, of course she does. Sure, it will get easier with time, but she doesn't want or need to hear that. I debate on

74

going to get Kendall but quickly dismiss the idea. I want to be the one she leans on.

"I can't keep falling apart like this," she cries into my chest.

"Yes, you can."

"No." Her voice is stern. "I have to live. I can't walk around crying all the damn time."

"Look at me." I place my finger under her chin and lift so her eyes connect with mine. "You're grieving. You lost both of your parents in a tragic accident. There is no time limit on your healing."

"W-What if I never heal?" she whimpers, her voice soft.

"You will." I say the words with conviction. I'll do everything in my power to make sure it happens. She just needs time.

"You don't know that."

"I know that you're strong and that you're a fighter. I know that your heart is broken, and it needs time to accept the loss."

"I don't want to accept it."

"I know, baby, but you have to. If I could bring them back to you, I would." I mean every word. I would give anything within my power to not see her hurting like this.

"I miss them so much." Her voice is faint, but I still hear her.

"Climb in bed," I say, stepping back. She does as I ask. I quickly turn off the light and slide in next to her. "Come here," I say into the darkness. She wastes no time curling up next to me and burying her face in my chest. "I've got you." I feel her body shake as her sadness breaks loose from her chest. "I'm right here," I promise. This is not how I saw this night ending, but she's in my arms all the same. That's all that matters. She needs this. She needs to let herself mourn her family, because she lost her sister that night as well. I can't ever imagine a scenario where she would willingly let her sister back into her life after what she did.

"I'm sorry." Her soft cries are muffled against my chest. She wipes at her tears, and I rub my hand down her back.

"Never be sorry for missing them. Never be sorry for feeling your loss, your pain. Never be afraid to fall apart with me."

"You're going to get sick of this," she says.

"Never. I'm going to be here, no matter what."

"I'm tired of falling apart."

"Don't be. No matter how far you fall, I'm going to be right here to help you pick up the pieces." My confession only makes her cry harder. I tighten my hold on her and let her cry. That's all I can do. Be here. Hold her. Love her. One day, I'll tell her. But right now, when she's grieving, when I'm trying to comfort her, it's not the time to tell her. She'll always wonder if I truly meant the words, or if they were simply to make her feel better. To make her feel less alone.

I mean them.

Which is why I'm going to wait.

I lie awake for hours and hold her, my buzz long since gone. She's no longer crying, and sleeps peacefully against my chest, but I can't seem to do the same. I've never felt for someone the way I do her. I've never cared enough for a woman to feel her pain deep in the pit of my soul. It breaks me to see her like she was earlier tonight, but at the same time, I know she needs to be able to release her sadness and her anger, and every other emotion she's going to walk through as she heals. She mumbles something I can't understand, and I wrap my arm a little tighter, holding her just a little closer. She sighs as if that's all it takes to make things right in her world, and my chest expands.

*Love.*

I'll do everything in my power to love her through this.

# Chapter 11

## Dawn

"How is it possible that the twins are already a year old?" I ask Kendall. We're in Tyler and Reagan's kitchen helping her set up all the food for Ben and Beck's first birthday party.

"Right? I swear the older I get, the faster time flies."

"The last year has been a blur."

Kendall stops what she's doing and looks up at me. "I know it's been a hard year for everyone. How are you holding up?"

I shrug. "Good days and bad days."

"I'm here for you, you know that, right? I've been trying not to push you, but I'm here."

I know that she is and I love her for it. "Thank you. I've been doing okay. It's been several weeks since my last breakdown." Not since New Year's Eve. Each day is a struggle, but I'm pushing through. Taking each day as it comes.

"I'm so sorry. That took forever," Reagan says, coming into the kitchen carrying three boxes.

"Let me help you." I grab the two smaller ones from the top.

"Thanks. The bakery line was a mile long and then traffic is crazy with the snow." She sets the large box down on the counter. "These are cupcakes for us and the kids. I thought that would be easier. Those—" She points to the two smaller boxes that I just took from her. "Those are for the boys to dive into," she says, smiling wide. "I can't believe my babies are turning one." She wipes a tear from her eye.

"We were just talking about that," I tell her.

"I don't know if I'm emotional because they're growing up so fast or because they're both here alive and healthy," she confesses.

"I'd say a little bit of both," Kendall says. "Last year was a tough one, for all of us."

"We never would have made it through it without all of you," Reagan tells us.

"We're family." Kendall shrugs.

"And I feel the same way," I confess. "I'm... alone now, but you all, your husbands, kids, and the guys, you all make me feel less alone."

"That's because you're not alone," Reagan says, like it's the gospel. "We're your family. It takes more than blood to form that bond. You're in tight." She crosses her fingers in a display of how tight we are.

"Who's tight?" Kent asks, laughing.

"Do you ever think with the head on your shoulders?" Kendall teases.

"Umm... is this a trick question?" he asks.

"Hey, you need any help?" Mark appears beside me.

"No, I think we have it. I thought you were all helping Ridge and Tyler with the kids?"

"Knox is entertaining all three of them. We're just kind of standing by and watching."

"That kid." Kent shakes his head. "He's a character."

"He's just like his daddy," Kendall says fondly.

"Nah, I can't ever remember Ridge being that entertaining," Kent jokes, causing us all to laugh.

"I think we're good," I tell Reagan as I place the stack of paper plates on the counter.

"Come and get it!" she calls out. Ridge shuffles in with Knox hanging off one leg, and with Everly on his hip. Tyler and Seth are right behind him, each carrying one of the twins. "Dive in," she tells them.

Kendall makes a plate for Knox and Everly, and Reagan does the same for Beck and Ben. We set the kids up in their high chairs, well, everyone besides Knox who's in a booster seat that usually ends up on the floor. He likes to sit in the "big boy" chair. The guys pile in and fill their plates before sitting at the table with the kids.

"Now, girl time." Reagan grins. The three of us make our plates and settle in the living room.

"So, who's having the next ankle-biter?" Kent asks.

The girls and I stop talking so that we can listen to their conversation. The kids are babbling to themselves. "I'm in," Ridge says without an ounce of hesitation.

"Obviously, I have superior swimmers," Tyler boasts.

"He's got you there," Seth chimes in.

"They're ridiculous," Kendall whisper laughs.

"Damn right." This from Tyler.

"Meh, I could do better," Kent quips.

"Dear Lord, let's hope not. Twins are exhausting. I can't imagine triplets," Reagan says, and it's as if you can hear the exhaustion in her voice, but that takes nothing from the smile on her face. She's tired, but she wouldn't change it for anything. Of that, I'm certain.

"Sounds like you're up," I tease Kendall.

She grins. "I don't know if we're ready just yet, but practicing…" Her voice trails off as a light blush coats her cheeks.

"What about you?" Reagan asks.

"Me?" I'm still learning to live with the fact that I have no family, none that I care to speak of anyway.

"Yes, you. You been practicing?" Kendall dishes it right back.

"Oh, we practice," I confirm, and we all bust out in laughter.

"What did we miss?" Seth calls out.

"Oh, nothing," I say through spurts of laughter.

"No wonder y'all didn't answer the door," Amelia says, entering the room. "What did I miss?"

"Oh, nothing. Just talking about practicing making babies." Reagan tries to sound innocent but fails as laughter sputters in her chest.

"Is it in the water? You have any bottled? I do not need that in my life right now." Amelia shudders.

"What?" Kendall asks. "You love kids."

"Yeah, I do, and I want them… someday. I just need to find a man who wants to stick around long enough to not only make them but raise them."

Something happened with the last guy she dated, but she's been pretty tight-lipped about it. She'll talk about it when she's ready, and the three of us will be here when she is.

"Anyway, sorry I'm late. I was helping Mom clean out her closet and lost track of time."

"You didn't miss anything. Go grab a plate," Reagan tells her.

Amelia stands and makes her rounds hugging all the kids and jabbing at the guys. She joins us a few minutes later with a plate of food. "Those cakes are too cute."

"Thanks. They're into construction. Ty's influence." Reagan laughs. "So I figured might as well indulge them."

Each of the boys' individual cakes are yellow with black stripes. The top says *Caution: Beck is One* and *Caution: Ben is One*. They are really cute, and I can't wait to see them dive into them.

"Babe," Tyler calls out. "Are we ready for cake?"

"He's worse than the kids." Reagan chuckles. "In a minute," she calls back.

The four of us chat for a few more minutes while Amelia finishes her food. We make quick work of cleaning up the kitchen and setting the cupcakes with little individual containers of ice cream out on the counter. Reagan and I each hold one of the small cakes, and Kendall lights the candle.

"Here we come," Amelia says loudly, and we all start to sing "Happy Birthday."

The kids are clapping and smiling, and when Ben and Beck dive into their birthday cakes, it's just as cute as I imagined it to be. They both have cake all over their face and hands. Ridge unwraps two cupcakes. One is placed in front of Knox on a plate, and the other on the high chair in front of Everly. All four kids are covered in cake and icing while the adults take pictures and watch with amusement.

It's a great day with lots of memories created. Thoughts also plague my mind that my parents will never be able to witness this with my children. My chest tightens, but I don't break down. I'm getting better at that—not breaking down at every thought or memory. I'm taking it one day at a time.

"Just think," Tyler says with a laugh, "we get to do this again next weekend with the grandparents."

Reagan smiles fondly at him, and then their twins. We started doing our own family thing once Knox was born and Ridge and Kendall got together. As our clan grows, so do our gatherings. I try not to think about what will happen if Mark and I ever split. How awkward it would be for us, and then there's the fact that I'm the new girl. Mark and the guys, Reagan, and even Amelia and Kendall all have history. I'm Kendall's friend, who they've only known for a couple of years. I'd be the odd man out. I'd lose the only family— I shake out of my thoughts. I'm not willing to go there today. I refuse to make this day about me.

"Let's get these kiddos cleaned up and move on to presents." Reagan laughs as Ben shoves more cake into his mouth. There are tears in her eyes, and as I survey the room, everyone is watching him and thinking the same thing. There was a time we weren't sure we would ever get the chance to see him celebrate this day. The fact that he's here and healthy, it's a blessing.

We gather in the living room. Ridge and Kendall take the loveseat, with Everly cuddled between them. Knox, already a ladies' man, is on Amelia's lap talking her head off and lapping up all her attention. Tyler and Reagan are on the floor with Beck and Ben, their gifts piled between them. Seth, Kent, and Mark are on the couch, which leaves me. I'm getting ready to settle on the floor next to Mark, but he pulls me into his lap.

"This is where you belong," he whispers in my ear.

"D, you can sit here," Seth says, patting his lap. I look over at him and he's wearing a shit-eating grin.

"Fuck off," Mark mumbles.

"Marcus." Kent places his hand to his chest as if Mark has just offended him. "There are children present."

"Tell him to keep to his side of the couch." Mark nods to where Seth sits on the opposite side of Kent. Seth and Kent dissolve into laughter, and Mark tightens his hold on me.

This possessive side to him has been happening more since the night I lost my parents. At times I think it's because he feels bad for me that I have no one but him, and our friends, until times like now, when his hand rests on my thigh and the other slips under the hem of my shirt and rubs my back. Only he and I know that's what he's doing. It's just for us, not for show. I've dissected his intentions a million times, but what it comes down to, is I refuse to ask. I can't handle it right now. Good or bad, I think it might break me. So instead, I pretend that this new affection he shows me in front of the group is not new, and it's how we've always been with each other.

I pretend that I have my shit together, and I know the exact path my life is taking me.

Fake it until you make it.

"Your place or mine?" Mark asks a few hours later.

I glance over at him where he sits behind the wheel of his truck, waiting for me to tell him which direction he needs to go. "I-I don't want to be alone." After all day with our friends and their kids, going home alone sounds like the worst kind of torture.

"Let me rephrase my question. Are *we*," he places emphasis on we, "going to your place or mine?"

I smile at him. "Yours."

"You got what you need for work tomorrow at my place?"

"Yes." At his insistence, I keep clothes and toiletries at his place. It does come in handy on the nights I don't want to go home alone. I'm spending more and more time at his place. I don't hate it.

He nods and turns right out of Tyler and Reagan's driveway. "Those little buggers are exhausting," he comments, settling his arm beside mine where it rests on the center console of his truck. He loops his pinky through mine.

"They definitely have a lot of energy," I agree. "However, they all did have cake."

"This is true. That's the best part about being Uncle Mark. I get to spoil them, sneak them extra cupcakes, and then leave them with their parents to fight off the sugar high."

"You're terrible." I laugh.

"Hey, it's part of the Uncle's Code of Ethics."

"Who wrote this particular Code of Ethics?" I ask. "Seth?"

"It was a group effort, and it's not so much as written as assumed. However, Ty was in on it when we started it. Knox was the only little one at the time, so my guess is that Ty would like to amend it." He chuckles. "Sucks for him. There are still three remaining childless uncles. Majority rules."

I just shake my head and smile. These guys and their antics never cease to amaze me. "I bet Kendall and Reagan can veto."

"The Uncle's Code of Ethics is sacred. No moms allowed."

"So you're telling me I'm privy to private man-child inside information?"

"Man-child?" he scoffs, making me throw my head back and laugh.

"Just calling it like I see it," I volley. He mutters something under his breath about no respect for the uncle, and I don't need to look in the mirror to know that I'm grinning like a fool.

❈❈❈

"I think I'm going to take a shower," I tell him once we're in the house. "I feel sticky." I hold my arms out as if you can see the sticky.

"Okay, babe," he says, kissing the top of my head.

I disappear into his bedroom, strip out of my clothes, toss them in the dirty laundry basket, and head to the bathroom. I'm standing outside of his walk-in shower waiting for the water to heat. This shower is one of my favorite parts of this house. It's huge, no door, no curtain, just lots of tile, and multiple showerheads. There's a bench in the corner that I use when I shave my legs. It's no wonder I spend more time here than my place. The company is number one, but this shower is a close second.

"Hey." His deep timbre greets me as his hands rest on my bare hips. "You good? You look pretty deep in your thoughts." He's been so cautious with me the last few months. I've pulled from his strength more than I care to admit.

"Sorry. I was just thinking about this shower. It so makes staying over worth it."

He moves closer and his naked body aligns with mine. "Is that all?" He bends to kiss my neck.

"You've seen this shower, right?" I goad.

His answer is to press his hard cock into me. "You've seen my cock, right?" he counters.

I was trying to be funny, but the heat in his voice has me rubbing my thighs together. I turn in his arms, resting my palms against his chest, his thick length straining between us. I make sure he's watching me, and make a point to look down and then slowly back up. "Sure. You've seen one, you've seen them all."

He growls as he grips my hips and lifts me. Instinctively, I wrap my legs around his waist as he steps us under the hot spray. "You're rough on a man's ego," he says, moving his hands to my ass and giving it a gentle squeeze.

"Meh." I go for nonchalant. "Maybe you should prove me wrong."

"Pixie." He breathes his hot breath at my ear. I yelp when we step out of the shower and he stalks to the vanity, yanking open the drawer and pulling out a condom. He sets me on the counter while he rolls it down his hard length. In a matter of seconds, I'm back in his arms and we're back under the hot spray. "Hold on tight," he says as he pushes inside me.

My head falls back and my hands lock tight around his neck. "Damn" falls from my lips. No matter how many times we've done this, it's still a shock to my body. Nothing compares to Mark inside me.

"So fucking tight," he moans as he pulls out and pushes back in.

*So fucking big,* I think it, but don't get a chance to voice the words as he quickens his thrusts. He turns and reverses up until his back rests against the shower wall. Hands on my hips, he lifts me and pulls me back down. Over and over he repeats this, driving me crazy.

"Mark," I moan his name as my body tingles.

"Give it to me, Pixie. I want all your pleasure. I want to hear you scream. I want to feel your pussy squeezing the fuck out of my cock." His hands move to my ass and I tilt my hips, making him growl.

Lift. Slam.

Lift. Slam.

"Oh, God," I moan when my legs start to quiver.

"No God, baby. It's just me," he says with a pant, never missing a beat in his ministrations of my body. "Come for me," he demands.

It's as if his voice is a trigger for my orgasm. I call out his name. My nails dig into his neck as my body convulses around him. A roar tears from his lips and with one final thrust, he holds himself deep inside me as he loses control.

"Want to change your answer?" he asks, kissing under my ear.

"What?" I'm still coming down from my orgasmic paradise.

"Why you like to stay over," he reminds me.

Lifting my head, my eyes find his, and he's watching me intently. We're both breathing heavily. Looping an arm around his neck, I use the other to place my hand on his chest, over his heart. "This," I whisper hoarsely. "This is what keeps me here."

"Fuck," he murmurs, and crashes his lips to mine. He kisses me lazily, moving us to the bench where he sits with me still wrapped around him. Slowly, he makes love to my mouth, his hands roaming my body. When the water eventually runs cold, he shuts it off and steps out of the shower. He makes sure I'm steady on my feet before releasing his hold on me. Towel in hand, he wraps it over my shoulders and hands me another for my hair before grabbing one for himself.

Quietly, he leads me to his bed, pulling back the covers and waiting for me to climb in. He wastes no time following in after me, tugging me into his arms. "It's yours you know. It will always be yours."

My heart slips a beat at his confession. "I'll keep it safe," I whisper into the darkness. These moments with him cause my heart to swell with so much love. I can easily picture this being our life. It's a vivid movie reel in my head, and it gives me something to hold on to.

Hope for the future.

New beginnings.

Now we just need to say the words and make it true.

# Chapter 12

## MARK

"Mark!" Knox shouts as Dawn and I walk around the house to the backyard. He comes running at me full speed. I let go of Dawn's hand, bracing for impact from the little dude. He launches himself at me, and I pick him up in my arms, settling him on my hip.

"Happy Birthday," I say, bouncing him.

"Dad gots fire that goes boom," he says excitedly.

"He does?" I ask, barely containing my laughter at his excitement.

He nods, his head bobbing up and down. "For my birfday and memory day," he tells me.

"Memorial Day," I correct. His third birthday was a couple of weeks ago, but Ridge and Kendall decided to wait until today to celebrate with everyone's schedules.

"I said that," he says, wiggling to get down.

I place him back on his feet and expect him to run back to the party; instead, he holds his arms up for Dawn. She doesn't hesitate to pick him up. "Happy Birthday, handsome." She kisses his cheek.

He wraps his little hands on her cheeks and places a sloppy wet kiss on her lips. She giggles, which makes him smile. "Wuv you, D," he says, resting his head on her shoulder.

"Why do all the littles keep trying to steal my girl?" I ask him.

He scrunches up his little nose and gives me his best evil-eye. "My girl," he states possessively.

Dawn shrugs, and carries him to the deck and sits down with him in her lap. That lasts about two-point-five seconds before he's off running and playing with his sister and his cousins.

"There's a new little," I say as I watch a little girl with dark curls chase after Everly.

"That's Mara's little girl, Finley," Kendall says. "She and Amelia went to college together. She's in town for a job interview." She points to the side yard where Amelia and Mara are standing and watching the kids run and play.

"She's adorable," Dawn says.

"She's the sweetest little girl," Reagan agrees.

"So, does the little man get his own cake to demolish?" I ask.

"No," Kendall says adamantly. "However, I did go with the cupcake option. It's so much easier."

Reagan holds her hand up for a high-five. "Exactly. It's all about easier with this group." She laughs.

"What can I do?" Dawn asks.

"Nothing. We've got it all under control. My dad and Ridge's are manning the grill. Our moms are inside putting the rest of the food together and have given us all strict instructions to take a break and let them take care of it," Kendall explains.

"Who are we to fight them?" Reagan laughs.

"Hey, guys," Amelia says, joining us. "This is Mara. We were roommates in college."

We all take turns saying hello and shaking her hand, as Ridge's mom, Heidi, calls out to tell us it's time to eat. The kids' plates are made, and they're set up on the miniature picnic table on the deck before the rest of us filter through piling our plates high with burgers, hot dogs, chips, baked beans, and potato salad.

Dawn's smile has been a permanent fixture on her face today. No sadness in the depths of those hazel eyes. I know she still struggles, but each day she seems to be coping better than the last. I've yet to tell her that I'm in love with her. Every time I start to, something happens, like we end up tangled in the sheets. That one happens more often than not. I can't seem to get my fill of her. I don't want to tell her for the first time when I'm balls deep. Although, one of these days, I might not be able to bite my tongue from shouting it out.

She's easy to love.

"You down for a game of football with the kids?" Tyler asks.

"Definitely." Standing, I drop a kiss to Dawn's temple, and follow him to the yard. Ridge is already there with the kids gathered around. Knox is the oldest at three, and the only one who really understand the concept of what we're doing. The others just seem to be excited to be involved.

What was intended to be a game of football, turns out to be the kids chasing the adult with the ball, and whoever that is drops to the ground and lets the kids crawl all over him until handing it off to the next guy. Rinse and repeat.

⁂

"How's she doing?" Ridge asks with a sleepy Everly resting on his shoulder.

We've just finished our football game with the kids, and they're tuckered out. I tear my eyes from Dawn, who's sitting and chatting with Mara, and look over at Everly. Her eyes are drooping. "She's almost out," I tell him.

"I meant Dawn."

"Good, man. She's doing better each day. Still sad at times, but that's to be expected."

"What about you? How are you?"

"Me? I'm fine."

"It's hard to watch the woman you love go through that," he says pointedly. "When Kendall was struggling with Knox, and her sister, it fu— freaking killed me," he says, catching his slip up. Not that Everly would notice since she's so tired.

"I just didn't know how to help her, you know? I mean, what do you say to someone who lost their family at the hands of their drug-addicted sister?" I shake my head in disgust thinking about Dawn's sister, Destiny. She's been out of rehab for months and we've not heard a peep from her. Not that I expected any different, but I know Dawn was hoping to hear from her. Hoping that rehab stuck this time. Although she struggled with letting her back into her life, I know that hope was alive and well until the months started to trickle by with no word.

"Any word from her sister?"

"Not a word." My gaze goes back to Dawn, who's smiling as she and Mara laugh at something Kent is saying. "It's good to see her like this," I say, nodding toward her.

"It's also good to see this one," he looks down at Everly in his arms, "like this." He laughs softly, breaking our serious moment. "She's been going all day fighting off a nap, afraid she's going to miss something."

"Looks like Daddy has the magic touch."

He grins. "It's the best, man."

I nod. "Fatherhood looks good on you. Tyler too."

"You ever think about what's next?"

"Every day."

"Does she know that?"

"Not yet."

"You need to handle that."

I nod. He's right. We both know it. I've been walking on eggshells as far as my feelings and hers since the night we got the call about her parents' accident. I've been dragging my feet, not wanting her sadness and pain to be mixed in with the happiness and joy I hope she'll feel when I tell her how much she means to me. How she owns my heart. I'm frustrated at not having that ability to tell her how much she means to me. I detest keeping my feelings a secret, keeping the truth of my emotions beyond my actions close to my chest. Even though I've not said the words, I make damn sure to show her every day with a touch or a look... with my actions. I'm waiting for the right time, and I'm starting to figure out there may not be a right time. I might have to just blurt the words out. I've bitten my tongue enough these past few months. I just want her to know it's my heart and not the situation that's speaking for me.

✼✼✼

I rouse to the sound of a ringing cell phone. Peeling open my eyes, I blink once, twice, three times to clear the sleep haze and look at the clock. Just after one in the morning. The phone stops and I roll over to see Dawn is still sleeping soundly. Rolling back over, I reach for my phone and tap the screen.

No missed calls.

Climbing out of bed, I make my way to her side of the bed in the dark and feel around for her phone on the nightstand and tap the screen.

One missed call.

It's not a number programmed into her phone, and inwardly, I curse fucking scammers and telemarketers. It's the middle of the damn night. Before I can move to get back in bed, it rings again. I scramble to pick it up and answer.

"Hello," I whisper, not wanting to wake Dawn.

"Hi, I'm looking for Dawn Miller."

"Who's this?" I ask, not bothering to hide my annoyance.

"My name is Jasmine. I'm calling from Mason County Memorial. We have Destiny Miller here asking for her sister, Dawn. Is she available?"

"You do realize it's the middle of the night?" I ask.

"Yes, sir, I'm sorry for waking you, but Ms. Miller is listed as our patient's next of kin."

"Is she alive?" I ask rudely.

"Mark?" Dawn's eyes flutter open. When she sees that I'm on the phone, she sits up and leans against the headboard. "Who are you talking to?"

"She's here," I tell the caller. "Baby, it's Mason County Memorial. They have Destiny there and you're listed as her next of kin." I hand her the phone, then sit on the edge of the bed, resting my hand on her thigh.

"Hello," she says, eyes now wide open and fear etched in her features. "Yes, this is Dawn," she says into the line.

I watch her closely as her face goes pale and her hand that's not holding the phone reaches out and grips mine. "Are they— are they okay?" she asks hesitantly. "Okay, should I come there?" She listens intently. "Okay. Thank you." She ends the call, letting the phone fall into her lap.

"What's going on?"

"That was the hospital," she says, staring wide-eyed. "They have Destiny there." She pauses, and I'm about to ask why Destiny's there despite already having a pretty good idea when she continues. "She just had a baby."

"What?" I ask, not expecting those words to come out of her mouth.

"My sister, she just delivered a baby. They're both doing okay. She said Destiny asked her to call me."

"What does she want?"

She shrugs. "I don't know. They're both resting. The nurse said not to rush there, but that Destiny was asking for me."

"Wow." It's not much as replies go, but I'm pretty much speechless.

"I guess it's a good thing tomorrow is a holiday and I'm off work."

"What time do you want to leave?" No way am I letting her go on her own. Not to deal with the crazy that is her little sister.

"You don't have to go." She's quick to decline.

"Where else would I be? My plans are to spend the day with you. So, where you are, I am."

Leaning forward, she rests her palm against my cheek. "You're a good man, Marcus Adams."

"Shh, you're going to ruin my street cred," I say dramatically. Moving, I crawl over her and plop down on my side of the bed. She snuggles into my chest and I hold her tight. I'm not sure how much more she can handle.

"I should have asked if she was clean," she says into the quiet of the room.

"She said they were both doing well, right?"

"Yeah, I guess that's a good sign. Maybe rehab stuck this time and she got her shit together?" she asks, and I can hear the hope in her voice.

"We'll find out soon enough," I say, kissing the top of her head. Once again, I'm in yet another situation where I'm not sure what to say. I have a very strong dislike for her sister.

"You really don't have to go," she says again over a yawn.

With my fingers, I gently trace up and down her spine. "I'll be there," I promise. I feel her body relax into me and her breathing evens out. It's then, I let sleep claim me.

# Chapter 13

## Dawn

The drive to Mason is quiet. Mark doesn't try to get me to talk, instead allowing me to get lost in my thoughts. I'm not sure how, but he always seems to know what I need. Today, what I need is time to process the fact that I'm an aunt. I need time to process my sister, the drug addict, as a mother, and the fact that our parents aren't here to see it.

"Dawn." I feel a soft caress on my arm and let it pull me from my thoughts. "We're here." Mark nods toward the entrance of Mason County Memorial. "You ready for this?"

"I'm not really sure," I confess. "I guess all this time, I hoped she was clean, but assumed when I didn't hear from her that she wasn't. Then there's the timeline. How far along was she? Was she pregnant that night?" I swallow hard. "The night of the accident?"

"Only one way to find out," he says, pulling the keys from the ignition and climbing out of the truck. He's at my door in a flash, pulling it open and helping me down. Once my feet hit the pavement, his strong arms clamp around me, holding me tightly against his chest. "Whatever happens, you've got me right here by your side."

I smile up at him. "You've already done so much."

He tucks a strand of hair blowing in the wind behind my ear. "That's what you do for those you care about. I've got strong shoulders, Pixie, lean on them."

I inhale a deep breath and slowly exhale. "Okay, let's do this." I hold out my hand and he tangles his fingers with mine. Side by side, we make our way into the hospital.

"Hi, can I help you?" an older lady greets us from the welcome desk.

"I'm looking for my sister, Destiny Miller."

She types on her computer and smiles up at me. "She's in the maternity ward." She rattles off her room number and proceeds to give us directions to the elevator.

"At any time you want to leave, we're gone," Mark says in the elevator.

"I just don't understand after all this time why she's asking for me."

"Maybe she wants to make amends? Apologize?"

"I highly doubt it. Destiny doesn't apologize."

"Maybe she's turning over a new leaf?" he suggests. We can both hear the doubt in his voice, but I appreciate the effort. If anything, it's helping to calm my nerves.

When the elevator doors slide open, my stomach twists with unease. Forcing one foot in front of the other, I watch the numbers on the doors as we pass by until we reach Destiny's room. I stop and stare at the number, delaying going inside.

"You want me to wait out here?" Mark asks.

"No." I tighten my grip on our joined hands. "I mean, unless you don't want—" He stops me by bending to kiss my temple.

"I'm with you, Pixie. Whatever you need. I just wanted to offer. You ready?"

I shake my head and say, "Yes," making him chuckle.

"I'm going with," he says, lifting his hand that's not holding mine and rapping on the door. We wait for acceptance to enter, but it never comes.

I knock again, and still nothing. "Excuse me," I say to a passing nurse. "Is it okay if we go in?"

"Are you family?" she asks.

"Yes. She's— Destiny's my sister."

"Just let me check with Mom." She pushes open the door, and it's not five seconds later, she's opening the door. "She must be down at the nursery. Have a seat in the waiting room." She points down the hall. "We'll round her up and come to get you if she wants to see you," she adds, scurrying off to the nurses' station.

Mark leads us down the long hall to the room at the end clearly marked Waiting Room, and pushes inside. It's a small room with couches and chairs that look more comfortable than any waiting room I've ever been in. There is a TV on the wall and a row of vending machines in the far corner.

"And we wait," I say, taking a seat on the couch. Mark settles in next to me, placing his arm around my shoulders.

"We just got here. Isn't it too early to complain about waiting?" he asks.

"No. This is my sister we're talking about. Hell, she probably planned it all out. I'll summon for Dawn in the middle of the night, and then I'll make sure I'm not in my room when she gets here so she has to sit and wait on me. Keep her in suspense," I mutter, and he chuckles.

"I doubt that, babe," he says as the nurse we spoke to enters the waiting room.

"Ready?" I ask, standing.

"Have you talked to your sister today?" she asks me.

"No," I answer. "It's been months since I've heard from her. I didn't even know she was pregnant."

"Oh, dear," she says.

"What's going on?" Worry takes over the dread of seeing Destiny after all these months, after her confession of what really happened the night our parents died.

"Well, I'm not sure, but it appears that we can't find your sister."

"Excuse me?"

"She's not in her room, and she's not been signed into the nursery today to see the baby."

"She has to be in this hospital somewhere," I say as I begin to pace the room. Of course she's gone. This is classic Destiny. "The baby?"

"She's doing just fine."

"She?" I say, even though I heard her just fine.

"She. You're listed as her next of kin, the baby's too, so I can tell you. She was born at thirty-seven weeks. She's tiny, but she's breathing on her own."

"And is my sister clean?" I ask.

She shakes her head and my heart plummets. "She tested positive for opiates."

"Fuck," Mark mumbles.

"The baby?" I ask, feeling as if my heart is in my throat.

"She's doing well, all things considering. She's tiny at four pounds and one ounce. She's crying a lot, which causes her to gasp for breath, so we have her on oxygen as a precaution as we help her through this." She rattles on about hyperirritability, jaundice, bili lights, and increased chances for infection.

"What happens to the baby? What happens if we can't find my sister?"

"The courts and social services will be involved. They already are due to her addiction. We'll survey immediate family, including yourself, and see if anyone is willing to foster the child."

"It's just me," I tell her. "Our parents—" I choke on the words.

"Their parents passed a few months ago," Mark answers for me, pulling me into him.

"Right, I'm sorry for your loss," she says, and I can see the pity in her eyes. "So, if you are willing, there will be lots of red tape, but the baby is going to be here for a while, so hopefully by the time we discharge her, you'll have gotten the approval from the judge for temporary custody, and you'll be able to take her home."

"Then what?" Mark asks.

"Well, then it will be up to you to petition the court for permanent custody if that's what you choose to do."

"I can't believe this is happening." I rest my forehead against Mark's chest. Just when I thought I was starting to find my new normal, my sister strikes again. This time in the form of an innocent baby who's fighting withdrawal symptoms because my sister can't stay clean. Even for her unborn child.

"Can I see her? The baby?"

"Yes. Right this way." The nurse turns on her heel, and we follow her out of the waiting room and down the opposite end of the hall. She leads us to a long window that showcases babies with names all done up on pretty cards. I spot my niece right away. Her card says *Baby Girl Miller*.

"What's her name?" I ask, peering through the window, trying to get a better look.

"She hasn't been given a name yet."

I stare through the glass at the miracle that is my baby niece, and the hatred I have for my sister grows. She's so tiny, and she's in what looks like an incubator, whereas the other babies are just in regular beds. "Can I hold her? I mean, are we allowed to do that?"

"You can. You have to be mindful of her IVs and oxygen, but you can hold her. Come with me." We follow her a few steps to a door that's locked and clearly states authorized personnel only. "We'll need to see some identification, to match it with her file to verify you are indeed listed as the next of kin. I'm sorry, it's procedure."

"Sure." I rummage in my purse, pulling out my wallet and handing her my ID.

"Thank you." She disappears behind the door, leaving us standing in the hall.

"I can't believe this. She's so tiny and fighting, and Destiny just what...? Skipped town? Left the hospital? What the hell is wrong with her? How is it that the same people raised us? It's not normal, Mark."

"Here you go." The nurse is back, handing me my ID before Mark can get a word in. "I'm sorry, sir," she says to Mark. "It's family only."

"He's my fiancé," I blurt before thinking. I can't do this alone. I need him there with me.

"Fiancé?" she asks skeptically, eyes darting to my left hand.

"Yes," I say, my voice strong. Mark moves to stand a little closer, placing his arm around my waist. I fight the urge to sigh that he's going along with this.

"Okay. I need some ID and will need to enter you into the system."

"Sure." He retrieves his wallet from his back pocket and fishes out his ID, handing it to her.

"I'm sorry," I rush to say as soon as she disappears behind the door. "I just don't want to go in alone, and you're here, and I need you, and I'm sorry."

"Hey." He cups my face in his large hands. "I'm right here. Whatever you need, it's yours." His blue eyes are warm and filled with reassurance. He didn't even flinch when I told her that he was my fiancé.

The door opens and the nurse peeks her head out. "Come on back." She motions for us. "We're going to need you to wash up and slip into these." She hands us some scrubs to place over our clothes. "She's prone to infection, so we're doing everything we can to limit her exposure until her lungs are more developed and she's stronger."

Mark and I take turns washing up and slipping into the provided clothes. "Right this way." She motions for us to follow her through yet another door, and then another. "I'll go get her. I'll be right back."

"I'm nervous. Why am I nervous?" My voice pitches high.

"Because you're about to hold the best part of your sister in your arms."

My mouth falls open and then closes. "You continue to amaze me, Marcus Adams." I don't know what I did to deserve a man like him, but I'm thankful for him all the same. When I met him, I never would have guessed this is where we would be. Me, madly in love with him and afraid to tell him, and him? Well, I never guessed from our first meeting he would be this loving and supportive guy. I never would have fathomed he would become my rock and the glue that holds me together. I had no way of seeing the fall I was about to take or that he would be the one there with open arms to catch me. Regardless, I'm glad he's here.

My safety net.

"All right, little lady," the nurse coos, as she's pushing the incubator holding my niece into the room. "There are some people here to meet you." I watch with rapt attention as she opens the lid and lifts her from her bed, holding her tiny body with such care.

"Why is she in this bed?" Mark asks.

"The light. She's jaundice and needs the light to help even out her bilirubin levels." He nods like he understands and we both go back to watching intently.

"She's going to be okay?" My voice catches with emotion.

"She's a fighter this little one," she says, not really answering my question. "Go ahead and have a seat," she tells me.

I do as I'm told, and she places the sweet baby girl in my arms. "Hi," I whisper. Hot tears prick the back of my eyes. Emotions threaten to overwhelm me. My parents are missing this, their first grandbaby. My sister, this little angel's mother, has disappeared. She's hours old, and already all alone in this hospital.

"You're a natural." Mark's deep timbre surprises me.

"Yeah?" I ask, never taking my eyes from the baby.

"Yeah," he says, crouching down next to me to get a better look. "She's beautiful."

"I can't believe she left her here," I speak my earlier thoughts.

"We don't know that," he tries to reason.

I get what he's doing trying to stay optimistic, but I've dealt with my sister and her disappearing for too many years. I feel it in my gut. She ran.

"Unfortunately, we do know," the nurse interrupts. "As of about fifteen minutes ago, security footage shows her leaving out a side entrance. They told me while I was entering your information into the computer."

"I'm so sorry," I whisper to my niece. "Who will name her?" I ask the nurse, without taking my eyes of the little bundle in my arms.

"She'll be Baby Girl Miller. I'm not privy to all the legal that needs to happen. I know that whoever takes this little one home, whether it be social services or family, will name her. If she's placed for adoption, her new family has the right to change that name."

I look up at Mark, who's watching me intently. I feel tears burn my eyes thinking about this baby girl going to an unknown family. She's my family, all I have left. "I want her," I say, never taking my eyes off Mark. He doesn't even flinch at my confession.

"Okay," the nurse says. "We'll get someone from social services to talk to you and start the process."

I nod and turn my attention back to the tiny human in my arms, who is fighting for her life, all on her own. There's been no one here to love on her and tell her she's a fighter.

Until now.

That person is me.

I lose track of time as I hold her, slowly rocking her in my arms. She fusses and jerks, which the nurse tells me is the drugs in her system. I thought I hated my sister after her confession the night my parents died. I thought that was her lowest low, but this is… I'll never be able to forgive her for this. The nurse said she was addicted to pills, but not out of her mind that she didn't know what she was doing to her unborn baby. She simply stated she needed them. As far as I'm concerned, she has no right to this beautiful baby girl. I'll fight her with everything I have to keep this little one safe. My sister has burned her final bridge with me. I thought maybe she had cleaned up and I could learn to forgive her. That's what Mom and Dad would have wanted me to do, but this… there is no coming back from this.

Sure, I could say that there is a semblance of redemption. She had enough care to call me, and bring me here. She knew I would take her baby. She knew that I would care for her. That's what my parents and I have always done. Fixed her screwups. Although, it's impossible for me to think of that baby alone without a mother to comfort her as a screwup. She's innocent in all this. My sister though, she's a screwup. Letting the drugs rule her life, choosing her next fix over her own flesh, her newborn baby. I'll be there for this baby; she's my family. My sister, however, I'm finished. She has to want to get clean, to mean it to make it happen. Until then, I want nothing to do with her.

She's dead to me.

# Chapter 14

## MARK

I'm out of my element here. For the second time in the last year, the woman I love is faced with the unimaginable, and I don't know what to do to help her. We've just finished talking to the social worker who explained all the red tape that goes along with the process of Dawn obtaining guardianship of the baby. Luckily, being the only living relative, and with no father listed, there won't be anyone to contest. At least not that we're aware of. Even if Destiny shows up, she won't get her baby. Not until the court runs her through counseling, rehab, and a host of other hoops she'll have to jump through.

"I can't believe this is happening," Dawn says, slumping down in the waiting room chair. "I guess I need to find an attorney."

"Maybe call Ridge and Kendall. I know they had a good attorney who helped them with the adoption."

"Good idea." She pulls her phone from her purse and dials her best friend. Kendall answers and she begins telling her what's going on.

I decide to call Ridge and fill him in. Before I get the chance, my phone rings. His ears must have been burning. "Hey, man."

"What's going on?"

"We got a call in the middle of the night to come to the hospital. Dawn's sister had a baby."

"No shit?"

"Yeah, but it's more than that. She skipped. She just fucking left," I say, keeping my voice low.

"What the fu— crap?" he says. "What's that mean?"

"Dawn's going to try and get custody. The baby is small, so damn tiny, could fit in the palm of my hand." I run my fingers through my hair. "I don't know how long the baby has to stay here, but I can't leave her alone."

"I wouldn't want you to. What do you need?"

"Honestly, right now, your attorney."

"Done. I'll text you and Dawn the number. You guys need anything?"

"I don't really know. We just drove down here first thing this morning and we weren't expecting this."

"How could you?"

"Yeah," I agree with him. "I'm going to be off for a few days at least."

"Done. Take the time you need. I've been there, brother. Dealt with the unexpected."

"Thanks, Ridge."

"Take care of your girl."

"Both of them," I say without thinking.

"Huh?"

"The baby, she's a little girl."

"Both of them," he agrees.

"Thanks. I'll keep you updated as I know more."

"Sounds good. We're here, man. Whatever you need."

"Appreciate it," I say, and end the call. Sliding my phone back in my pocket, I take a seat and watch Dawn pace back and forth in front of the window as she talks to Kendall.

"Thanks, Kendall," she says, and by the sound of her voice, she's fighting tears. "I'll let you know," she says, ending the call.

"Well?"

"She gave me their attorney's number. I'm going to call them now." She taps the screen of her phone and dials the number. After asking to speak with the attorney, she's put on hold and she's back to pacing. Back and forth. Back and forth. She doesn't stop until she begins to introduce herself and tell her story. I wait patiently, trying to decipher their conversation only hearing one side. "Really?" she asks, her voice hopeful. "Thank you. Thank you so much. Yes, yes. I'll see you then." She ends the call and looks at me with a smile.

"Well?"

"He's here, in Mason. He had a hearing, and he's at the courthouse. He wants me to meet him there now."

"Okay." I stand from my chair. "Let's go."

"No. Wait. We can't leave her here all alone. What if... what if Destiny comes back? I mean, I don't think she's stupid enough to do that, but we can't leave the baby here all alone."

"I'll stay."

"I-I'm sorry."

"Why are you apologizing? I'm here for you, and whatever you need. You want me to stay, I'll stay."

"Okay, and you're on the list as my fiancé," she says, and an embarrassed flush coats her cheeks.

"I'll stay here with the baby. I won't leave the nursery waiting room. You go, do what you need to do. She and I will be here when you get back."

"Mark, I— thank you."

"Come here." I hold my hand out for her and she places hers in mine, letting me pull her into my chest. Wrapping my arms around her, I comfort her in the only way I know how.

Touch.

"I should go. I don't want to keep him waiting." She stretches to press a kiss to my cheek and backs away. "I'll hurry."

"Go. Be safe and do what you need to do." With a nod, she's gone.

"How is she?" I ask the nurse when she comes out of the Authorized Only door. I've been sitting here in the waiting room for two hours. Every once in a while I go to the glass window and peer in at the babies. Baby Girl Miller has been there every time I checked until the last time I checked. That was about ten minutes ago. I was giving it five more minutes before I beat the door down to find out where she is.

"She's doing okay, considering."

"Where is she?" I stand. I'm an intimidating fucker with my height and my ink. I'm not against using it to make sure that little girl is safe.

"She's fussy. We have volunteers who hold the babies and rock them. She's coming down from the drugs, and well, she's struggling," she says sadly.

"What can we do?" I ask. I feel helpless at this point. That tiny baby girl is suffering. My girl is suffering and damn if I can fix it. I want to fix it and I can't. I don't know what she needs.

"Well, there is something."

"Anything."

"Babies, they need the comfort, and skin-to-skin contact is good for them. It calms them, stabilizes their breathing, their heart rate, and many other things."

"Okay, what does that mean exactly?" Skin-to-skin can mean a lot of different things. She's not my baby, so I'm not sure what the rules are. "I'm not her dad," I add as an afterthought.

She nods. "But you are approved to have contact with her."

"So what do I need to do?"

"We'd bring you in. Have you remove your shirt and hold the baby against your chest."

"That's it? I just hold her?"

"Yes."

"Let's do it."

"You sure?"

I give her a look, one that tells her not to question me. "Lead the way," I finally say. She turns and swipes her badge, opening the door, and I follow along behind her.

"We need you to remove your shirt and then wash up. Place these over your jeans." She hands me a pair of scrubs. "Once you're suited up, we'll move you to a small private room. Due to her condition, someone will stay with you. Do you have any questions?"

"Nope." I get to work stripping off my shirt and washing my arms. I go a step further and wash my chest as well. No way do I want to hurt her in any way. Once I'm done, I slip on the scrub pants and pull the booties on over my shoes. "Ready."

The nurse, whose name I still don't know, leads me through another door down a small hallway and pushes open another door. It's a small exam room. The lights are dim. There is a rocking chair in the corner and two other chairs on the opposite wall. "Have a seat. I'll bring the baby to you."

I debate on calling or texting Dawn to make sure she's okay with this, but they said it will help the baby, so I have to try. I'm sitting here helpless; it's the least that I can do.

"How do we do this?" I ask once the nurse is back, pushing the bed the baby girl is in.

"You'll need to be mindful of her tubes. I'll place her on your chest, and cover her with a blanket. All you need to do is hold on to her, and rock," she says as she lifts the baby from her bed.

"I can do that." I open my arms and wait as she lays her against my chest. My hand cradles her back, and it almost covers her entire body. "She's so damn tiny," I say as I lift half my hand and let her cover the baby, and then the other half.

"Just hold her close and rock her," the nurse says soothingly.

I start to rock slowly, pushing the chair with my feet. "I'm not sure what your aunt Dawn is going to call you, but I've had a lot of time to search the Internet today," I tell the baby. "Don't worry, we'll fill you in on what that is when you're a little older. Anyway, I was looking for names to call a baby girl, and the one that sticks out to me is Daisy. So, until Aunt Dawn chooses a name for you, I'm going to call you Daisy. You okay with that?" I ask her. She twitches in my arms and I freeze, halting the rocking and stare wide-eyed at the nurse.

"She's okay. That's her body reacting to the withdrawal. Just keep talking to her. It's soothing."

"I'm so sorry," I tell this innocent baby in my arms. With two fingers,

I gently rub her back as I continue to rock her. "So, Daisy," I say, clearing my thoughts, "that's my name for you. Aunt Dawn will give you a name that will be yours, and as unique as you are. I just hated calling you Baby Girl Miller. You're more than that," I explain like she actually understands me. "Daisies are beautiful flowers, my mom's favorite in fact. They symbolize new beginnings and that's what you are. A new chapter in our lives."

I'm so lost in my conversation with the baby, I didn't hear the door open. But when I hear sniffles, my head jerks up and I find Dawn standing with her hands over her chest, and tears coating her cheeks. The nurse, standing next to her with her hand on her shoulder, tears shimmer in her eyes as well.

"What happened?" I ask. I've seen enough of her tears to last me a lifetime.

"Nothing." She smiles and wipes at her cheeks. "I mean, something. The judge granted me guardianship. I have to have my place inspected before I can bring her home, but I'm allowed to make medical decisions for her, and I'm not worried about the inspection, so I get to bring her home. When she's ready," she adds.

"That's good news, baby." I look down at my chest. "You hear that, Daisy? Aunt Dawn is going to take good care of you." I turn my attention back to Dawn. "Why the tears?"

"You." She shakes her head. "You're an amazing man, Marcus Adams." She must read my confused expression because she laughs, a loud "throw your head back" laugh, which startles Daisy. "You're here, holding this tiny baby, talking to her, giving her a name all your own. I don't know any other man who would be here doing what you're doing right now."

I don't tell her that I know of four immediately, not to mention our fathers. "I hated to keep calling her—" She nods, cutting me off.

"I heard you tell her. I think it fits her."

"Yeah?"

"Yeah, Daisy it is."

"Wait. That's what you want to name her?"

"I do. I was already thinking a D name since that's what my parents did for Destiny and me, and your explanation of Daisy, I'm sold on the idea."

Something happens in my chest, almost as if my heart flips over. This little girl, this tiny bundle in my arms, she isn't mine, but she needs to be someone's. A flash of my life with her and Dawn, raising her as ours flashes through my mind.

"What is it you're doing?" Dawn asks, pulling me out of my thoughts.

"Oh, she— I'm sorry. I still don't know your name," I admit to the nurse.

"Lynn." She smiles.

"Right, Lynn said that skin-to-skin is good for her. Her heart and breathing," I explain.

Lynn picks up. "Skin-to-skin contact has proven to regulate body temperature, breathing, and heart rate. It's also been proven to relax the infant. She's had a rough afternoon, jerky, but she's only done it once since he's had her," Lynn explains.

"We've got this cuddling thing figured out, don't we, Daisy?" I ask the baby. I tear my eyes away from her to look at Dawn. "You want a turn?" I ask her.

She nods with tears in her eyes. "Yes."

Lynn jumps into action, leaving me alone with Daisy to get Dawn sorted. A few minutes later, Dawn's in the room wearing a gown. Carefully, since I'm carrying precious cargo, I stand and Lynn takes her from me. I watch as Dawn opens her gown, and Lynn rests the baby against her chest. Daisy jerks and a whimper comes from her tiny form. Dawn is quick to soothe her, running her hand gently over her back over the blanket.

"She's lucky to have both of you," Lynn says.

She steps away, and I take her place, kneeling next to my girls. That's what they are. Mine. Dawn has been mine, and by association, this baby girl will be as well. She already has her tiny fist wrapped around my heart. No matter what happens moving forward, I'll be there for both of them.

# Chapter 15

## Dawn

It's been four days since I got the call in the middle of the night that my drug-addicted sister had just given birth. Four days since she fled the hospital. Four days since she's been seen. Four days of watching her baby girl go through withdrawals. Four days of falling in love with a tiny human.

During the four days of living in this hospital, Mark hasn't left my side. He's been here every day and every night. I've been selfish needing him here with me, not wanting to go through this alone, but this is my new life. It's unexpected, but mine all the same.

"She's out," I tell Mark. He's sitting in the private room with Daisy on his chest. He's done this twice a day since we've been here. The doctors and nurses say her stats are great and she's gaining weight. They say they contribute these changes to us being here. That she knows she's loved.

"Good. I hate that she had such a rough night. I wish they would have come and gotten us."

I nod my agreement. I wish they would have too. The thought of her suffering causes a twinge in my chest. "Kendall's bringing me some more clothes," I tell him. She drove here that first day and brought us each a couple of changes, but I'm not leaving until Daisy does. I've already talked to my work and filed for family medical leave. Thankfully, I have some time, so I'll get paid for the time I'm off.

"Yeah, Ridge was stopping by my place to do the same."

"Mark." I sigh. This is not the first time we've had this conversation. "I can't thank you enough for being here with me, for helping me through these first few days. However, I know you have a life to get home to."

"Aunt Dawn is talking crazy again, Daisy girl," he says to my sleeping niece.

"Marcus," I playfully scold him and he chuckles.

"I'm where I'm supposed to be."

"Stubborn man," I grumble.

He chuckles. "She thinks I'm charming," he says to the sleeping baby.

"Knock, knock." Lynn sticks her head in the door. "Looks like Uncle Mark has the touch." She smiles when she sees that Daisy is nice and cozy against his chest.

"What can I say? The ladies love me." He grins.

"Well, how about we put her down so the two of you can go talk to your friends. They're just outside in the hallway waiting for you."

"Thank you, Lynn." She's been amazing. Hell, the entire hospital staff has been stellar and doing everything they can to help us. They even "overlook" the fact that we're practically living here. Not that we're the only ones to have ever done that, but they find us empty rooms to shower in, and when that's not available, they sneak us into the staff lounge. That feels like special treatment, but what do I know.

"All right, Daisy, we have to go see Aunt Kendall and Uncle Ridge, but we'll be back soon." He kisses the top of her tiny little head before standing and placing her in her bed. My heart stalls in my chest as I watch him with her.

There is nothing like seeing a man be affectionate with a child, and in this case, a tiny baby girl. Her pale complexion is a huge contrast to his dark tan and colorful ink. He handles her as if he's been doing it for years, not just a matter of days. I watch him as he places her in her bed and gently runs his finger over her forehead.

"You sure she doesn't need a blanket?" he asks Lynn as his brow furrows.

"I'm positive. The lights keep her nice and warm." He's asked this same question every day. The answer never changes, but that doesn't keep him from expressing his concern.

I walk to where he stands next to her bed. "We'll be back soon, sweetie," I tell my niece, clasping Mark's hand and pulling him from the room. We strip out of our scrubs and he pulls his T-shirt over his head before walking out to the hall to find Ridge and Kendall.

"Hey." Kendall rushes me. "How are you?"

"We're good. Daisy is growing and gaining weight. The skin-to-skin seems to be doing her a lot of good. Although she responds better to Mark than to me," I confess.

"Do you blame her?" Kendall laughs, and I can't help but crack a smile. "Come on, we brought lunch." She links her arm through mine and guides us to the waiting room at the end of the hall.

"What smells so damn good?" Mark asks from behind us.

"Margaret's," Kendall replies, and my mouth waters.

"I haven't eaten there since we move to Jackson."

"Me either."

"What's Margaret's?" Mark asks.

"This small little diner in town. They have the best homecooked food." I take in the small table that's set up, and my eyes mist with tears. I pull my best friend into a hug. "Thank you for this. For driving all this way to bring us clothes, twice in a week, for bringing us what's sure to be the best meal we've had in a week. I just— Thank you."

"We're family." She gives me a watery smile. "Now dig in."

That's exactly what we do. The four of us sit here at a small round table in the hospital waiting room and have lunch. We catch up on life, work, and the rest of our family. It's a nice break from the hospital food and the conversation of the medical staff.

"So, how's she doing?" Ridge asks.

"Great, man," Mark answers before I can. "She's gaining weight, and her vitals are stable. We've been doing that skin-to-skin thing and they say it's really helping her."

Kendall gives me a look, one I can't really decipher before it's gone. "Do you have pictures?" she asks.

"Of course we do," Mark says, and he and I both pull out our phones and start flipping through images.

"He's good with her," Kendall whispers, just for me.

"He is. He's been great." So great in fact I've been leaning on him too much.

"Cute, right?" I hear Mark say, which pulls my attention to him. He's still swiping through pictures on his phone.

"She's tiny," Ridge says, sitting back in his seat.

"Yeah, I was afraid I'd break her at first." Mark laughs.

"She's gaining weight, so that's good. She has to be five pounds and go three days without oxygen before I can take her home," I explain.

"At the rate she's going, it won't be long," Kendall replies.

I nod, answering a text from Amelia, and sliding my phone back in my pocket. She and I are not as close as she is with Kendall and Reagan, but I didn't grow up with them. However, she's been great reaching out to see if we need anything. That leads me to now, and I know Mark's not going to like what I have to say.

"So, Amelia should be here in a few hours. That means you can go home and get back to your life," I tell Mark from across the table.

He drops his napkin to the table and glares at me. "What are you talking about?"

"I know you don't want me here alone, and Amelia is still looking for a job. She just wrapped up her last temp job she was doing and volunteered to come and sit with me."

"We don't need her here."

"You're right," I agree with him. I hate that this is upsetting him, especially in front of our friends, but I needed them as a buffer. "I'm doing okay now. I can't tell you how much it means to me that you were here for me, but you have a job to get back to."

"As his boss, I've put him on indefinite family leave." Ridge leans back in his chair and crosses his arms over his chest.

Closing my eyes, I take a deep breath. I knew this was going to be a fight. "I appreciate that, I do," I tell Ridge, before turning my gaze to Mark. He's sitting the exact same way as Ridge, his arms crossed over his chest, gearing for an argument. "I couldn't have done this without you. You've been my rock since we've been here, and I'll never be able to tell you how much that means to me. I'll never be able to return that favor to you. I needed you and you were here, no questions asked." I pause to gather my thoughts. "I appreciate you, but I can't let you put your life on hold because my sister made bad choices. You have a job, bills to pay, family, friends. You need to go back to your life."

"I've told you, I'm where I'm supposed to be. And I could say the same for you. You have a job, bills to pay, and friends to come home to."

"I've taken a leave of absence."

"So have I," he counters.

"Mark," I sigh.

"Dawn," he mimics my tone.

"We're just going to clean this up and try to go sneak a peek at Daisy." Kendall stands and Ridge follows suit. They quickly gather our trash, toss it into the trash can, and disappear out of the room.

It's just the two of us.

"Why are you fighting me on this?"

"Why are you fighting me?" he challenges.

"This is something that I need to do. I need to learn to handle these kinds of situations on my own. I need to be able to take care of her. Me. I'm her legal guardian. I'm the one with a sister for a fuck-up. I'm the one now responsible for a little girl who has no one else. That's all on me. Not you. You didn't sign up for this."

"Neither did you."

"She's the only family I have left."

"Really? Am I not your family?"

"You know what I mean," I say, exasperated.

"No, actually, I don't know what you mean. What I'm hearing is that I'm nothing to you. That we're not building a life together. That you want to do it all on your own. What about what I want? What about me, Dawn?"

"You're such a good man," I say softly. "You're honorable and dependable, and I know you well enough to know that you will never walk away from us."

"You're damn right. Why would I?"

"Because we're not yours," I whisper the words to hide the crack in my voice. Although the crack in my heart is just as loud, I'm sure he can hear it from across the table.

His face turns to stone. "That may be," he says, his voice gruff, "but you, and that little girl in there, you're mine. I might not be yours, but you're mine and I want to be here."

Oh, God. I knew this was going to be hard, but I never imagined this is how things would end up. I don't want to push him away. I just want him to go back to his normal life. I don't want my sister's actions to control his future too. "Go home, Mark." The words taste sour in my mouth.

"You can't make me leave."

"I can. I'm going to remove you from the list. You won't be able to have access to her. There is no reason for you to stay."

"What the fuck?" He stands, his chair flying back to hit the wall. "Why are you doing this? Why are you pushing me away?"

He knows me too well. "It's better this way. You need to go back to life as a single guy. You didn't sign up for a girlfriend with an infant niece she's responsible for, who's coming off her mother's addiction to pills."

"I signed up for you," he says. His voice is deathly calm, but his hands that are fisted at his sides and the tic in his jaw tells a different story.

"It wasn't supposed to be this way."

"That's life, Dawn. It's messy and complicated, but that doesn't change how I feel about you."

I see Ridge, Kendall, and Amelia through the glass heading toward us. "Please, just go," I say, rushing out of the room. I hear Kendall and Mark both call out for me, but I don't stop. I keep going until I'm in the bathroom at the other end of the hall.

"Hey." Amelia approaches me where I stand with my hands braced against the sink, head hanging down as I try to hide my tears. "What happened back there?"

I look up at her and a sob breaks from my chest. "I'm in love with him."

She nods. "Then why are you pushing him away?"

"Because I love him. He didn't sign up for this. My fucked-up family, my fucked-up life. He deserves to find a woman he can have kids with, not a ready-made family with a little girl who could have a host of issues due to her mother's drug use. It's going to be hard, and I can't ask him to stick around for that."

"Did you ask him?"

"What?" I wipe the tears from my eyes.

"Did you ask him? Did you say 'Mark, I need you to stay?'"

"No, of course not. I mean, yes, I asked him to come here with me that night. I thought I was seeing my sister and her baby for the first time. Thought I would say hello and we could go back to our lives. That all changed the minute my sister skipped out."

"I know. I'm sorry that you're going through this so soon after losing your parents. If anyone knows what you're going through, it's me."

"How could you possibly?" I scoff.

"Let's just say life is complicated, and I've learned firsthand how that messes with you. I can also see that you're hurting yourself and him, for no reason. He wants to be here."

"Okay, I'll give you that," I say, wiping more tears as they fall. "But what about a month from now? What happens when he wants to go out and I can't because Daisy is having a bad day, or I don't have a sitter? What happens when he wants to spend the day lazily in bed, and she's sick or crying or... I don't know... anything? The life we had is not the same. Not anymore."

"I get that. I do. However, did you give him the chance to choose?" she questions.

"No. You know him. Hell, all five of them. They're honorable and dependable and he would never walk away from me."

"I agree with you, but I think you have it wrong. Sure, he's honorable and dependable and I agree with you that all five of them, the group, they've been thick as thieves my entire life. They're the kind of guys you want forever with. Which is why I'm baffled that you're doing this, but even more so—" She pauses, shaking her head. "Even more so, that man loves you, Dawn. He loves you and you're ripping his heart out. He's not here because he's honorable or dependable. He's here because his heart tells him this is where he needs to be."

"I love him too much to let him stay." Pulling a tissue from the box on the counter, I blow my nose and wipe my eyes. "Thank you for being here. I needed someone here or else I know he'll never leave. Once he's gone, you can go. Thank you for making the drive and being here. I know you don't understand it, and honestly, I'm not sure that I do either. What I do know is that this hurts. The only other time I've felt this kind of loss was lo-losing my parents." I choke back a sob. "I have to do this now before he does it later."

"You're making a mistake."

"I know. He's never going to forgive me, and my heart, it won't either." Tossing my tissue in the trash, I wash my hands and walk out the door. I don't look for him, or for Kendall or Ridge; instead, I go straight to the nursery, knock on the door, and wait for them to let me in. I change into my hospital-issued attire and go sit next to Daisy's bed. The tears flow freely. I know this is a mistake. Nothing that makes your heart hurt this bad is a good idea, but I love him too much to saddle him with this.

I just wish I would have told him how much I love him before I forced him to leave.

# Chapter 16

## MARK

What the fuck just happened? One minute we're laughing and showing off Daisy's cuteness, and the next, she's telling me to leave. Telling me I can't see either of them anymore.

"Did that just happen?" I ask, staring after her as she races down the hall and disappears into the bathroom.

I feel Ridge's hand land on my shoulder in silent support. "She's scared," Kendall defends.

"Of what? Of me?" I blanch at her words.

"Yes, but not the way you're thinking. She's afraid of needing you."

"I want her to need me."

Kendall's eyes soften. "I know you do, but she's been through a lot these past few months. She lost her parents at the hands of her sister, and now here she is again, in this situation because of her sister. She thinks she's bringing you down with her. She's afraid that if she leans on you too much, that when you walk away, it'll break her. Not just break her heart, Mark. It will break her. She won't come back from that and she has to stay strong for that little girl in there."

"Did she tell you that?" I ask.

"She didn't have to. She's my best friend."

"I love her. I'm not leaving her."

Kendall nods. "I know that too. She needs time to process what she just did. She's scared. She's going to be a mom to a baby who was born to a drug-addicted mother. That's a huge undertaking. We're her only support system. While you and I know that's enough, that we are here for whatever she needs, she sees it differently. She sees it as her responsibility and that she has herself to rely on."

"She has me." I slam my hand against my chest, trying like hell to keep my voice calm, remembering where I am.

"I'm glad to hear that."

"What?" I ask, confused. I look over at Ridge. "Are the women in our lives losing their damn minds?" Ridge chuckles.

"She's going to realize what she did was wrong. She's going to realize that she made a mistake. I'm glad to hear that you're going to fight for her."

"How do I do that, Kendall? How do I fight for them when she's pushing me away? She said I couldn't see Daisy. She needs me. The skin-to-skin thing, that helps her and I know she knows my voice," I say, trying to control my emotions.

Kendall steps forward and wraps her arms around me. "I love how you love her," she whispers.

"I can't leave them here," I confess, wrapping my arms around her.

"Then don't," Ridge speaks up.

"She said she was taking me off the list. I can't see Daisy, and she won't see me."

"She was saying whatever she needed to push you away."

"So, what do I do?"

"Get a room," Ridge says. "You stay here close by."

"Hey." Amelia approaches.

"How is she?"

"Broken."

I nod.

"She's not thinking clearly, and when she finally does, she's going to have some regrets. Namely you," Amelia says pointedly.

"Help me." My voice is pleading.

"You're staying?" she asks. I'm sure she overheard our conversation.

"Yeah, I'm going to get a room nearby."

"Okay, I'll have her do the same. Make sure you're in separate hotels."

"And?" I ask, hope bubbling inside.

"And I'll convince her to let us take shifts. She knows she's not keeping me from anything, so when she goes to the room to sleep, I'll call you."

"Will they let me see her?"

"I'm sure they will. If she does take you off the list, use your Mark Adams charm."

"You mean his brooding 'give me my way' charm?" Ridge jokes.

I crack a smile. Fucker. He's no more sunshine and roses than I am unless it's his wife and kids.

"Okay. So, I come here to see Daisy when Dawn's not around? The staff is going to be suspicious."

"So you tell them the truth."

"And they kick me out," I counter.

Amelia shrugs. "They've seen you with the baby, and with Dawn. Explain her losses, and they're already aware of the situation with the baby's mom. I think you're good."

"So what? I just visit the baby and never see Dawn? I hate this idea."

"It's the best I've got. She's going to need you. She's going to crack and you're going to be close by when that happens."

"How do you know?" I ask.

A haunted look comes over her. "Let's just say I had a friend, in college, that had some medical issues. She did something similar. She regretted it."

"Mara?" Kendall inquires.

"No, but that girl, she's been through her fair share of heartbreak."

"What do you have to lose?" Ridge asks. "You don't want to leave, and you know the baby is responding to you. You hang out, visit when you can, and be ready."

"And if she never changes her mind?" I ask. That's the issue here. We're going on the assumption that she regrets pushing me away. And no matter how much I want to believe that, my heart is also cracked wide open and bleeding from her words. I'm not convinced she's going to change her mind.

"Then you know you've done all that you can," Kendall says. "I've known her since our freshman year of college. She's always been independent. Hell, she moved to Jackson with me, away from her family. Sure, she wanted to get away from the drama that was her sister, and now she has to live with that. She has to live with the fact that she left and wasn't here." She swallows hard. "She loves you, Marcus. I promise you that. She's just been through hell and back and she's trying to brace herself for the impact of this latest fall."

"Come on. We'll get you a room, and get you settled in," Ridge tells me. "Amelia, we're going to grab you and Dawn a room as well. Kendall will text you the details."

"I'll handle it," Amelia assures me.

"Thank you." I give her a hug. "Take care of them for me," I whisper, before letting her go. Then I turn and walk out of the hospital. I thought the day I walked back out these doors, Dawn and Daisy would be with me.

Lying on this bed in my hotel room feels wrong. The bed's too soft, and the room's too quiet. I've grown accustomed to the chairs in the hospital waiting room, and the constant hustle and bustle of the medical staff and visitors. I miss her. I miss both of them.

Amelia texted me about an hour ago and said that she finally convinced Dawn to go to the room and get a good night's sleep. She's taking the night shift with Daisy. So, here I am, waiting for the message that tells me I can come back to the hospital. I have one more hurdle to jump, and that's convincing the staff not to tell Dawn about my visits and to still let me snuggle Daisy.

Needing a distraction, I pick up my phone and dial my mom. "Hey, honey, is everything okay?" she asks immediately.

"No."

"Marcus, what's going on?" Her voice is soft and filled with concern.

"It's been a week," I say, and then proceed to fill her in on everything that's happened up to this point.

"Wow. Your dad said he texted you about borrowing some tool and that you were in Jackson with Dawn's new niece. We had no idea."

"I'm sorry. I should have called and explained, but it's been a rough few days."

"I get that, but that doesn't explain the sadness I hear in your voice. You said the baby, Daisy, that she's doing well? I love that name," she says.

"She is. She's gaining weight and her vitals are strong. And as far as her name…" I explain to her how I was searching for a cute name to call her, and when I saw Daisy and considered the meaning, doubled with the fact that it was my mom's favorite, I started calling her that. "Then Dawn, she loved the name. It goes with the D theme that her parents used for her and her sister. I guess that's what she's naming her. I don't know about her middle name. I assume her last name will be Miller. Destiny wasn't married, at least not that we're aware of. She was checked into the hospital as Miller."

"It's a beautiful name," she says, and I can hear the smile in her voice.

"Am I messing up here, Mom? Should I just come home?" I can't help but feel as though I'm betraying Dawn.

"Only you can decide that."

"Tell me from a woman's perspective."

"Well, it sounds to me as if Dawn is letting her head rule her heart. She's been through so much, and I can't blame her for not thinking clearly."

"Would you be pi— ticked off when you found out?"

She's quiet and I'm starting to worry what her answer will be. "Honestly, I can't say. I can tell you that she knows you and knows the kind of man you are. You're not trying to hurt her or the baby. I think she'll see that."

"I hope so."

"Hey, why don't Dad and I come up there tomorrow? We'll grab lunch and visit for a while."

"Yeah, that sounds great, Mom. I'll text you my hotel info."

"Give that baby girl a kiss for me," she says, ending the call.

I drop my phone on the bed, but it rings immediately.

Amelia.

"Hey," I greet her.

"Took me some time, but I finally convinced her to go shower and sleep in a bed for a few hours. I don't know how long you have, but I told her to text me before she comes back, that the hospital coffee might not cut it. That's the best I can do for a warning."

"Thank you, Amelia. I'm on my way there now." Grabbing my coat from the chair, I make sure I have my room key and I'm out the door.

I don't know why that little girl tethers me to her the way she does, but it kills me to think that she misses me. That she wonders where the man who has been a constant this week has gone. Do babies even know these things? Regardless, I know, and I need to be there for her, for both of them. I just hope Dawn comes to her senses soon.

It didn't take much to talk the nursing staff into letting me see Daisy. As Kendall and Amelia suspected, Dawn hadn't removed me from the authorized list. I only got a few short hours with her before Amelia got a text saying that Dawn was on her way back. Even though my time was short, my heart felt lighter. I knew Dawn got some much-needed rest, and hopefully some food, and Daisy, well, my little snuggle buddy was having a good night. Her jerking was getting less and less. Her crying has increased, though. They tell me she's colicky. I'm not really sure what that means, but apparently, when she's skin-to-skin, it soothes her. I'm glad she was able to get a couple of hours rest with me, and I'm sure Dawn will do the same.

My girls are getting what they need.

I went back to my room and was able to catch some sleep, and now I'm in the hotel lobby waiting for my parents to arrive. I'm watching the door when I spot them. They're wheeling a luggage cart with a big white box on it.

"What in the hell are they doing?" I mutter to myself.

Mom sees me and waves, a smile on her face. "Come here," she says when they stop next to the couch I'm sitting on. I stand and bend down, wrapping her in a hug.

"Hey, Dad." I give him a one-armed hug as well. "What is that?" I ask, barely able to contain my amusement.

"Oh, this is a car seat and the stroller came with it. You're going to need this, or Dawn is to bring Daisy home. We just wanted to help," Mom rambles.

My dad looks at her with his heart in his eyes. It's always been this way between them. Keith and Theresa Adams have a love for the storybooks. Met in high school, married right after graduation. Not long after Meghan came along. The rest, as they say, is history.

"Yeah, I'm guessing there's going to be a lot that she needs. We haven't really thought further than just getting her well enough to come home." At least I haven't. Maybe Dawn has and she just hasn't said anything. I mean, she did push me out of their lives without me having any idea it was coming.

"Thanks. I'll uh, I'll keep it in my room, you know, until she's ready."

"Have you seen her today?" Mom asks.

"No, I did go over there last night. Dawn went to the hotel to shower and sleep, but she was only gone a couple of hours."

"You think she knows you're still in town?" Dad asks.

"No, not unless one of the nurses have slipped up and said something. Amelia is Team Mark, well, Team Mark and Dawn, so I know she's not going to say anything. Not until she thinks Dawn is ready to hear it."

"Right, well, let's get this up to your room, and then we can grab some lunch."

"Thanks, I'll run it upstairs and meet you guys in the restaurant." I point across the lobby to the hotel restaurant.

"Sounds good, son," Dad says, slipping his arm around my mom and heading in that direction.

I push the cart onto the elevator and ride to the third floor. My room is just down the hall and to the right. I leave the cart in the hallway, and grab the box, placing it on the small table in my room. The image on the box is now facing me. It's pink and dark gray, with small pink and white daisies etched onto the fabric. I've never been an overly emotional man.

I love my friends, my family, but getting choked up, that shit's not something I do. However, here I am swallowing back the lump in my throat. She's not even a week old and that little girl has wormed her way into my heart. Just like her aunt.

Dawn says I didn't sign up for this and she's right. I didn't, but that doesn't mean I don't want it. That I don't want them. That little girl needs someone in her corner, a man to show her how a woman should be treated, how she should be loved, and Dawn, well, she already knows. That man is me and I'm not going to stop fighting.

For either of them.

An idea begins to form, and I fire off a text to Reagan and Kendall.

**Me:** *I need your help.*

**Reagan:** *I'm in.*

**Kendall:** *Anything.*

Sliding my phone back in my pocket, I head back downstairs to my parents. I'm going to need Mom's help as well. I told Dawn that I would always be there to catch her. Actions speak louder than words, and I'm about to be real fucking loud.

# Chapter 17

## Dawn

I have to admit, a hot shower, and a soft bed did me some good. Though, I slept maybe an hour. I couldn't seem to shut my mind off from what I'd done. Pushing Mark away felt like the right thing to do, but now being here without him, it feels wrong. All of it.

"She's awake," Mary, the nightshift nurse, says from the doorway of the waiting room.

"Thanks, Mary." I stand and follow her back to the nursery. When I got here during the early morning hours when sleep evaded me, they told me she was resting peacefully and had been for a few hours. I nodded, peeked in on her, and then went to the waiting room. The small yellow room felt cold and empty without Mark.

Just like my heart.

Robotically, I scrub up and slip into a gown and the hospital-provided scrub pants. By the time I'm done, Mary has Daisy in her arms ready and waiting for me. "She had a good night, and she's gained another ounce," she says, handing her to me once I've settled into the rocking chair. She helps me settle the baby against my bare chest and covers her with a blanket. It's one of those hospital-issued ones, not soft like those the twins have. No, these seem… impersonal. That brings together another set of issues. This little sweet pea is going to need so much. Pushing that out of my mind for now, I dip my head and breathe her in.

She smells like Mark.

I know that's not the case, but I swear I can smell him on her. A musky, woodsy scent that is uniquely him mixed with sweet baby girl. Even though my senses are messing with me, it's comforting. I can pretend that I didn't push the man I love away for reasons that I know are half-assed at best. I don't want him to feel like he has to be here. I want him to have that carefree life he was living before we got that phone call in the middle of the night. Shaking out of my thoughts, I focus on Daisy.

"You think she can come home soon?" I ask Mary.

"She's doing wonderful and gaining weight like a champ. Hopefully soon," she says, not really committing.

"You hear that, Daisy? You're doing so well, and soon we'll be out of here. It's just you and me, kid." She's snoozing away, not a care in the world, and that's how it should be. Her tremors and jerks are so much better, and I pray that she's one of the lucky ones. That she's able to make it through what my sister did to her. I'll do everything I can to keep her safe and away from my sister. However, with her little disappearing act, it looks as though she couldn't care less what happens to her daughter. She knew Dawn was coming and bailed, leaving her to pick up the pieces. I guess at least she called. Thinking of this little girl with no one here for her, it's a thought that would bring anyone to their knees.

I rock her for as long as they'll let me before going back to the waiting room. I almost expect to see Mark there waiting for me, but I know better. I pushed him away and broke both of our hearts. I just… I don't know what I'm doing. I have this tiny human that depends on me, and then I have him. I love him with everything I am, but I was too damn chicken to tell him, and now, now he'll never know. My phone buzzes in my purse.

**Amelia:** *Just woke up, you need anything.*

**Me:** *No, thank you.*

**Amelia:** *Can you talk?*

**Me:** *Yeah.*

A few seconds later, my phone is ringing. "Hey," I greet her.

"How's she doing this morning?"

"Good. She gained another ounce."

"That's great news," she replies.

"It is. Hopefully I can take her home soon."

"Mark called," she informs me.

"I assumed he would. How is he?" Part of me doesn't want to hear it and the other part wants any little morsel of information I can get about him.

"He's hurting. He misses you."

I sigh. "I miss him too."

"Then why?"

"I don't want to hold him back."

"Look. I know you're coming from a good place. Trust me, I do. I also know from experience that pushing those that you love away is hard on everyone involved, and really, all it does is cause unnecessary pain."

"Want to talk about it?" I ask her.

"No. We're talking about you."

"Is this where you tell me I'm making a mistake and that I'll never be able to forgive myself?"

"No. This is where I give you the facts, and I just did that. I'm not in the position to pass judgment. We are all entitled to our feelings and we all deal with them in our own ways."

"I-I didn't expect that."

"We all have shit in our lives, Dawn. We deal with it the best that we can. With that being said, I'll also tell you that Mark loves you. I don't know if he's said the words, but regardless, it's true."

"I miss him," I confess.

"Then call him. He'll be right there."

"I know he would be. I just need to think about why I pushed him away. Even to me my reasons seem farfetched."

She laughs. "Always when it comes to the heart."

"You seem like you're speaking from personal experience yet again." I know she's hiding something, but I'm the new girl, so I don't know if she'll open up to me.

"Yeah," she says softly. "Let's just say that I was once presented with a situation that both wrecked me and scared the hell out of me. I pushed. I ran, and looking back, I know that wasn't the best of choices."

"I'm here for you."

"I know. I appreciate that. Things are good, and I'm back on track, which I know sounds cryptic as hell." She chuckles. "Right now, let's worry about you, that baby girl, and Mark. Oh, and food. I'm going to grab a shower and bring you some lunch."

"Thank you, Amelia. I truly can't tell you how much you being here means. You can head home when you're ready. I just… I knew he would never leave if he thought he was leaving me here all alone."

"No thanks needed. That's what friends are for, and you're right. He wouldn't have left." Her voice sounds funny, but I don't question it. "I'll see you soon." The line goes dead, and instead of putting my phone back in my purse, I send an olive branch to Mark. I tell myself it's because he deserves to know since he's been here from that first night. To be honest, I just miss him.

**Me:** *Daisy gained another ounce.*

His reply is immediate.

**Mark:** *That's my girl. We'll have her home in no time.*

*We'll.* He has no way of knowing what that word does to me, or how badly I wish that he's our future. He probably doesn't even realize how he said it.

**Me:** *I hope so.*

**Mark:** *Say the word and I'm there, Dawn. I miss you. Both of you.*

Tears prick my eyes. I miss him so much my heart aches.

> **Me:** *I miss you too.*

> **Mark:** *Does that mean I can come back?*

I smile through my tears.

> **Me:** *How about you take a few days, then we can talk again? I won't keep you from the hospital, but I needed you to get back to your life.*

> **Mark:** *You're my life.*

Oh. My. God.

> **Me:** *Can we talk? In a few days? Just give us both some time?*

I don't know what I'm saying. I'm letting my heart rule when I need to be listening to my head. He needs to move forward. However, I can't help but think about what Amelia said. She pushed away too and the regret in her voice was tangible. I think a few days for both of us will be good. He can see that being away from us is not as bad as he thinks and me, well, I know it's bad.

I'm feeling his absence everywhere I look. If he still wants to be here in a few days, if he's still just as adamant that he wants to be a part of this, I'm going to let him. He deserves the right to make his own choices. I had no right to take that away from him, but fear does crazy things to you. The fear of needing him and then him leaving. The fear of loving him so completely that my heart will never recognize another.

> **Mark:** *I don't need a few days, but if that's what it takes to see you.*

> **Me:** *Thank you.*

> **Mark:** *Give her a kiss from me, and this one's for you.*

He adds a row of kiss emojis and I can't help but smile.

> **Me:** *Will do.*

I'm sure it's not what he was hoping for, but I need to give him these next few days. Give him time to think and ponder.

"Who's putting that smile on your face?" Lynn asks.

"Mark," I tell her honestly.

She nods. "He's one of the good ones."

"You think so?"

"Oh, honey." She laughs. "If you could see the way he looks at you and that little girl in there. How many men do you know would do what he's done for her?"

The guys in our small group flash through my mind. "Maybe a few, but they're his best friends." I shrug.

"Are any of them single?" she asks.

"Two of them are."

"How many are there?"

"Five."

"Do they all look like Mark?"

"Pretty much."

"Damn." She laughs.

"You have no idea."

"So, you said only two are single, that must mean that you're not letting him go so easily."

"I don't want to, but he's a single guy who until a week ago was dating a single girl with no baggage. I'm no longer that girl." I don't know why I'm pouring my heart out to this stranger. Then again, she's giving excellent care to Daisy and has been with us this week. She's no longer a stranger in my eyes. She's just… an outsider maybe.

"See, that's where you're wrong. He's not a single guy. You said it yourself. He's a man, dating a woman that he obviously cares about. Let him decide."

"Then what happens when he leaves?"

"Then you know." She shrugs. "You can live your life always worried about what's around the next corner. I know you've been through a lot with just recently losing your parents, and now this, but you have to remember something. Your life is what you make it. You have to fight for what you want, and live each day as if it's your last. You're going to fall, and most of the time, you're not going to expect it. You have to let those around you catch you until you can stand on your own two feet again."

I wipe the tears from my eyes. "Anyone ever tell you you're a smart woman?"

She laughs. "Helping people is what I do." She points to her badge that tells me she's a registered nurse. "It's easy to give advice to those you're not emotionally connected to. I can see the forest through the trees, so to speak."

"Thank you, Lynn."

"You're welcome. Now, here comes your lunch." She nods over my shoulder as Amelia approaches.

"Everything okay?" Amelia asks.

"Yeah, just someone else reminding me what a fool I'm being when it comes to Mark."

She nods. "Good. He's blowing my phone up worried about the two of you. He's a needy man when it comes to you," she says, making us all laugh.

The rest of the afternoon, Amelia and I cuddle with Daisy, and although she protests, I send her to the room that night. Sure, a hot shower and a soft bed are enticing, but I know I'll just sit and kick my own ass for being so stupid with Mark. When he calls again in a few days and wants to come to us, I'm going to let him.

Then, I'm going to tell him I love him.

Let the cards fall where they may.

# Chapter 18

## MARK

I spent the day with Mom and Dad putting my plan in motion. They were both a huge help, especially Mom. I sent Kendall and Reagan a text keeping them in the loop. I wouldn't be able to pull this off without everyone's help. I'm pushing the keycard into my door at the hotel having just said goodbye to my parents when my phone rings. "Hey, A," I say to Amelia.

"She's not leaving."

"What?" I ask, stepping into the room and tossing my room key on the small dresser.

"She's not going back to the hotel tonight. She told me to."

"Damn."

"Yeah, I'm not seeing her leaving there often enough for you to come by. I'm sorry, Mark."

"I should have guessed that this would happen."

"She's a stubborn one that woman of yours."

I laugh. "Don't I know it. That's why I'm in this situation."

"Give it a few days."

"Yeah, actually, I've been working on something. I think I'll head home tonight. At least at home I'll be able to be productive."

"I'd say that's a good call on your part. I plan on staying. I don't have anything going on really, and she needs the support."

"Thank you, Amelia. Keep me updated if there's anything I need to know?"

"You got it. Drive safe."

"Thanks." I end the call and quickly pack up my room, and head downstairs to check out. Once I'm in my car, I fire off a text to Mom and the girls letting them know what's going on and that I'm on my way home. Then I call Ridge.

"What's up?" he answers.

"I'm coming home."

"What? Why?"

"She's not taking shifts. Amelia says she doubts she'll leave long enough for me to sneak in another visit."

"I'd say you're right. She probably only left the first time to get herself under control from pushing you away."

"Ridge? Is that you?" I ask, laughing.

"Fuck off. My wife has a theory and I happen to agree with her."

"Oh, yeah, care to enlighten me on the rest of this theory?" I'm hoping it's the same as mine—she's scared. My plan could backfire, but at least I'll know I fought for her.

"She's having a tough time" is his reply.

Kendall is her best friend, well, outside of me. I'd like to think I take that top spot. "I know." I sigh.

"She's overwhelmed and worried about everyone and everything she loves, what she has left. However, my wife also thinks that this plan of yours is going to work."

"Yeah?"

"Yep. I have to admit it's a good one."

My fingers are crossed. "Hey, so I'll be in town this week, at least for a couple of days. You need me on site?"

"No, actually, we're supposed to get rain all day tomorrow, so we're out if that happens."

"Okay, well, keep me updated."

"We get rain, we'll be at your place. Help you get things in order."

"Appreciate, man. I'll talk to you soon."

We end the call, and I get lost in my thoughts as I make the drive home. It's only a couple of hours, but it gives me time to sort through everything in my head. I have a clear vision of what needs to be done. Now it's time to set the strings in motion.

It's been one hell of a week. Each day Amelia checked in letting me know that Dawn was staying at the hospital. I threw myself into my plans for winning her back. I finished up late last night with the help of our friends and family. Now, I'm headed back to Mason. She said give it a few days and it's been a week today since I've seen her. That's too damn long, so I'm going to her.

We've texted off and on this week, but it's been seven long days since I've heard her voice or held either of them in my arms. Time's up. I'm prepared and ready for a fight.

My first stop is the hotel. This time, it's the one where she and Amelia have been staying. "Staying" is putting it lightly when it comes to Dawn. Amelia convinces her to leave the hospital to shower, but she always comes right back. I'm staying at the same place. I'm not hiding that I'm here. She needs to know that I'm not giving up. That she can push as much as she wants, I'm going to push right back. At least as long as I still see the love in her eyes. When she can look at me without it appearing like she's tearing her own heart out and tell me that she no longer wants me in her life, then I'll accept defeat. I'll always love her, but I'll let her go.

The drive is uneventful, and I spend the majority of my time planning my speech to win her back. Check-in at the hotel is a breeze since I already had a reservation. I dump my bags and rush back out the door to the hospital. I'm just walking through the main entrance when my phone rings. Glancing at the screen, ready to send whoever it is to voice mail, I stop when I see Dawn's name. It's like she read my mind.

"Hey, beautiful," I greet her.

"Mark." She sobs the word and I take off running to the elevators.

"Dawn, baby? What's wrong?" I jab the button for the elevator, willing it to open faster. Finally, the doors slide open. "Dawn, I might lose you, but I'm almost there. I just got onto the elevator."

"You're here?" she asks.

"Yeah, baby. Where are you?"

"The nursery." She sniffs.

"Okay. I'm coming to you. I'll be right there," I say, but silence greets me. "Fuck." I shove my phone back into my pocket and watch the numbers climb, praying that it takes me straight to the top floor. Luck is on my side, and as soon as the doors open to the top floor, I'm jogging out and down the hall. When I reach the nursery, Dawn is coming out of the door, tears streaking down her face.

My heart thunders in my chest from both adrenaline and fear. I open my arms and she rushes into me. I hold her close as tears continue to fall from her eyes. "Baby, you have to tell me what's wrong," I urge. Her grip on the back of my shirt tightens as her cries grow louder.

"I can help," Lynn says. "Come with me." She motions for us to walk down the hall and into a room that says Staff.

Dawn has a tight grip on me, and I'm lucky I got her to move down the hall, so we stand, declining Lynn's offer to sit. "Is it Daisy?" I ask Lynn. My mind races with the possibilities of what could have happened.

She shakes her head. "Dawn got a call from the Emergency Room about fifteen minutes ago. Seems her sister has been brought in for a drug overdose."

*Motherfucker.* I tighten my arms around her. "You don't have to go see her," I whisper to Dawn.

"I-I have to. I'm her next of kin," she mumbles into my shirt. "I hate her, Mark. I hate my sister and I know that's a terrible thing to say." She pulls away and sad eyes peer up at me. "I hate her."

"I know, babe." I kiss her forehead. What I want to say is that I hate her too. I hate her for causing the accident that killed their parents. I hate her for what she did to the little girl who's stuck in this hospital because she didn't care enough to take care of herself and her unborn child. I hate her for everything she's done to Dawn. Everything she's put her through.

"How's Daisy?" I ask.

A small smile tilts her lips. "She's growing and doing so well."

"Good. Let's go down to the ER, see what's going on. She's safe here." I look to Lynn who nods.

"I'm not leaving her side. The ER has already called up to us, letting us know birth mom is in house. I promise you she's going to be fine."

"Let's go." With my arm around her shoulders, I lead Dawn to the elevators, hitting the button for the bottom floor where the ER is located.

"I don't know how much more I can take," Dawn whispers on the ride down. "I don't know how to help her."

Not knowing what to say to that, I don't say anything. When the elevator doors open, the chaos that is the ER greets us. Making our way to the receptionist desk, we ask for Destiny.

"Dawn," a masculine voice says from behind us.

Turning, we see a guy who's about six foot, thin as a rail, and has sunken eyes. His hair is a greasy mess, and his clothes look like it's been weeks, maybe longer since they've been cleaned.

"C-Cal? What are you doing here?" Dawn asks. I feel her stiffen beside me.

"I brought Dest. She wasn't acting right," he says, his head twitching. His eyes roam all around the room as if he's nervous to be here.

"Not acting right?" Dawn asks. "She fucking overdosed, you idiot. What did you give her?"

"Just a few pills. She was hurting from that kid. Just gave her something to take the edge off."

"That kid is upstairs fighting the effects of the drugs her mother did while pregnant," she seethes.

"Fuck, I thought it was dead. She didn't tell me."

Dawn freezes. "Are you...? Is the baby yours?" she asks.

"Nah, not this one."

"What do you mean not this one?"

"She got rid of one a couple of years ago, said it was mine. This one though, it's hard to tell. She's been around, doing ah... favors to get what she needs. Right out of rehab she was jonesing for a fix."

"Oh my God." Dawn breathes the word.

"What?" He raises his hands in a "what do you do" manner. "You know how it is."

"Leave," I say, my voice low and deadly.

"Hey." He backs up. "I don't want no trouble."

"Now."

"I'll just be over here. She owes me, and I ain't leaving until I collect."

With more calm than I feel, I guide Dawn to the waiting room, and just so happen to see an officer. He catches my eye, and I nod toward the jackass we were just talking to where he sits in the corner of the room. Eyes still wild and roaming. When he sees the officer, he stands but doesn't move. I would remember him anywhere. He's strung out, looking a hell of a lot worse than the last time I saw him, but I remember him. The day he showed up at Kendall and Dawn's apartment with the letter from Melissa. I can't believe he's the one who has been supplying Destiny with pills. When they say it's a small world, they really mean it.

"The family of Destiny Miller," a nurse calls out.

Together, we stand and walk to the door. "Destiny is my sister," Dawn says.

The nurse nods. "Come with me. The doctor would like to speak with you." Quietly, we follow behind her. "Have a seat," she says, once we're in a small private room. There is nothing in here but four chairs. It's small and uninviting.

"I have a bad feeling," Dawn says.

I do too, but I don't tell her that. "Come here." I pull her chair closer to mine and lace our fingers together.

"How did you get here so fast?"

"I was coming to see you. I couldn't stay away any longer."

She wipes a tear from her eye before it has the chance to fall. "I've missed you, Mark."

"I've missed you too, Pixie. Daisy too."

"I'm sorry. I'm so sorry for pushing you away."

"I'm here, where I want to be. That's all that matters. We'll figure the rest out. Just don't shut me out again."

"Never." She shakes her head adamantly. "If this is where you want to be, with me and Daisy, we want you here too. More than anything I want you here."

I cup her face in my hands. "This is not where or how I wanted to do this, but I'm not letting another chance pass me by. I love you, Dawn. I want a life with you, whatever that is, however it looks, whatever it turns out to be. I want that. I want it with you."

She loses her battle with her tears. I'm not sure if it's from where we are or if it's from my admission. My guess is a little of both. "I love you too. So much," she says, just as there's a knock at the door.

"Hi, I'm Dr. Travis." He extends his hand to Dawn and then me.

"We've met," Dawn says sadly. "You were working the night my parents passed. Car accident," she adds.

"I'm sorry for your loss," he says kindly.

"Thank you. How's my sister?"

He shakes his head and I know we're in for another round of devastation. I can feel it. "I'm sorry. We did all that we could do. Her heart stopped. We weren't able to bring her back."

"W-What?" Dawn asks.

"I'm so sorry," Dr. Travis replies.

She nods. "So, what does that mean for her daughter?"

Recognition crosses his face. I'm sure Daisy's case is well-known around the hospital.

"We have custody of her, from the courts," I explain.

Again, he nods. "As her next of kin, it will be your responsibility to arrange services if you wish to do so. As far as the baby, that's up to you."

"Thank you, Dr. Travis." I hold my hand out for him and he accepts.

"Take all the time you need," he says, and leaves the room.

"Tell me what you need," I say, wrapping my arms around her once again.

"I'm not sure." She hugs me back, then steps away. "I mean, I'm sad. She's my sister and I wish I could have helped her. She didn't want help, you know? I mean, she was in rehab and was pregnant, knew she was pregnant and still used again. Daisy is paying for that decision."

"Our girl is strong," I assure her.

"I need to plan services I guess. Honestly, I'm not sure who would come, but it needs to happen. My parents would want that to happen."

"Okay. I'll call the funeral home that we used for your parents."

She nods. "I need to see Daisy."

"Let's go." I kiss the top of her head, and lead her out of the small room and back to the elevators. I catch a glimpse of the officer placing that Cal character in the back of his cruiser right by the door before we load.

"I can't believe it was Cal who was supplying her. Of all people."

"I was thinking the same thing. I'm glad you and Kendall got away from him."

"We knew he was toxic and he wouldn't accept that Kendall said things were over between them." The elevators doors open and we step out. "That's life. It just seems to have a way of working out."

"That it does," I say, kissing her temple. "Let's go see our girl."

Together, we head to the nursery, suit up, and for the first time in a week, I see Daisy. "Look at you," I say in awe. "She's grown so much." I look at Dawn. She has tears in her eyes as she watches me.

"She has," she agrees.

"You're going to be home in no time."

"You good with her?" Dawn asks. "I'm going to go ahead and call the funeral home and…" She swallows hard.

"I can call them." I start to stand.

"No, you stay. I need to do this. I appreciate the offer and you being here, but I need to take care of it."

"Okay. We'll be here waiting on you." She blows me a kiss and leaves the room. "And you, little lady, I missed our snuggles," I tell Daisy. Her breathing is even as she rests against my bare chest. It's a sad day for my girls, and I hurt for them, but at the same time, they're with me. Where they belong.

# Chapter 19

## Dawn

Today was hard. I'm emotionally and mentally exhausted. Never did I imagine that less than a year after burying my parents, I would also be burying my baby sister. It's not something I would wish on my worst enemy.

I hated that I had to leave Daisy at the hospital alone. I was struggling with it all when Amelia called and offered to come and sit with her. I thanked her about a million times then made sure she was added to the visitors' list at the hospital, and there would be no issues. She was listed, but I already knew that. It was more my worrying than anything. I just hate thinking of Daisy there all alone, without anyone who loves her close.

It's taken me time to come to the fact that these people, they're not just Mark and Kendall's friends, but mine as well. They're my family. The only family I have left. And I am so utterly grateful to them for everything they have done for me.

"You want to go home and change?" Mark asks.

That's something else that's new. Though the realtor has shown my parents' house several times, we have yet to get an offer. At first, I was frustrated but now, I see it as a blessing. Mark has convinced me to stay there, or at least shower there to save money on the hotel room. That's after I had to argue with him about paying for my room for me. This was my compromise. My parents' home is in a subdivision about ten minutes from the hospital, so I'm still close. Not only am I close, but Daisy is doing great. She's off her oxygen, gaining weight, and eating like a champ. My theory is that Mom and Dad knew I would need a place to stay close by. That's why we haven't had a buyer yet. Call me crazy, but that's what I'd like to believe.

I wasn't sure I could handle staying here, but it's been okay. Mark has been with me every step of the way. I'm worried about his job, but he assures me he's fine. Kendall even went as far as to have Ridge call me and tell me himself. I guess that's the perks of working for your best friend. I'm still worried about money. Mark said that his condo rental is bringing in income, and he has some savings. I think his exact words were "Babe, I was a bachelor for far too long. I've saved. I'm okay." I didn't argue after that. It's selfish, but I want him here. He wants to be here, and I'm not strong enough—or foolish enough—to push him away again.

"I'm sorry." I reach over and rest my hand on his shoulder.

"For what?" he asks, not taking his eyes off the road.

"Pushing you away. I feel like we've barely had time to talk since you've been back. I'm sorry. I just didn't want to be a burden to you."

"You could never be," he says, placing his hand over mine and giving it a gentle squeeze.

"You signed up for a baggage free girl."

"Well, a lot has changed. You're no longer single." He looks over and grins. "And we have a baby girl who needs us."

"You do that a lot, you know."

"What?"

"Call her ours or refer to us as your girls."

He shrugs. "Is that not right? Are you and Daisy not mine?"

"I mean, I'm your girlfriend, but Daisy, she's my niece."

"She's a few court documents away from being your daughter, Pixie."

"I know that. It's kinda freaking me out," I admit.

"Why?"

"I'm her sole provider. It's up to me to care for her, provide for her, raise her to be a strong, confident woman. That's a lot for me to process."

"We'll get her through it."

It's as if he doesn't even realize he's doing it. Every time he includes himself, he makes my heart flutter in my chest. I love this man more than I ever knew was possible. "I love you," I tell him, because he needs to know.

"I love you too. We changing or no?" he asks again.

"Definitely. I want to get out of these clothes." I'm wearing the same black dress I wore the day that I said goodbye to my parents. I never thought I'd be wearing it again this soon, at least not to another funeral.

"What are you doing?" Mark asks, motioning to the phone in my hands, before putting his eyes back on the road.

"Making a list."

"Care to elaborate?" He chuckles.

"There is so much that I need. I'm not ready for a baby. Daisy is growing and getting stronger every day. I need clothes, and bottles, and blankets, and a bed and see…" I turn my phone, showing him the list. "It goes on and on. Most people have nine months to prepare and a baby shower. I have an infant niece and a couple of weeks at best."

"I picked up a few things."

I turn in my seat as much as the seat belt will allow to look at him. "What do you mean you picked up a few things?"

"I knew you would need a bed, and bottles, and stuff. I wanted you to have what you needed to bring her home. Oh, and my parents, they bought a car seat that has a stroller with it. Mom assures me it's got the highest safety ratings."

He says it so casually, as if he didn't just incinerate my heart. "I— Really?" I ask.

"Yes, really." He glances over at me and smiles. "You have a lot going on, and I wanted to be ready when she comes home. When we get to the house, I'll run through your list and mark off what we already have."

"I…" I'm at a loss for words. He's so loving and caring and thoughtful. He pulls into the driveway of my childhood home and we climb out of the truck, making our way inside. As soon as the door is closed, I turn and wrap my arms around his waist.

"What's this?" he asks. "Not that I'm complaining," he amends, and I can hear the smile in his voice.

"This." I pull back just enough to look up at him. "This is thank you. This is I love you. This is I'm sorry for pushing you away." I bury my face in his chest and just hold on tight.

"Love you too, Pixie."

"I don't know what I would do without you. I can't believe you bought stuff for Daisy." Standing on my tiptoes, I place a kiss on his chin.

"And you," he says, tucking my hair behind my ear. "You don't have to do this on your own."

"I know. I just didn't want you to feel like you were expected to stay with us."

He chuckles. "Baby, do I look like a man who does something he doesn't want to do?"

"Good point." I smile. "Truly, Mark, thank you for everything. This last year, I couldn't have made it through it without you."

"Go get changed," he says, tapping my ass. "We have a little girl to go see." He pecks me on the lips and I pull away. "Hey, let me see that list," he says as I start to walk away.

I toss him my phone. "You know the code. It's in the notes app," I say over my shoulder.

Ten minutes later, he walks into my childhood bedroom—where we've been staying—and tosses my phone on the bed before stripping out of his clothes. "Amelia called to check in. Everything is good. Daisy is sleeping. Everyone is still here, and she's going to meet us as well. We're going to grab something to eat before heading back to the hospital."

"That actually sounds great. Thank you." I pull my tank top over my head, slide my feet into some flip-flops, and sit on the bed. Grabbing my phone, I open the notes app and see almost every item checked off.

"Um… Mark, this is more than just a few things." I hold up my phone, showing him the list even though he's already seen it.

"Maybe." He shrugs. "I didn't want you to stress over having what you needed."

"I'll pay you back," I tell him.

"Now, you're just talking crazy." Leaning down, he kisses me. "Let's go, Pixie, before we're late."

"Mark," I say, trying to get his attention.

"Chop-chop, woman," he calls over his shoulder.

Collecting my phone, I follow after him. He may think I'm not paying him back, but he's wrong. It might not be right away, but I'll make sure I do.

"What are we doing here?" I ask Mark as he pulls into the church parking lot.

"Well, I know the service today was small," he starts.

"By small you mean the only people who showed up was us and our friends?" Destiny has burned so many bridges the attendance was low. Sure, I'm exaggerating and a few of her friends from high school attended, but the number was low, and if not for our core group of friends, it would have been much smaller.

"Anyway," Mark says, moving on, "we know she didn't have a lot of people in her life, and before you comment, we also know that was her doing. However, she's still your sister, and getting together after the services is a thing," he says.

"A thing?" I ask, trying to turn the conversation light. I've cried enough tears in this lifetime.

"Yes, a thing." He rolls his eyes. "So we asked the minister if we could use the community room, and the girls put a little something together." He pulls the keys from the ignition. "Now let's get moving." He pushes open his truck door. I follow suit and meet him at the front of the hood. He reaches for my hand and that's how we enter the church. It's been years since I've been here. Destiny and I would come with our grandma before she passed away. I tug on his hand to stop him. "I feel bad. This isn't my church."

"Don't worry about that. Come on." He pulls gently on my hand and we step through the side door of the church that leads to the community room. I stop and take a look around. Our friends are here, their kids. Kendall's parents, who have become so much my own since we've been friends. Mark's parents are here as well.

Kendall pushes through the crowd and pulls me into a hug. "I'm sorry for your loss," she says, and my eyes mist with tears. Reagan is next, then Amelia. Followed by Kendall's mom, Sonia, and Reagan's mom, Heidi, as well as Mark's mom, Theresa By the time the men take their turn, I'm a crying, sobbing mess. The last hug is from Mark. His is the strongest and the longest.

"We're here for you," he whispers, just for me.

I nod and wipe my eyes with the tissue that appeared a few hugs ago. I don't know who gave it to me, but I'm thankful. "I don't know what to say," I admit.

"There's nothing to say," Heidi says. "You're family."

"Come make a plate." Heidi links her arm with mine and guides me to where a spread of deli sandwiches, fruit, and vegetable trays are waiting.

"Thank you for this, for today. I know you didn't get to meet her, but she was... this vibrant little girl. We used to play dress-up and make mud pies," I say with a smile, thinking back to when we were younger. "Dest always had a mind of her own and marched to the beat of her own drum. We just didn't know that would lead her down the wrong path." I wipe under my eyes to keep the tears from falling. "We tried so many times to help her. My parents—" I swallow hard. "My parents did everything they could. They died trying to help her." Mark leans over and puts his arm around my shoulders.

"I went through this... phase I guess you could call it where I felt sorry for myself that I have no living relatives. Well, except for a tiny baby girl. I know now that I was wrong. Family is not just blood. It's heart. Everyone in this room has a piece of my heart. I can't tell you what it means to me to know I have you in my corner. I love you all. Thank you for being here." I grab a napkin and wipe the tears that I couldn't stop from falling.

Mark leans in and kisses my temple. "I love you," he whispers, before going back to his plate of food.

My pain glossed over the fact that I do have a family. We may not share the same bloodline but their hearts are connected to mine. Family is what you make it, and sitting here, I know I've made a good one. Surround yourself with good people, people who share your heart, your fears, and your goals. Open up to them, let them see you for who you really are, and they will forever be your family.

Before today, I was scared of raising Daisy on my own. But looking around this room, I know I don't have to be afraid. I have a huge support system, and I've finally accepted that. Daisy and I are lucky to have them in our lives, and not a day will go by that I'll ever take that for granted. I look over at Mark, and he's laughing at something Kent just said. I'll never push them away again.

These are my people and I need them more than ever.

# Chapter 20

## MARK

I stayed in Mason a few more days after the funeral. Daisy is doing well, growing and getting stronger every day. Now that she's out of the woods, Dawn started staying at her parents' place. I think it's been good for her to be surrounded by them in their place. Fortunately, she'd left most of the furniture to stage the house as the realtor thought that would be best. There are only a few pieces that she kept and took back to her place. The photos and other personal items she wanted to keep have been packed up and moved to her place as well. Still, it's the home where she grew up filled with memories. I know it's hard for her, but my pixie is holding strong.

"How're the girls?" Seth asks.

It's early Monday morning and I'm back on the job. I got home late last night. "They're doing good. Daisy is growing and gaining weight. She should be able to come home soon."

"Glad to hear it," Kent says, joining the conversation.

"You ready for this?" Tyler asks.

"Ready for what?"

"A baby around all the time."

"What the fuck, man? Why would you ask me that?"

He holds his hands up in defense. "I'm not trying to be a dick, Mark. I'm just saying she's going to be a single mom. She's not just that little girl's aunt. She will be her mother. That's a lot to take on."

"What? You think I'm just going to walk away from her? From both of them?"

"Not at all. I know you love her. I also know you love that baby. I'm just saying, be sure before all three of you are too far in. It's three hearts you'll be breaking."

"I don't plan on breaking any hearts," I say through gritted teeth. I know he means well, but I'm too raw from Dawn pushing me away. In the back of my mind, I'm worried she'll do it again. And honestly, Tyler knows better.

"We're on your side," Ridge defends. "We just thought you might want to talk about it. Ty and I, we've got kids, man. We know the work it takes."

"You think I don't know that? Fuck, what is this? You think I'm not good enough to be in their lives?"

"It's the opposite. They're damn lucky to have you. We're on your side, Mark. We're just putting it all out there," Tyler says.

"Well, let me put it out there for you. I love her. I love that little girl who has wrapped her tiny fist around my heart. I'm not going anywhere."

"Good," Kent says. "Now that everyone is on the same page, can we talk about how Seth's been quiet lately. Too damn quiet," he adds, giving our friend an inquiring look.

"Fuck, why you gotta turn the tables on me?" Seth complains.

"Serves you right," I mumble.

"What's up with that?" Tyler asks. "You have been quiet lately."

"Care to elaborate?" Ridge asks.

"Nope."

"Come on, man. You all dig into my life like it's your fucking job," I tell him.

"It is," Seth replies.

"And mine, when I was dating Kendall," Ridge adds.

"I feel left out. Y'all didn't meddle with Reags and me," Tyler says.

"That's because you two were inevitable," I tell him.

"Come on, man. You've gotta give us something," Kent says, almost pleading.

"Fine. I might be interested in someone. She has a past, lots of baggage, and I don't even know if she's interested."

"Where did you meet her?" Tyler asks.

"When did you meet her?" Ridge adds.

"That's all you're getting. And... I've only met her once, but she's the kind of woman who makes you think about life. About where you've been and where you're going."

"You got all of that from one meeting?" Tyler asks.

"Pretty much. Can't stop thinking about her."

"Damn," Kent mutters. "That's some deep shit, Seth. Who knew you had it in you," he says, losing control of his laughter.

"This." Seth points at Kent. "This is why I didn't want to tell you."

"Come on." Tyler nudges him in the shoulder. "You know we're just fucking with you."

"You've got it easy," Ridge announces. "Y'all were relentless when I first started dating Kendall. None of you have gotten it as bad as you gave it to me."

Seth winces. "I'll give you that one. You were the first to fall, brother. We learned from you and Kendall."

"Yeah, what not to do," Kent agrees.

"Then why in the hell are you harassing me?" I ask, annoyed all over again.

"And me," Tyler counters.

"Do you have short-term memory loss? Do you not remember you started all of this? Asking if I'm ready to be with a single mother. You did that shit." I point at him.

He nods. "I wasn't giving you shit, more like something to think about. It's a lot of responsibility. If Dawn's your girl, then that baby girl is yours too, by default. It's important to make sure you've thought it through."

"You let me worry about me. And for the record, of course I've thought it through. I know what it means, and I'm all in." I look over at Ridge and Tyler. "She's my Kendall, my Reagan." They immediately nod their understanding.

"Why didn't you just start with that?" Kent says, grinning mischievously.

"Fuck off," I say, laughing too.

"So, poker night?" Seth asks.

"Can't. I'm leaving here Friday and spending the weekend with Dawn, then driving back late Sunday night."

He nods. "Okay, well, we're planning a night when she comes home."

"Sounds good, man. We can have it at my place."

"I'm holding you to that." Seth points at me.

"I'm not backing out." I'm also not telling him it's because I know without a doubt that I'm not going to be ready to leave them more than I have to once I get them home.

"Get to work," Ridge says, with absolutely no heat in his voice.

I've missed these guys, the banter, giving each other shit. I've always known they had my back, but even more so now, with all of their support of Dawn. I'm lucky to have them in my life. Family is what you make it and I couldn't be prouder to call these four misfits my brothers.

I'm not even out of the parking lot before I'm dialing her number.

"Hello," she answers.

"I miss you."

She laughs. "It's not even been twenty-four hours."

She's right. I left there at ten last night to make the long trek home. I didn't want to leave them. However, with Daisy being out of the woods, and her being settled at her parents' place, it's the right thing to do. Ridge, although, he said it was okay, depends on me as a part of his small crew. "Too long," I mumble into the phone.

"Long day?" she asks.

"Yeah." I yawn. "We worked late. We're trying to wrap up this job. They're calling for rain toward the end of the week, so we're getting in what we can now."

"Makes sense," she agrees.

"Is it wrong I'm keeping my fingers crossed for a rainy day on Friday?"

"I don't know. I am a little biased. That gets you here sooner."

"Woman, it's like you read my mind." I chuckle.

"So, what's on the agenda for tonight?" she asks.

"I'm headed to Mom and Dad's for dinner, then home to crash. You?"

"Amelia surprised me with a visit. Something about a friend of hers had something done. When she's ready, we're going to go grab dinner."

"Good. I hate the thought of you spending all week alone. How's Daisy?"

"Great. Vitals are strong, she's eating well, breathing on her own. Her tics are pretty much gone. We're still doing skin-to-skin. The staff says that's helping her, the connection or whatever. It makes me feel useful, if that makes any sense. She's this tiny little thing, and I just want to make it better for her."

"Spoken like a momma bear," I reply softly.

She sucks in a breath. "I-I guess I haven't really considered that."

"Baby, you're the only mom she's ever going to know. You're going to adopt her. I know we just laid her to rest, but you're the best thing to happen to that baby girl. You're going to give her a life full of love and laughter."

"I've cried enough," she says quietly.

"I'm sorry. I didn't mean to upset you. The opposite actually. I want you to know I'm there for you, for both of you. I know what it means to be involved with a single mom, which is what you now are." My earlier conversation with the guys filters through my mind. I assume she knows this, but it's better to get it out there. Leave nothing to interpretation. "I know that you're a package deal, and I want the whole package."

"I love you."

"I love you too, baby."

"Amelia's here," she says, clearing her throat.

"You girls have fun. Give Daisy a kiss from me."

"Will do. Get some rest."

"Not likely until I'm with you, but I'll try."

"You." She chuckles softly. "You know how to hit a girl with all the feels."

"What's that? You want me to feel you?" I say, lightening the mood.

"That too," she says, this time it's full-on laughter.

"Music to my ears," I say in regard to her laughter. "Tell Amelia I said hello."

"Will do. I'll text you later." She ends the call.

I already feel lighter by just talking to her and hearing the sound of her voice. I have to admit talking with the guys earlier helped. I knew I was all in and have told her this, but telling her again, reminding her that we're in this together can't hurt. Repeating that I want Daisy in our lives as well, reassuring her is always a good thing. Pulling into my parents' driveway, my stomach rumbles, already calling out for whatever it is my mother is creating in her kitchen. I don't know what it is, but I know if Mom's making it, it's going to be delicious.

Climbing out of the truck, I check to make sure I have my phone in case Dawn needs me, and head inside. I don't bother knocking, instead calling out my arrival.

"In here," Dad calls from the kitchen.

I let his voice and my nose guide the way. "Is that... roast?" I ask.

"Sure is."

"My stomach thanks you," I say, kissing Mom on the cheek. "Can I help?"

"You know how she is, son. This is her domain." Dad laughs.

I raise my hands, backing away, and Mom tosses a dishtowel at me. "What did I do?" I ask, laughing.

"You two." She points between the two of us. "I'll be glad when we can bring Daisy home. Then you two are outnumbered. Finally, the women will rule." She holds up the tongs she's using to plate the roast as if she's the victor.

My chest tightens at their automatic acceptance of Daisy. I know they love Dawn; they've both been telling me for months to stop beating around the bush and make us official. Then that night happened—the night she lost her parents—and things spiraled, but we made it to where we're supposed to be. She knows I love her and support her. That's what matters.

Dad and I clean up after dinner, forcing Mom to sit and relax. We catch up on life, and everything would be perfect if my girls were here.

They'll be home soon.

# Chapter 21

## Dawn

It's been five long weeks, but finally today, Daisy Elizabeth is coming home. I chose Elizabeth because it was my mom's middle name. I filed for adoption, and the attorney has told me he sees no obstacles that would prevent that from happening.

I'm a mother.

To my niece.

I have a daughter.

It's all new, and I'm scared as hell to leave this hospital with her. To know that her care is in my hands. If it were not for the fact that I know I have Kendall and Reagan to rely on, I'd be freaking out more than I am. Oh, and then there's Mark. My amazing boyfriend, who has accepted this new change in my life. He's been there every step of the way with his never-wavering support. I'm lucky to have him.

"I'm going to miss her, and you," Lynn, the pediatric nurse who's been with us since day one, says. She's currently going through our discharge paperback.

"I know. We're going to miss you too," I tell her. "However, I'll be glad to be home and get settled. Get into a routine."

"Routines are important with little ones," she agrees.

"Okay. I think we've gone over everything. The social worker has signed off on the release so you're free to go."

"That's it?" I ask. After all this time, it's hard to believe we're going home.

"That's it. Mark's pulling the car around front, right?"

I work to not roll my eyes. "He is. I explained that I didn't give birth, which means walking to the parking lot is fine, but he insisted."

"From first glance, I'd have pegged him for a fighter more so than a lover." She laughs. "But he's all heart when it comes to the two of you."

"He is," I agree. There's not much I can say that she hasn't already witnessed firsthand over the past few weeks.

"You girls ready to go?" Mark asks, walking into the room. He's carrying a baby seat. It's black with pink and white daisies on it.

"Your mom." I smile and shake my head.

"This is nothing. She bought her a blanket online with her name on it and it's covered in daisies too." He shrugs.

"She's too sweet." I smile up at him.

"Come here, sweet girl," he says, taking Daisy from my arms.

I don't even try to stop him. Instead, I admire this man—all tattoos and muscles—cuddle the pink bundle. It melts my heart to watch him with her like this. To know that regardless of what life has thrown at us, he's here for the long haul. I've seen him with his twin niece and nephew, and of course our friends' kids, but this feels different.

"Thanks, Lynn," Mark says, pulling me out of my thoughts. "Ready, baby?" he asks.

He's standing before me, diaper bag—that he bought, which is pink and gray, not manly at all—thrown over his shoulder, and the car seat in his hand. Daisy is snoozing away, all bundled up with her pink fuzzy blanket that Reagan brought her last weekend.

"Yes."

I hug Lynn and then turn back to him. He holds his free hand out for me, and I don't hesitate to put mine in his. Together, we make our way to the elevator, and out to the parking lot. Mark places Daisy in the middle of the back seat of his truck, placing her seat in the base as if he's done it a million times.

"Up you go," he says, turning to me and placing his hands on my hips, lifting me into his truck.

"Mark." I laugh. "I'm capable of getting into your truck."

"Probably." He shrugs. "But I needed my hands on you. It's been too long, Pixie."

I don't bother to argue with him. I know it's not going to do me any good. He waits until I'm buckled up in the back seat before closing the door and rushing around to the driver's side.

"Homeward bound, ladies," he says, adjusting his rearview mirror.

"This day seems like it took forever to get here." I glance at the sleeping baby.

"Glad it wasn't just me. I'll be glad to have the two of you home, where you belong."

My heart does that thing again where it squeezes in my chest when he says things like that. Words can't describe how much I love this man.

✦✦✦✦

"I thought we could swing by my place first, if you don't mind," Mark says from the front seat as we get closer to my place.

"Sure," I say, because being alone with this little angel beside me for the first time is freaking me out.

"Mom stopped by earlier. She left us her crockpot lasagna, and some other stuff."

"That was sweet of her. She didn't have to do that," I tell him.

"She's been there with me and my sister. Taking care of a newborn is exhausting. Her words, not mine," he's quick to add. "She wanted the first day home to be less stressful. I told her to just take it to my place."

"I'm suddenly starving. Your mom is an outstanding cook," I say, even though he already knows.

"That she is," he agrees, pulling into his driveway.

"What in the world?" I say, looking at the front porch. It's decorated with pink balloons and a big stork that's in the flower bed that says Welcome Home, Daisy. I try but fail to fight the tears.

"Did you do this?"

"Not directly." He smiles over his shoulder at me.

"Meaning?" I ask, wiping my tears and smiling at the same time. I'm such an emotional roller coaster you would think I'm the one who just gave birth.

"I might have helped orchestrate it. And by that, I mean, I bought everything and my parents took care of it when they dropped the food off."

"What am I going to do with you?"

"Love me?" he offers with a boyish grin.

"Done."

He throws his head back and laughs, which causes Daisy to startle, but fall right back to sleep. "I'll get her," he says, climbing out of the truck and opening the back door. "You remember the garage code?"

"Yes." Grabbing the diaper bag, I rush to open the garage door so they can get inside.

"You know, my truck not fitting in this garage is an issue. Not now, but it will be this winter when we take her out. I should look into getting an SUV or something."

"We have my car," I remind him. I don't ask why he assumes Daisy and I will be here this winter. I've accepted that he wants to be in our lives and it thrills me. I don't know what I did to find him, to have his love and attention, but I'm forever thankful for him.

"You should probably look into something bigger too," he tells me. "By the time you put that stroller in the trunk, it's full."

"I've been thinking of a new car, but not with baby paraphernalia in mind." I hold the door open for him. "Times, they are a changing."

He bends to place a kiss on my lips. "Let's change with them," he says, stepping into the house.

I follow along behind him. "Where are we going?" I ask when he doesn't go to the living room or even the kitchen. Instead, he heads to the opposite side of the house where the bedrooms are. "Mark?" I ask, and he keeps on walking, Daisy's seat in his arms until he reaches one of the bedroom doors.

"Close your eyes," he instructs.

"What's going on?" I ask, confused.

"Please? Just close your eyes."

"Okay," I say hesitantly. My eyes flutter closed. I hear the door open and feel his arm slide around my waist.

"I've got you. Just step forward," he says, his lips next to my ear. Once we're in the room, he releases his hold on me. "Give me just a second. Keep them closed."

"You know this is killing me, right? What are you doing?" I can hear him moving around, but the sound gives nothing away.

"Almost ready."

I wait, shifting from one foot to the next, antsy for what's about to happen. I have no idea what he's up to, but I'm sure whatever it is, it involves the baby. He's been adamant the last couple of weeks making it known he wants the package deal. It's hard to tell what he's done.

"I'm going to count to three and you can open your eyes. Are you ready?" he asks, teasing me.

"Really?" I laugh.

"Thought so." His deep chuckle washes over me. "Okay, open," his deep timbre whispers.

I blink my eyes open. Immediately, my hand flies to cover my mouth. We're standing in the middle of the most beautiful nursery I've ever seen before. Each of the four walls are painted in soft pastel colors of purple, pink, yellow, and green. There's a white crib, a changing table, dresser, and a rocking chair. The white wood stands out against the colors on the wall. Over the baby bed, hangs the letters of her name. The strings are white, and each letter is painted bright colors of blue, orange, pink, green, and yellow.

"Crazy daisies," he says from behind me.

"How did you? When did you?" I turn to look at him, and he has Daisy in his arms.

He shrugs. "I had some time on my hands when you asked me to leave, and later when I was here without you. I used it wisely."

"Mark, this is— It's incredible." I turn, taking in every detail. "I can't believe you did all of this."

"I told you I picked up a few things," he says.

"This is more than a few things. This is everything she needs."

"The changing table has diapers and a wipe warmer. The sales lady assured me it was an essential item. There are some clothes of all sizes in the closet. Those are from Mom, Reagan, Kendall, and Amelia. The guys helped with painting and assembly. Reagan, Kendall, and Mom made me a list of what we would need, and I went shopping. This is what I came up with. I know there is a lot more that we're going to need, but this will get us started."

"You think?" I go to him, wrapping my arms around his waist, careful of the baby. His free arm wraps around me, hugging me tightly. "This is a lot of work for her to have a place to stay when we're here. I can't believe you did all of this." I look up at him. "I love you. My heart is full."

"I love you too." He drops his arm from around my waist and walks to the bed where he places Daisy. "You're home now, Daisy girl," he whispers, leaning over the edge to kiss her tiny forehead.

Tears sting my eyes. "Mark," I say, but it comes out more like a sob.

"I got her a shirt. You want to see it?" he asks. I nod because words aren't possible at the moment. "Come here." He motions for me to join him by the crib.

One step at a time, my feet carry me to them. Mark steps back and gives me a clear view of Daisy in her bed. Peering over the bed, I take in her sleeping form. Her little lips are puckered as she sleeps. She makes the cutest faces. My eyes scan her shirt and I read it. Then read it again.

## MUMMY AND DADDY'S
### *Angel*

I turn to look at Mark, only to find him down on one knee holding a gorgeous sparkling diamond ring. "I love you, Dawn. I love that little girl, and I'm tired of being in limbo. I'm tired of worrying if where I want us to go is where you want us to go. I want forever, Pixie. I want to know that at the end of each day, you and Daisy are going to be here, in the home I bought for us. I didn't get a chance to tell you that. This place, I want it full of Daisy's brothers and sisters. I want a swing set in the backyard and lounge chairs on the deck for us to watch our children grow." He smiles, and it lights up his face. "My love for you and for that little girl, that was my unexpected fall. It came out of nowhere, but I want it. I want you both in my life, in my home, in my arms. I promise that I'll always be there to catch you."

Tears are falling and my vision is blurry. My heart, it beats for this man. "Yes," I say through my tears.

"I didn't ask you yet." He smiles up at me.

I drop to my knees before him. "Mark Adams, will you—" I start, but he places his hand over my mouth.

"No way, sweetheart, you are not stealing my thunder." He drops his hand and takes my left hand, ring poised at the tip of my finger. "Dawn Miller, will you do me the incredible honor of becoming my wife?"

"Yes." I launch myself at him, fusing our lips together. He falls back onto the floor, me on top of him, never breaking our kiss.

"I love you," he says, finally pulling away. He smooths my hair back out of my eyes from where I'm staring down at him. "I love her too. I want us to get married and adopt her together. I know that means this will have to happen fast, but…" He trails off, not sure of what I'm going to say.

"Yes. Yes, to all of it. Yes." He pulls me into a hug, and just like that, the worry and the fear are gone. I know that no matter what I do in my life, with this man by my side, we can conquer anything.

# Chapter 22

## MARK

She said yes. My arms are locked tightly around her, holding her close. In the back of my mind, there was this fear she would say no. That she would struggle to prove she can raise Daisy on her own. I was prepared to change her mind. To fight to prove to her that she's never going to be alone as long as I'm still breathing.

My hand slips under the back of her shirt, feeling her soft skin. "We need to pack up your place," I tell her. "I was going to do it for you, but I didn't want to overstep, and to be honest, I wasn't sure you would say yes."

She lifts her head. "Seriously?"

"Yeah." I cup her face in my hand. "You've been through so much, I wasn't sure. I was hopeful." I give her a smile.

"Thank you for not giving up on me."

"Never." I roll us over on the floor, so I'm hovering over her. "I'm always going to be right here." Sliding my hand under the front of her shirt, I run the pad of my thumb over her nipple. Even through the silky material of her bra, I can feel the pebbled peak.

"Should we move?" she asks, motioning her head toward the crib.

"She's sleeping, and even then, she has no idea what I'm about to do to you."

"It feels… weird," she says, scrunching up her nose and looking cute as hell.

"Right." Standing from the floor, I turn the baby monitor on and offer her my hand, helping her up. "This thing is pretty cool. We can see and hear her in our room. Come on. I'll show you." I guide her down the hall to our bedroom.

*Our bedroom.*

"See." I go to the nightstand and point to the small screen.

"Aww," she says, picking it up to get a closer look.

"I read a lot of reviews online, and this is the best rated one I could find. I liked the video option so we can see her and not have to go into her room and risk waking her up."

"You thought of everything."

I fight the urge to puff out my chest at her recognition, and the fact that I'm taking care of my girls. That's all I want. "Not everything. I'm sure there are things that I'm missing."

"Maybe, but that's going to be our life as she grows."

"I like the sound of that." I snake my arm around her waist. I need her close.

"Me too." She looks up at me and then holds her left hand out in front of her. "We're getting married."

"Mrs. Adams," I say, kissing her softly, tracing her lips with my tongue.

"Tell me I'm not dreaming. Is this really happening?"

"As soon as we can make it happen."

"How soon?" she asks, kissing the underside of my jaw.

"How soon can you plan a wedding?"

Sadness crosses her face. "I-I don't really know. I always imagined that when I was married, they would be there, you know? All three of them."

"I wish they could be here too. They will be. They're here." I place my hand over her heart.

"They liked you. They'd be happy for us."

"There is no one who will love you the way that I do." I give her my truth.

"I believe that," she says. "I guess we should talk about what we want and when."

"Soon," I say again. "I want us to adopt her together. I never want her to feel as though either of us didn't want her."

"Mark." She closes her eyes and takes in a deep breath. "I don't know how to tell you what that means to me. I don't have the words to tell you how my heart feels. You're a gift, to both of us, one I will forever cherish."

"You just did," I tell her. "Besides, you're my fiancée now. That ring on your finger is all I need. The entire world will know you're mine, and not a day will pass that you and our little girl won't feel it."

Her hands wrap around my neck and she pulls me into a kiss. She's so short that she has to strain to reach me. Bending, I place my hands on her thighs and pick her up. She laughs, but wraps her legs around my waist and keeps her lips pressed against mine.

Spinning us, I press her back against the wall and devour her. My tongue explores every inch of her mouth, while my hands squeeze her ass.

"More. I need more," she pleads, resting her head against the wall.

"Tell me what you want, baby."

She lifts her head and smiles. "You, Mark. I want you. Any way I can get you."

Turning from the wall, I stalk to the bed. I'm ready to put her down and ravish her when a small cry comes through the monitor. We both freeze and turn to look at the small screen. Daisy's little arms are moving and she lets out another cry.

"I'll get her," I say, setting Dawn down on the bed.

"I can go."

"I'll get her." I kiss her one more time before rushing to the other side of the house to get our little girl.

"Hey, sweetheart." I pick her up and she shudders, but her cries stop. "What's going on, huh? You hungry?" I ask as I rub her back.

"It's time for her to eat," Dawn says, appearing in the doorway.

"I'll change her. You want to get a bottle ready?" I ask.

"I can change her."

"I got it, babe. This little angel needs a bottle. Stat. Go." I shoo her away and take Daisy to the changing table. "All right, sweet girl. Take it easy on me this go round, will ya? This is my first time with no one here to supervise. We need to show Mommy that we can do this."

*Mommy.*

It's not hard for me to refer to Dawn as such. She's got the loving, nurturing gene, and well, that's who she is. It's not official, but it will be soon. And I'll be Daddy.

"So, Daisy, your mommy and I are going to get married, which will make me your daddy. You okay with that?" I ask as I remove the soiled diaper and quickly slide the new one under her. "I promise to love you for every day of forever. I'm even going to talk to Mommy about having you a few brothers and sisters to play with. Would you like that?"

She just stares up at me like she can't figure me out.

"There," I say, finishing the final snap on the pink sleeper we brought her home in. "You ready to eat?" I lift her from the changing table. With Daisy in one arm, with the other, I wrap up the soiled diaper and toss it into the diaper bin. "It's supposed to keep the stink out. I guess we'll see if they sold me a gimmick," I tell her.

Turning, I find Dawn leaning against the doorjamb just watching us. "There's Mommy," I whisper to the baby.

"You're so good with her."

"I've had lots of practice. Meghan's kids and then Knox, Everly, Ben, and Beck. There's no shortage of babies in our family." I hold my hand out for the bottle. "I can feed her. Why don't you go take a bath or a long hot shower?"

"I—" She stops and bites her bottom lip. "Are you sure?"

"You were ready to argue with me, weren't you?" I ask, shaking my head.

"I caught myself." She sticks her tongue out at me.

"Don't be like Mommy, Daisy. She has bad habits."

"Hey!" Dawn laughs.

Some of the light is back in her eyes. I know she's still grieving, and we have a lot to learn, obstacles to face with the adoption and raising this little girl, but there is no one else I'd rather face them with. "Go," I say, reaching for the bottle again.

She steps forward and hands me the bottle, running her hand over Daisy's baby fine hair. When her eyes meet mine, I never could have imagined how the words out of her mouth would make me feel. "Be good for Daddy," she says with a smile.

*Daddy.*

Before I can comment, she turns on her heel and rushes from the room. "Well, it looks like Mommy's on board, kiddo," I tell her. I settle into the rocking chair and offer her the bottle. She sucks greedily. "I hope you like your room. When you get older and can tell us what you want, we'll change it however you want it. When my sister was younger, she was changing her room all the time. It must be a female thing, because I couldn't have cared less."

I watch her watch me, and my chest tightens. It's still surreal Dawn said yes, and this little lady is going to be my daughter. Our lives are falling into place, finally. Sure, it's not how we imagined it would go, but to be honest, I wouldn't change it. This little girl and her aunt, soon-to-be momma, have my heart in the palm of their hands.

"I think we should talk about dating," I tell Daisy, pulling the bottle from her mouth to burp her. She protests with a whine. "I know you're not ready, but if we don't do this, then your belly will hurt and we can't have that," I say, placing her on my shoulder and rubbing her back, softly patting too. It takes her a few minutes, but she finally gives me a burp that would rival the guys.' "Goodness, how does something so sweet and tiny do that?" I place her back in the crook of my arm and offer her the rest of her bottle.

She almost finishes the bottle before she's snoozing away. I bring her back to my shoulder and work another manly sounding burp out of her before returning her back in her crib. I watch her sleeping, giving Dawn some more time alone. After making sure the monitor is turned on, I head to the living room and check that the second camera receiver is turned on so I can hear her if she wakes up.

Part of me wants to crash Dawn's bath, but she deserves time to herself. With nothing to worry about and just soak and relax. She's probably lived at the hospital the past few weeks, and I know her showers could have broken world records for the world's fastest. So, instead of joining her, I start pulling the salad fixings from the fridge and place the garlic bread Mom left in the oven.

Dawn joins me about fifteen minutes later. "That smells so good," she moans and my cock twitches.

"You ready to eat?"

"Yes. How did Daisy do?" she asks.

"Great. Almost the entire two ounces before she fell into a full-belly coma." I laugh.

"Did yo—"

I interrupt her. "Yes. I burped her twice. All is good. There's a monitor there." I point to the receiver in the living room. "There are two, so no matter where we are, we will be able to hear her."

"You thought of everything."

"I tried to make this as easy as possible for both of us. We didn't get time to process that we're going to be parents, and slowly gather everything we're going to need. We didn't get time to let the realization that we're going to be responsible for a tiny human to sink in. I know Ridge was a fish out of water those first few days until he got everything organized for Knox. I was just trying to make life easier for us."

"And that?" She points to the plate of lasagna I just dished from the crockpot. "Did you beg your mom to cook for us?" she teases.

"Nope. That was all Mom. She insisted she made us something easy to heat through."

"Remind me to thank her," she says, taking a huge bite.

"They want to come over to meet her. Daisy. Knowing my mom, she has another gift for her."

"Sure, whenever. I was worried about getting what we needed. I mean, I know you said you picked up a few things, but you pretty much took care of it all."

"I'm sure I missed something. You should go through her room and see what we still need, and we can get that this weekend. Maybe we can have Mom and Dad come over and watch her while we go out. I don't think taking her out to a store with her being this little is a good idea."

She smiles wistfully. "Look at you being a protective papa bear," she says.

"Always when it comes to my girls."

"Do they know?" She motions toward her ring finger.

"They knew I was going to ask you. They didn't know when."

"What about the gang? They know?"

"Nope. They know I love you. They know that there is never going to be anyone for me but you, but they don't know I bought a ring, or that I was going to ask."

"Why not?"

I shrug. "I kind of just wanted it for us, you know? I mean, I told my parents, because well, I didn't have a choice. Mom was dropping off some clothes for Daisy and saw the bag from the jewelry store on the counter. I had just gotten home."

"Were they okay with it?" she asks hesitantly.

"What kind of question is that? Of course they were okay with it. But you need to understand that if they weren't, that wouldn't change my decision to marry you. My heart"—I point to my chest—"it's yours."

"What if we do it here?"

"Do what here?"

"The wedding. What if we get married here?"

"Is that what you want?" It's important to me that she has her special day. I know it won't be the same without her parents or sister, but it still needs to be a day she will always remember.

"Sure." She shrugs.

"No."

Her head whips up. "No?"

"Nope. Not with a reply like *sure*. I want this day to be all you hoped it would be. I know it's going to be hard as hell for you, but we're a family, us and Daisy. You deserve a day of your dreams to celebrate that. So yeah, my answer is no. Try again."

"You're... let me think about it," she concedes.

"Better. Now eat before it gets cold. I have something I want to show you."

"There's more?"

"Yep. It was my backup plan," I admit.

"Backup plan?"

"Yeah, in case you said no. A man's always gotta have a backup plan to win over his girls."

"You're too much." She smiles, and it warms me from the inside out.

We finish eating, then clean up the kitchen. I can't help but think that I'm glad that I got to propose here instead of at the hospital like I had planned. I hate that she lost her sister so soon after her parents, but I'm glad I could be there for her.

"You ready?" I ask her.

"Yes." She sits up straighter on the couch and watches me as I stand.

"So, I thought if you said no, I would have this big reveal to prove to you that I was all in, but since you said yes, I've got nothing so I'm just going to show you."

"Enough already. Let me see. Where is it?" Her eyes scan the room.

"Close your eyes."

"Mark," she groans.

"Close 'em, baby."

"Fine."

I wait until her eyes are closed to remove my shirt. Turning, I stand with my back to her. "Open," I say. I stand still, letting her look at my back. I have lots of ink, but there was still some real estate on my back, and my girls have now claimed that spot.

"Pixie?" I ask when I hear nothing.

"I don't, I mean, when did you? Mark, this is amazing," she says and her voice grows closer. "When did you do this?"

"Earlier this week. It's still healing, but you can make it out, right?"

She laughs. It's a light and airy beautiful sound that fills our home. "Yeah," she says with a tremble in her voice. "It's easy to see the daisies growing in the dawn of day. This is incredible and no one has ever—" She chokes on a sob.

I turn to face her. "I love you. Both of you. You both already own my heart. I thought it was only fitting to have you etched into my skin as well."

"It's beautiful and incredible, and I— Turn around so I can see it again," she says, making me laugh. Her arms wrap around me from behind and she rests her head against my back, the side opposite my tattoo. "I love you, Marcus Adams."

"I love you too, future Mrs. Adams, and our daughter." Moving us to the couch, I kiss her as if my last breath depends on it.

Daisy wakes up soon after so we cuddle with her before it's time for a bath, another bottle, and bed. I want to ravish my fiancée, but we're both exhausted. We fall into bed with full bellies and full hearts, and let sleep claim us. It was the perfect night at home with my family.

# Chapter 23

## Dawn

Life is passing by like a freight train. Daisy turned three-months-old last week. It's hard to believe. My sweet baby girl is growing and thriving. She smiles constantly, and she has Mark and I both wrapped around her little finger. However, it's not just us. Mark's parents are just as bad as we are. Theresa has always been a stay-at-home mom and has volunteered to watch her for us. She refuses to let us pay her so we do other things like this weekend. It's Labor Day, and we got them a weekend away at a bed-and-breakfast a couple of hours away. Their friends Jim and Tammy are going with them.

They took to her as their granddaughter without question. Theresa even went as far as to pull me aside and assure me that she will love her for my parents and her, and that we'll keep their memory alive. Of course, I cried. I've cried more tears in the last year than I have my entire life. Each day it gets a little easier, but there will always be a hole in my heart that they left behind.

I'm in the kitchen packing up some bottles for our outing today.

We're headed to Tyler and Reagan's for a cookout.

"Phew-ee baby girl, what have you been eating?" I hear through the monitor and stifle my laughter so I can hear more. "Bleh," he says, and I have to put my hand over my mouth. "Ew, you're stinky," he says, in the voice he uses just for her. I hear baby laughter, which is new. "You think this is funny? Daddy needs a clothespin," he tells her.

I stand here and listen until I hear him tell her it's time to come and find me. I get back to work packing up the extra bottles for the day.

"What can I do?" he asks, holding Daisy in his arms.

"I'm good, just packing up some extra bottles and formula."

"This one," he says, jostling her in his arms and making her smile, "she about stunk up the entire house."

"Did she?" I ask as if I didn't hear him.

He shudders. "How can someone so tiny and so cute produce that?" he asks as if he's truly appalled.

"You've smelled the formula she eats, right?"

"When can we give her baby food again?"

"Not for a few more months, but that's not much better."

"When is she out of diapers?"

I throw my head back and laugh. "We have lots of months before that happens."

"What? Like seven?"

"Usually two and a half to three. Kendall started Knox at two and a half."

"So, years, that's what you meant to say."

"Pretty much."

"Damn," he mutters under his breath.

"Still want to add to this brood?" I ask him, remembering his proposal and the promise of brothers and sisters for Daisy.

"Pft, you think a few sh— poopy diapers are going to keep me from knocking you up? Think again, beautiful." He leans down and kisses the corner of my mouth, and Daisy squeals her delight.

There's not really anything I can say to that, so I don't. I focus on closing up the diaper bag after another check that we have diapers, wipes, clothes, blanket, binky, and the rest of the items on my list.

"Pack 'n Play is in the back of your SUV," Mark says, coming in from the garage, Daisy still in his arms.

"She's going to be spoiled if you keep packing her around like that."

"Okay?"

"Okay," I repeat. "We don't want her to cry because she wants to be held."

"If she wants to be held, I'll hold her."

"What if it's at 2:00 a.m.?" I ask him.

He shrugs. "Whatever she needs she gets."

I can't believe how incredibly in love with her he is. I knew he loved her, but he will stop at nothing if he thinks she needs or might want it. I'm warning him to not spoil her when the reality is, it's too late. She's spoiled rotten and to be honest, I wouldn't have it any other way.

✶✶✶✶

"So, when's the wedding?" Kendall asks. "I would have thought Mark would have made you pick a date by now."

We're sitting in the living room. I came in to change Daisy and ended up feeding her while I was in here. Kendall came looking for me and here we sit. Daisy has long since finished her bottle.

"I don't know," I confess. "I can't decide where, and Mark vetoed when I said our house."

"Why?"

"At the time, it was just an idea that popped into my head, and when he asked if it's what I really wanted, I said sure. Apparently, that was the wrong thing to say. He said no, and to figure out where my dream wedding would be and he would make it happen."

"And now?"

"I keep going back to it. I mean, it makes sense. I want something small, and our house is set up for the kids and people to stay if they wanted to."

"So tell him again. This time don't let him tell you no. Tell him it's what you want."

"I just... the day is going to be hard enough without them there, and I like the thought of starting forever in our forever home. It's going to be small, just all of you, your parents, and his, so it's not like there's not enough space. Hell, I'd be good with one of the guys marrying us."

She laughs. "Oh my God! That's perfect. Which one?" she says, her eyes lighting up.

I shrug. "Who do you think?"

"I'm thinking Kent."

"You think he'd do it?"

"I know he would. You should totally do it."

"The more I think about it, the more it makes sense. No outsiders, you know? Just those we are closest to."

"I think your wedding should be what you want it to be. If you don't want all the fanfare, then don't do it. If you want it to be Kent, or whoever, then that's what you should do. Just explain it to him."

"I admit when he asked me, I was still reeling from the proposal. I was still trying to process that we were actually getting married. That he wanted this crazy life with me."

Kendall reaches over and runs her index finger over the top of Daisy's foot where she's sleeping in my arms. "He's so good with her."

"They all are. I can still remember that first day when we saw Ridge with Knox at the office. It was like an ovary explosion to see this big strong guy covered in ink doting on his little baby boy, but damn. When I found out there were four more just like him, and that all of them treated the women and kids in their life as if they were a precious gift, I'm surprised my ovaries are still there," I say, and she laughs, nodding her agreement.

"Yeah, they're a great group of guys. Speaking of, has Mark mentioned anything about Seth?"

"Not really, just that he thinks he's interested in someone but won't dish the details."

"Damn." She chuckles. "That's all Ridge will give me too."

"He'll tell us when he's ready." I say the words, but I can't help but wonder who it is. He's with our group all the time. Sure, it's not twenty-four hours a day, but there's not even been a mention of this woman. I'm intrigued for sure.

"What are you two doing in here?" Reagan asks, taking a seat on the

178

couch next to Kendall. Amelia follows her and takes the chair.

"Just chatting. I fed this one and she zonked out on us."

"You feeling okay?" I ask Amelia. She looks a little pale.

She waves me off with a smile. "It's hot as hell out there. I just need to cool off."

I don't really buy her excuse, but I won't force her to talk. If there is anything that I've learned about Amelia is that she's a vault and she only opens the doors when she's ready.

"We were just talking about the wedding," Kendall chimes in. "Dawn is thinking about having it at their place." She looks over at me and grins. "What do you ladies think of them having one of the guys marry them?" she asks.

"Love it," Reagan says with a smile.

"Which one?" Amelia asks, already starting to get some color back in her cheeks. Maybe it was the heat, but I wouldn't think that would make her pale, the opposite in fact, but her coloring is coming back all the same.

"Guess," I tell her.

She looks over at Reagan. "Let's say our pick at the same time." Reagan nods.

"On the count of three." Kendall wiggles in her seat. "One. Two. Three."

"Kent," Reagan and Amelia say at the same time.

Kendall throws her head back in laughter and Daisy jumps in my arms. Her little eyes pop open and she looks around, surveying what might have woken her up. She starts to fuss, so I stand and rock her in my arms.

"I'm sorry," Kendall says softly.

"Wasn't the first time and won't be the last," I tell her. "Weren't you the one who said don't keep the house quiet, let them learn to sleep through everyday noises?" I ask her.

"That was my mom, but I passed it on to you and Reagan."

"Best advice ever." Reagan nods. "Why the laughter? You don't think Kent will do a good job?" she asks us.

"That's who we said too. All four of us are on the same page."

Daisy is still fussing and it's getting louder. "Hey," a deep voice says from behind me. "What's going on?" Mark asks. His hands rest on my hips as he offers Daisy his hand. She whimpers, sticking out her bottom lip. I can already see where this is heading. "Come here, sweetie. Daddy will make it better." He releases his hold on me and steps around me to take her from my arms. She shudders and then rests against his chest. Her cries long forgotten.

"Baby whisperer," I mumble.

"Nice." Seth holds his fist out to Mark. "Daddy's got skills."

I swear Mark puffs his chest out with pride. "You know it."

Knox climbs up on Kendall's lap. Everly is asleep in Ridge's arms. Tyler has Ben, and he looks like he's losing the battle with fighting his nap. Beck, who is in Kent's arms, is ahead of his twin. His eyes flutter as he rubs them.

"Nap time," Tyler says.

"We put an air mattress in the spare bedroom. Knox and Everly can sleep there. That way if they roll off, they don't have far to fall. I wouldn't risk them rolling out of our bed," Tyler says.

"Ready, Momma?" Tyler asks Reagan. She nods and stands. Kent hands Beck off to her, and they disappear down the hall.

"I'm going to take Everly on back," Ridge says, following along behind Tyler and Reagan.

"And this guy, he fights n-a-p-s." Kendall spells out the word.

"Hey, Knox." Kent bends down to his level. "The little kids are having a hard time going to sleep. You think you can pretend and show them how it's done?"

"No naps," Knox grumbles.

Kent laughs. "No, not for you. We just need to do this." He closes his eyes and tilts his head and pretends to be sleeping. "You're the older one, so you have to show them how it's done."

"Okay," he says reluctantly, but holds his arms open for Kent and lets him carry him back to the bedroom.

"Sometimes the men in our lives make me feel inadequate," Amelia says, and we laugh with her.

"Don't hate, A," Mark says. "It's not our fault we have the touch."

A few minutes later, Reagan and the guys join us. "They're all out," she says, taking her spot next to Kendall.

"So, we going to start poker night back up or what?" Seth asks.

"Yeah, we can have the first one here," Mark says. "You okay with that?" he asks me.

"Sure, I can pack Daisy up and—" I can't exactly invite myself to anyone's home, not even his parents. Now mine, on the other hand… A pang of sadness hits me.

"No, you don't have to leave," Kent says adamantly. "That's not what poker night is about. It's just us hanging. This is your home," he reminds me.

"Or," Kendall says, "we can hang out at our place. The kids can have a movie night, and we can catch up." She looks at Reagan and Amelia. "You ladies in?"

"Yes," they quickly agree.

"Perfect. Then we'll plan a girls' night where the guys get to keep the kids."

Oh, my best friend is a smart one. "Brilliant." Reagan laughs.

The guys just nod, and some of the wind in our sails deflates. It's not a hardship for them to be around the kids. That's a great thing. In fact, I find it rare in a lot of instances, at least in my line of work. Ninety percent of the kids seen in our office are brought in by their mom. If a dad brings them, they usually end up on the phone with mom to get answers to the questions. I'm confident that wouldn't happen with our group. These guys, even the uncles, are involved in the kids' lives.

The guys settle on next weekend for poker night, and we're doing a girls' night the following weekend. We spend a few more hours just catching up. Daisy soaks up all the attention being the only kid awake. Seth passes her to Kent, who passes her to Tyler who passes her to Ridge. Mark steps in when Ridge is about to pass her to Kendall, grumbling about getting cuddle time with his own daughter.

"Today was fun," I tell Mark. We're back home, and just got Daisy to sleep.

"Yeah, this is nice too," he says, pulling me next to him.

"You'll get no complaints from me." He grins at my words and kisses my forehead. "So, I've been thinking."

"Uh-oh, should I be worried?" He laughs.

"Possibly. I was thinking about the wedding."

"Okay."

"Well, the more I think about it, I really do think we should do something small here, and before you say no," I rush to get out when I see him opening his mouth to speak. "I've thought about it. I don't want something big or elaborate. I never did. I just want a forever love like my parents had. I can't think of a better place than the home we're making together for that to happen."

"When?"

"Well, we have to get a marriage license, and then just make sure our friends and your parents are available. Maybe order some food, and..." I bite my lip, not sure how he's going to take this next part.

"And what?" he prompts.

"Well, Kendall and I were talking and we had this crazy idea, but it's really not that crazy and I kind of like it. I'm just not sure how you're going to feel about it."

"Lay it on me, Pixie."

"Okay, but just keep an open mind."

He cups my face. We're lying in bed facing one another, bodies aligned, and I'm pretty sure I could convince him with sex, but I want him to agree on his own free will. "You can tell me or ask me anything."

"Right. Well, Kendall and I were talking," I start.

"So you've said." He grins.

"Shush, let me get this out. So, Kendall and I were talking and how would you feel ifKentmarriedus?" I rush to get it all out.

"Come on, baby, you can do better than that. Say it so I can understand you." He's grinning, which means he heard me. He's just torturing me.

"How would you feel if Kent married us? He's perfect. All laidback and chill. I think it would be fun."

182

He smiles. "You know, out of all of us, I can see him doing that. Well, I can see Seth as well, but I can't see him taking it serious."

"Exactly. Kent is perfect. I'm pretty sure he can get ordained online. You think he'd do it?"

"Yeah, I do. Is that what you want?"

"It is. I want those we love around us. Just something small and simple."

"I'll make it happen." He rolls over and grabs his phone. I watch as he taps away on the screen and holds it between us.

"What's up?" Kent's deep voice answers.

"Need a favor," Mark says. "Oh, and you're on speaker. Dawn is here with me."

"Hey, gorgeous," Kent says sweetly.

Mark grunts.

I laugh. "Hey, Kent."

"What's the favor? Need a sitter?" he asks.

"No, but Dawn and I were wondering if you'd be willing to become ordained and marry us?" Mark just throws it out there.

"Sure, I can just do that online or something, right? I love you both, but I am not going back to school."

We both laugh. "Yeah, online. I'll look into what you need exactly," I tell him. "We'll cover the cost."

"Nah, don't worry about it. So, when's the big day?"

I glance over at Mark.

"Soon, the next month or so maybe?" he tells him.

"I'm in. I'm honored. Where is this shindig taking place?"

"Here, at our house," I say.

"Seth is gonna be so jealous," he jokes.

"Nah, he knows he can't be trusted." Mark laughs.

"Just let me know what I need to do."

"Thank you, Kenton," I say sweetly, using his full name.

"You're welcome, doll," he says, and Mark hits End.

"Hey, you hung up on him."

"He deserved it."

"He's going to marry us."

"More talking about that, less talking about him," he says, pretending to be put off. "Come here." Hand on my hip, he tugs me closer. He slides his leg between mine and kisses me. It's slow and teasing. His tongue lazily duels with mine.

"Are you teasing me on purpose?" I ask against his lips.

"Yes."

"How much longer until the good stuff?" I manage to ask without laughing.

"Woman." He rolls on top of me and settles between my thighs. He presses his hard length into my center and I moan. "This what you want?"

"More," I say, gripping the sheets.

"I'll give you more." He trails kisses down my neck just as Daisy lets out a scream.

We both freeze waiting to see what's next, and it's full-on crying. He sighs and rests his forehead against mine. "Daisy girl has impeccable timing." He moves off me and climbs out of bed. "I'll go get her," he says.

With a huff, I wait for him to come back to me with an unhappy baby. Instead, he calls for me through the monitor.

"Uh, babe, can you come in here?" he asks.

I try to see what's going on, but Mark is just standing by the crib and Daisy is still crying. He's trying to console her but not making a move to pick her up. Jumping out of bed, I make my way to her room. As soon as I enter, the smell hits me.

"Oh, girlie, what do we have going on in here?"

"It's everywhere, Dawn. Ev-er-y-where," he says dramatically. "What do we do?"

"We clean her up."

"She's covered in shit," he exclaims. His eyes go wide. "Don't talk like Daddy," he tells her.

"Move, you big baby." I hip check him and lift our soiled daughter from her crib. "Phew-ee, let's get you to the tub." Grabbing a blanket, I wrap it around her and then head to the bathroom. I admit I gag a few times during the process. As soon as she's cleaned up, I hand her off to Mark while I take care of the crib.

"I should have done that," he says apologetically. "That would have been more useful than standing there watching you."

"You handed me a towel and the three extra wash cloths," I remind him.

"Right, huge help," he says sarcastically. "Is she sick? Should we take her to the doctor?"

"I don't think so. No fever. She seems to be feeling fine. It's time for her to eat, so feed her and see if she takes it. Babies just sometimes have explosive diapers."

"You're such a sweet little thing to have all that," he tells her as they walk toward the kitchen to get a bottle.

I watch them go with a smile on my face. This isn't how I thought my life would go, raising my infant niece as my own. I don't regret that decision. As far as Mark, I love him with everything I am. He's accepted Daisy as his with no hesitation. Late-night exploding diapers and all, I'm a lucky woman.

# Chapter 24

## MARK

It's poker night for the first time at my new place. When I volunteered, it was more because I assumed my girls would be here, close to me, than it being at my place. I didn't think that through because they're packing up and headed over to Ridge's place for a girls'/kids' night.

"Babe, you can stay," I tell Dawn. I feel like I'm begging her.

"No way. Reagan is making that buffalo dip I love. I'm not missing out on that."

"You sure? I have wings and pizza being delivered."

"Hmm." She taps her finger to her chin, pretending to think it over. "Nope."

"So, what time will you be home?"

"I don't know, later. How late do you play?"

"Don't worry about that. You come back when you're ready. We want to keep Daisy on a schedule, right? So, nine or so?"

"Mark." She throws her head back and laughs. "It's seven thirty now.

We're just going to be at Ridge and Kendall's. It's a ten-minute drive from here."

"I know. I just feel like I'm kicking you out of your own house, and well, if I'm here, I want my girls here too."

"As soon as the guys get here, you'll forget all about missing us and be immersed in losing money."

"Who says I'm going to lose?" I ask, taking Daisy from her and kissing her cheek.

"I mean, maybe you'll win. We do have a wedding to pay for," she teases.

"Our wedding is going to be the cheapest in history. No venue, my mom and Kendall's are doing all the food. I can afford to lose a hand or two."

"Diapers. We have to buy lots and lots of diapers."

"And stinky formula," I say in a high-pitched voice, and Daisy smiles. There is nothing in the world better than knowing that smile is because of me.

"Be careful and if you need me to come and get you later, let me know."

"Mark." She stops to look at me. "It's poker night. Have a few beers. Relax. Enjoy a night with no fiancée and kid hanging around."

"I want you here. Always," I say adamantly.

"I know that, but you can still kick back and relax. We're not drinking because we'll have the kids. I'll be home in a few hours. Relax."

"Mommy says to relax," I tell Daisy. "You would think she would know by now I'm always going to worry about both of you."

"I love you." She smiles up at me. "I'm all packed. You want to walk us out to the car?"

"You need her Pack 'n Play?"

"No, Kendall has one I can use."

"All right, little lady, let's get you loaded up in the car." I carry her out to the garage and strap her into her seat, which we usually leave in the car unless we're going into the store or something like that. We try not to take her out much. She's still young and people have zero boundaries. They touch babies they don't know and we don't know where their hands have been. I shudder at the thought. "Be a good girl," I say, kissing her cheek.

"Come here." I pull Dawn to me and kiss the hell out of her. Desire washes over me and I'm close to canceling poker night to ravish her instead. I sleep next to her every single night, but we're usually exhausted from taking care of Daisy, a long day at work, and the ten million other things that life seems to send our way. It's been almost a week since I've been inside her, and that's too damn long. "You're mine tonight," I tell her, grabbing her ass. Have I mentioned that I love her ass? Round and tight. It's an ass that looks incredible in yoga pants, jeans, hell, even her scrubs.

"Promise?" she asks, breathless.

Internally I'm fist bumping myself knowing I did that to her. "Never broken one yet."

"In that case, I'll be home early."

"That's my girl," I say, kissing her one more time. "Drive safe, babe."

"Have fun." She gives me a pointed look.

"Impossible not to with the crew," I tell her with a laugh. "Love you."

"Love you too."

I wait until she's in her car and pulling out of the garage door, except I don't get the chance when Kent pulls in and he and Seth climb out. I wait for them to enter the garage before shutting the door.

"My contribution." Seth holds up a twelve-pack.

"You drinking?" I ask Kent.

"Nah. I'm his DD. Just talked to Ty. He and Ridge are leaving his place now."

"Come on in." I walk back into the house with them on my heels. "I ordered pizza and wings. Should be here soon."

"Where we doing this?" Seth asks.

"Basement. You can take that down to the fridge down there if you want? Unless you want to keep walking upstairs to grab a beer?" I chuckle.

"That would be a big, fat negative."

Kent and I share a look, but before we can discuss what might be going on with Seth, the doorbell rings. "Food's here." I happily pay the delivery kid for dropping off the four large pies and four pounds of wings, making sure to add a gracious tip.

"Fuck, did you invite someone else?" Seth asks.

"Nope. Just the five of us."

"Is Dawn not feeding you?"

"Like you can't devour an entire pizza on your own," Kent says.

Seth grins. "You know it." He opens the top of the first box and pulls out two slices, adding them to a paper plate.

"It's been ages since we've done this," Kent comments, helping himself to some pizza.

"Life," I say, "has a way of getting in the way."

"Our little group has had a rough couple of years," he agrees.

The doorbell chimes. "Come in," I call out, and Ridge and Ty come walking in. They immediately make themselves a plate.

"So, which of you two are next?" Ty asks. "We've got this one married off, or close enough." He points to me and I nod.

"Not against it," Kent says, before shoving another bite of pizza into his mouth. "Just need the girl," he says once he's swallowed. I don't think he even chewed.

"What about you?" I ask Seth.

"Believe it or not, you fuckers make it look like we're missing out," Seth says. "You're all fucking smiles, giggly babies, and 'gotta go home to my wife.' I admit I'd like to have what you have."

Kent nods. "You do make it look like it doesn't suck," Kent agrees.

"It doesn't suck."

"How's that going? With Daisy and Dawn, I mean? Is the adoption started?"

I nod. "It's in the works. I'm glad we're going to be married before it's official so we all have the same last name."

"You're a good man, Marcus Adams," Ridge says.

"Nah, man. I'm lucky to have them." I'm not just saying that. I'm honored to be able to call both Dawn and Daisy mine.

"What happened with that chick?" Kent asks Seth.

"What chick?" We all know he's playing dumb.

"The one you wanted. You met her once and she had you all tied up in knots."

"Not much. I haven't seen her since."

"Have you talked to her?"

"We've texted a few times," he confesses.

"And?" Ridge asks.

"Nothing to tell."

"I call bullshit." This from Tyler.

"Call it what you want. There's nothing there. Not yet anyway. We're getting to know each other slowly. If and when something happens, I'll be sure you four know first," he says, rolling his eyes. "Why the sudden interest in my love life?"

"We're all established," Tyler says. "Kent isn't seeing anyone, and you have this girl that we know nothing about. You can bring her around, you know. We won't run her off."

"Yeah, I won't even flirt with her," Kent says.

"Like you do my fiancée?" I ask him.

"Or my wife," Ridge adds.

"Or mine," Tyler chimes in.

"You guys are too easy. I can't resist," he says, grinning. He picks up the pizza boxes that are not yet empty. "Grab the wings and let's play some cards."

✸✸✸

Two hours later, I'm fifty-dollars richer. "Read 'em and weep, boys," I say, dropping my cards to the table and pulling in the pot of money.

I hear the garage door open and glance down at my phone. It's just after ten and Dawn is home. I want to rush upstairs to see her, to see Daisy before Dawn puts her to bed, but I stay in my seat. Seth drains his beer and announces he has to go to the bathroom.

"I'll be right back. I'm gonna go see if Dawn needs any help getting Daisy in bed." I don't wait for a reply before I'm rushing up the steps, taking them two at a time. Dawn and a sleepy baby greet me at the top of the stairs.

"Hey, Daddy," Dawn says, her voice low.

Hand on her hip, I lean down and kiss her, then Daisy. "How was your night?"

"Good. Ben and Beck were exhausted, and Knox and Everly were already in bed, so we called it a night. This little lady has been fighting sleep. I thought for sure she would crash on the way home, but no such luck."

"Come here." I take Daisy from her arms. "You want Daddy to rock you?" I ask her. She snuggles into my chest. Slowly I begin to rub her back.

"Seriously?" Dawn asks.

"What?"

She points to Daisy. "She just closed her eyes."

"What can I say? I've got the magic touch."

"Is she asleep?" I hear Kent ask.

Turning, I let him get a good look. Daisy must open her eyes because he smiles softly and jiggles her foot around. "You look tired, pretty girl." Leaning in, he kisses the top of her head. "Let your old man rock you to sleep." He winks at Dawn and she laughs.

"Old my ass," I mumble.

"I'm gonna head out. Reagan is on her way home with the boys, so I'm going to go in case she needs help getting them down," Tyler announces.

"They were fighting it when I left. Amelia was helping her to the car," Dawn tells him.

"Yeah, they've been doing this thing where they fight sleep. It's like they're afraid they're going to miss something. I'll see you guys later. We'll do it at my place next time," he says as he heads for the front door.

"We're all calling it a night," Ridge says. He kisses Dawn on the cheek, runs his index finger down the side of Daisy's face, and leaves.

"Thanks, man," Seth says. "I cleaned up downstairs. Left the cards on the table."

"That works. You didn't have to do that, but I appreciate it."

"Night," Kent and Seth say at the same time, and then they're gone.

"Sorry," Dawn says. "I didn't mean to break up boys' night."

"You didn't. We've been playing for two hours. I'm up fifty bucks." I wag my eyebrows and she laughs. "Let me get her down, and then I'll be in."

"Thank you." She covers a yawn.

"I'm coming for you," I tell her with a wink.

"I'll be ready," she says, kissing Daisy on the cheek and rushing off to our room.

It takes me longer to get our girl to deep sleep than I anticipated. Every time I thought she was sound asleep, I'd stand from the rocking chair and her eyes would pop open. So I snuggled and rocked her a little longer. She's growing so much compared to the day we brought her home. I hate that she's growing up so fast.

Finally, I'm able to place her in her crib and she stays asleep. "Night, baby girl," I whisper, and quietly step out of her room. When I reach our bedroom, Dawn is sound asleep, curled up in a ball on top of the covers. She's wearing one of my T-shirts and my guess is nothing else. My cock twitches, but he's not getting any action tonight. Grabbing an extra blanket from the closet, I cover her up, turn off the lamp, and climb into bed. Not exactly what I had planned, but at the end of the day, she's here in my bed, and Daisy is safe in hers. What more can a man ask for?

# Chapter 25

## Dawn

Girls' night ends up being a wedding-planning marathon. Kent came over last night and finalized his online submission to be ordained. We printed it off and he said he was going home to frame it. I wouldn't put it past him.

On Monday, Mark and I went during our lunch breaks and applied for our marriage license and the date is set. Two weeks from today I'll be Mrs. Marcus Adams.

"Okay, dress," Reagan says.

"I was just going to wear something I have."

"Really?" Reagan says, and I can hear the disappointment in her voice.

"Yeah, I mean, this isn't a big affair or anything." I pause and then tell them the other reason. "I always imagined my mom and my sister with me, and I don't know, I just decided something I have will work."

"What do you want, Dawn? Do you see yourself in a dress, not one that you already own? Hell, it doesn't have to be a wedding dress. Maybe just something new he's never seen before?" Kendall suggests.

"Yeah, I can see the appeal of him never seeing me in it before."

"Done. We're going shopping tomorrow." Her fingers start flying across the screen of her cell phone. "We would go tonight but everything is closed." She purses her lips as if the stores are wrong for being closed at nine thirty on a Saturday night.

"Who are you texting?"

"Mark and Ridge, letting them know they're on kid duty tomorrow."

"Might as well add Tyler to that message," Reagan tells her.

"And Kent and Seth, just in case they need extra hands." Amelia laughs.

"Good idea." Kendall goes back to her phone and again, her fingers fly across the screen. "Done," she says, finally looking up.

"Okay, dress is tomorrow. What about decorations?" Amelia asks.

"Meh, I figured some fresh flowers or something."

"Come on, Dawn, you can do better than that," Kendall says. "How do you feel about letting us take over the decorations?"

"Guys, you don't have to do this. It's simple," I tell them.

"Simple and elegant. It still needs to feel like a wedding. You and Mark deserve nothing less," she says.

"Oh." Reagan sits up straighter in her seat. "Add Daisy's dress to the list for tomorrow."

Kendall points her finger at her. "I like the way you think, sister of mine," she says, and they both laugh.

"So, how about it? You going to trust us with the decorations?" Amelia asks.

"Sure. Just don't go overboard and we want to pay for it," I say, making sure I make eye contact with all three of them.

"How about it's our wedding gift to you? Y'all combined two houses so you don't really need anything. What do you two think?" Reagan asks Kendall and Amelia.

"Love it," Kendall says.

"What else?" I ask. Although I'm almost afraid to.

"Food?" Amelia asks.

"Sonia, Heidi, and Theresa," I say, naming Ridge, Kendall, and Mark's moms. "Theresa said not to worry. They were taking care of it."

Kendall nods. "The best part is with those three, we know we're in for some good eats." She laughs.

"You sound like my brother." Reagan chuckles.

Kendall shrugs. "There are worse things. Besides, he is my husband."

"So, we're good, right?" I ask. I don't want this to get out of hand. I have to reel them in to keep it small.

"What about music? What are you walking in to?" Amelia asks.

"I-I'm not sure. I was thinking Mark and I could just kind of stand in front of Kent." My heart aches thinking of walking down the aisle without my father.

Kendall reaches over from her spot next to me and gives my hand a gentle squeeze. "I'm sorry," she says softly.

"Shit, I wasn't thinking," Amelia says.

I wipe a tear before it falls. "It's okay. It's my life."

"Do you trust me?" Kendall asks.

"Of course," I say, and I mean it.

"Let me handle it. The music, the walking, all of it."

"You have two kids, a husband, and a full-time job," I tell her. "You don't need to put this much effort into it."

"Dawn," she sighs. "You're my best friend. Of course I'm going to." She looks over at Reagan and Amelia. "I would do it for any of you. Please, I want to, and it's not too much. These two are in on the decorations, so that takes some of the load off."

"Are you sure?" I look at each of them. "I hate that you're all doing so much. It's just supposed to be small and simple."

"It will be," Reagan promises. "Let us handle it. We know it's hard for you, and it's easier not to than to feel the pain. Let us make your wedding day special."

"Okay." I nod, wiping at another tear.

"Shit, y'all better change the subject. Mark's going to be pissed if he finds out we made her cry," Amelia says, dead serious, and we all burst into laughter. She's grinning, which means her comment did what she wanted it to do. Break the tension and mask the sadness.

"Well, that's settled. Now, let's talk about something else." Reagan turns to Amelia. "You're the only single lady among us. What's going on with you? Seeing anyone?"

"No." Amelia shakes her head. "Still living with my parents and searching for full-time employment."

"Human resources, right?" I ask her.

"Yeah. To be honest, I haven't really been looking. I'm just… in a funk I guess. I mean, I want to be gainfully employed and move out of my parents' place, but I was gone for college, and I missed them. I don't hate it at the moment." Something flashes in her eyes that I can't read before it's gone.

"Nothing wrong with that," Reagan says.

"Hey, maybe talk to Ridge. He moans about all the HR stuff he has to handle. Maybe he'll be ready to let go and hire someone?" Kendall suggests.

"Yes. My dad was the same way growing up when the company was his. Mom would tell him over and over to hire someone, but he never did," Reagan tells us.

"I might do that," Amelia says, not really committing but knowing that will pacify Kendall and Reagan.

Maybe it's because I've spent a lot of time with her while she was with me in the hospital or maybe it's because I didn't know her then, but my gut tells me there's something going on with her. She fidgets in her seat and I know she's uncomfortable.

"Okay, enough of my wedding high-jacking girls' night. What next?" I ask.

"Well, we've already broke out the wine, so junk food and movies. Oh… dance party?" Reagan laughs.

"Really?" I ask.

"Hell yeah. Girls' night we let loose and act like we're fifteen again."

"All right." I toss her my phone. "It's already connected to the bluetooth speaker, pick whatever you want. I'm making some popcorn."

"We'll help." Kendall grabs Amelia's hand and drags her into the kitchen with us.

"There are only four of us," I say, looking at the chips, cookies, brownies, candy, and I know there are two cartons of ice cream waiting for us in the freezer.

"Girls' night, calories don't count," Kendall says.

"Good thing. We've already demolished two bottles of wine," I say, holding up the empty bottles as proof.

Amelia waves me off. "We'll burn that off with the dance party."

"That's a real thing?" I ask.

Reagan laughs as she joins us. "Yeah, we used to have them all the time, Amelia and me. She was two years older than me, like Ridge, but since she was the only girl, we hung out a lot. We had some kickass dance parties."

"I'm sorry I missed that," Kendall says, and she truly sounds disappointed.

"Okay, ladies, let's do this." Reagan turns the volume up and "Love Shack" by the B-52s blares through the speakers.

Junk food forgotten, we bounce around the kitchen and living room acting like fools, pulling out our cheesiest dance moves. I can't wipe the smile off my face, even if I tried. I needed this night more than I knew. It's a perfect reminder to live in the moment. You never know what tomorrow might bring.

# Chapter 26

## MARK

When I woke up this morning, I rolled over to an empty bed. I had to sleep alone last night, which is the craziest thing I've ever heard. But then I remembered why my lovely fiancée insisted on separate rooms, and my smile cannot be contained.

Today is my wedding day.

We're not going with the traditional "can't see the bride the day of the wedding," but she did insist we sleep in separate rooms. She also insisted she stay in the spare bedroom, which is finally furnished with a queen-size bed. I didn't fight her on it. Okay, not much. She's been pretty calm with all this wedding planning and easygoing. This is the first real thing I've heard her ask for, so after whining briefly, I conceded.

We're getting married at noon, which is apparently a time that works with the nap schedule of Daisy and the other littles. I don't care what time, just that it's finally happening. Glancing at the clock, I see it's just after six and Daisy will be up soon. Climbing out of bed, I go ahead and grab a shower, then throw on some basketball shorts and a T-shirt. I don't bother shaving. I know Dawn likes me with a few days' growth, and with my parents keeping Daisy tonight, I plan to let her experience it. All. Night. Long.

"Morning, beautiful." I kiss Dawn on the cheek then bend down to do the same to Daisy, who sits in her high chair. She likes to be where we are, which is a win since we always want her around. "You're a happy baby this morning." She grins when my beard tickles her cheek.

"Need any help?" I ask Dawn.

"Nope, just a basic eggs and toast for breakfast. Everyone will be here at around eight."

"Why so early?"

"Decorations, and apparently, I have to do my hair and makeup."

"You don't need it," I say, biting into a piece of toast. "Can I give her this?" I ask Dawn.

Her eyes are soft as they watch me. "No, she's still too little."

"Sorry, baby girl. Not today," I tell Daisy, offering her a small toy that she ignores and keeps watching me as I devour my toast.

"Yeah, so the house is about to be taken over."

I shrug. "End result is you're my wife. They can do their worst."

"Your parents are going to be keeping an eye on her today."

"I can do it."

"I know, but when you get ready and stuff."

"Babe, you put me in jeans and a button-down. It'll take me like two minutes."

She laughs. "You can duke it out with your dad. He's the one who suggested it."

"Baby hog," I say to Daisy, making a funny face which has her smiling. "Grandpa is a baby hog. He did it with Imogen and Isaac too," I grumble. I feel bad as soon as I say it. Dawn would give anything for her dad to be here. I glance at her and she's smiling, and I exhale. That's all I need to do is offend her or make her cry on our wedding day. She's shed enough tears.

We're barely finished with breakfast when the cavalry starts to arrive. My parents are the first and, just as I suspected, my dad makes a beeline for Daisy and scoops her out of her high chair. My baby girl giggles at the faces he makes and instead of giving him a hard time, I think about how lucky I am. They've accepted Dawn and Daisy into my life without question. They've accepted her as their granddaughter. It's sometimes those in your life that you love the most that you take for granted. I'll never do that again. Not when looking at my future wife allows me to remember the pain and tragedy of losing those you love and how you don't always get the opportunity to say goodbye.

"There's still time to back out," Kent murmurs. I give him a death glare and he chuckles. "Just needed to be said." He grins.

"You're supposed to be behind this union," I whisper back harshly.

"Oh, I am. I love Dawn and Daisy, but you know, as your friend and now the officiant of this blessed union, I wanted to throw it out there."

"All I need you to throw out is you may now kiss your bride."

He clamps his hand on my shoulder and nods.

"I can't believe what the girls did to the house," I say, looking at the arch of flowers we're standing under.

"They have no boundaries. All three of them have been slave drivers for the last two weeks. We kept if from you both, wanting it to be a surprise."

All of my earlier irritation fades away. "Appreciate it. Today is going to be hard for her."

He nods in understanding. "Showtime," he says as Matt Stell's "Prayed For You" begins to play.

I feel myself choke up, and I swallow hard. I haven't even laid eyes on her yet, and I'm already feeling the well of tears. Sucking in a breath, I slowly exhale. Our living room has been transformed into a wedding— small, intimate, complete with the flowered-covered arch I'm standing under. I know everyone wanted this day to be special for her. We all know how hard it's going to be.

There is no bride side or groom side; it's all one side. There are four chairs in the front row, and two of them have single red roses placed there. One for each of her parents. The other two I assume will be for mine. Again, I swallow hard thinking about them missing this day.

Looking toward the hallway, I see my mom appear and Daisy is in her arms. My little girl is wearing a light-pink frilly dress, with a matching bow on her head. Mom takes each step slow and steady. Daisy takes it all in. When she sees me, she smiles, and my heart beats like a drum in my chest. Heavy, steady beats as they draw closer. Instead of taking her seat, Mom brings Daisy to me. This wasn't the plan, but it was the one thing that I insisted on. Mom said she would make it happen. I'm not just marrying Dawn, but Daisy too. It's important to me that she's here and with us.

"Hey, baby girl." I kiss her cheek and she squeals, making everyone laugh. "Look." I point to the hallway just as Dawn appears. I choke back a sob when I see my dad by her side. She's gorgeous in a long-sleeve white dress. It stops just above her knees and is form-fitting. "There's Mommy," I tell Daisy.

Dad stops in front of me, Dawn on his arm, and I want to reach for her. "Who gives this woman away?" Kent asks.

"It's with incredible honor, in the memory of her parents, that I do," Dad says, his voice holding a bit of a wobble as he says the words. I watch as he brushes Dawn's tears away with his thumbs and kisses her cheek. He then turns to me. "I'm trusting you with her heart, son." I nod because my throat is clogged. I can't speak. He places her hand in mine and she steps closer. Daisy squeals again and reaches for her.

"Hey, baby," Dawn says, her voice cracking.

Needing my hands on her, I snake an arm around her waist and pull her into me. I bury my face in her neck and breathe her in. Daisy wiggles from being stuck between us. "I prayed for you," I whisper.

"Now, now, enough of that," Kent says, and everyone laughs. I pull away from her and we begin. We decided to just let Kent roll with whatever. That's part of what makes this day special. It's people we love and hold dear to us who are here. He surprisingly doesn't do anything outlandish. He sticks to the traditional vows as we exchange rings.

"Now, Mark, this is the part you've been waiting for." He grins wolfishly.

"Finally," I say dramatically. Again, our guests, our family laughs.

"Wait," Dawn says.

My heart drops.

"I-I wanted to say something." She looks up at me, then out to our guests. "To all of you." She takes a deep breath and slowly exhales. "The night I got the call, I was going to tell you that I loved you." She smiles, but the sadness in her eyes is powerful. "I was so scared, not sure if you felt the same way, but I felt it deep and wanted you to know. I was prepared for you not to say it back." She pauses and swallows hard. "Then I got the call, and instead of telling you that I loved you, I was leaning on you. Depending on you to hold me up, to catch me when I fell." Reaching out with my free hand, I wipe the tears from her cheeks. "I didn't even have to ask you. You were just there." She turns to our guests. "All of you were there. Supporting me, loving me through the worst day of my life. I know that there is no way I could have made it through without all of you." She bites her bottom lip as it begins to wobble. "Then, just when I was starting to feel like I could maybe learn to live this life without them, this little lady entered the world." She leans in and kisses Daisy on the cheek before her hazel eyes find mine. "Again, you were there. No stipulations, no pretenses, you just were." She again looks at our guests. "All of you were."

She looks at her feet, and my heart stalls waiting for what she's going to say next. When she doesn't speak, I say, "I told you," I whisper, "I'll always be there to catch you when you fall."

She smiles through her tears. "I never could have imagined that this is where we would end up. Raising this little girl to be our own. Your heart, Marcus Adams, is one of a kind. I will spend every day showing you what you mean to me, showing you how special you are to accept not just me and my crazy baggage, but this little girl. We love you so much." She takes in a few deep breaths. "I wasn't sure what to get you for a wedding gift. It's hard to find a gift for a man who has given me everything. That is until I got the mail yesterday." She turns to the crowd, and Kendall hands her a piece of paper. "This came at just the right time, and I don't know if my parents are up there cheering for us, but it's what I'd like to believe. Maybe even my sister." She whispers that last part. "Open it," she says, handing me the folded piece of paper.

She tries to take the baby, but I shake my head, opting to open the paper and read it. My eyes scan the page, and I freeze, going back to read the first line again.

*Congratulations! Your petition for adoption has been approved.*

My eyes scan the letter and it has my name at the top. I look up at her and she nods. "I got one too. I opened yours hoping this is what it would say." She shrugs with zero remorse for opening my mail. Not that I care. She's my wife, or she's about to be.

"D-Daisy?" I say, my voice cracking. I hug her to my chest and kiss the top of her baby-soft hair. I love this little girl with all that I am, and I'm officially going to be her daddy. "D-Daddy loves you," I tell her, my voice trembling. I look over at Kent and even his eyes are misty. "Let's do this," I tell him. Everyone laughs and the tension is broken. I should say something back to her, tell her that my heart belongs to her, but I can't. She's literally rendered me speechless.

"With the power vested in me by this great state of Tennessee, you may now kiss your bride," he says, and I waste no time pulling her into a kiss. Daisy wiggles and I faintly hear Kent say, "Not in front of the baby," as he takes her from my arms. My hands cup Dawn's face, and I kiss her as if it's the first time with the promise of all of our tomorrows.

When I finally pull away from this kiss, I can't find it in me to remove my lips away from hers.

My wife.

Resting my forehead against hers, I just stand here, letting that knowledge sink in. I'm married. I have a wife and a daughter and, without a doubt, my unexpected fall has been the greatest journey of my life.

# Chapter 27

## Dawn

Today has been incredible, emotional, and so many memories were made. The girls nailed the decorations and the music. Not that I expected anything less. I'm so blessed to have them in my life.

"How long until we kick them out?" Mark asks.

"Stop," I say, laughing. "They're our guests."

He aligns his body with mine, and I can feel how worked up he is. "This could get embarrassing, wife," he says, his lips next to my ear.

"Control yourself."

"We're going to go," my mom says. "This little angel is getting sleepy."

"We can keep her," Mark says.

"Nonsense. You're not going on a honeymoon. You deserve at least a wedding night with no interruptions." I can feel my face heat.

"Thank you, Theresa. We really appreciate it. I'll get her bag." I pull out of Mark's hold and head to Daisy's room. I already have her bag packed. I grab it and rush back out to the living room. "Here you go."

"Thanks," Keith says, taking Daisy from Theresa, making us all laugh.

"I swear he's going to spoil her," Theresa says.

"Mom, that's a good thing."

"I agree, but she's supposed to be grandma's girl," she says with a pout.

"Call us if you need anything," Mark says.

"She'll be fine."

She will be. Keith and Theresa have a room for their grandkids with three baby beds; they added a third when Daisy was born. We tried to tell them she could sleep in one of the other two, but they countered with they wanted to be able to have all three of their grandkids at once and since they were all still little, they needed a safe place to sleep. We didn't argue after that, not that it would have done any good.

"We're all heading out too," Ridge says. "Give the newlyweds some time together."

"You don't have to," I tell him.

He winks at me. "The girls chose noon for a wedding time on purpose. The plan has always been to leave, giving you all some time." He leans in and hugs me, then Mark. "Congrats, you two."

"Thanks, brother," Mark says.

Within twenty minutes, the food is cleaned up, the living room is back in order. The only thing remaining is the arch covered in fresh flowers. I'm glad they left it. It's beautiful, and we get to keep a piece of today just a little bit longer.

I watch as Mark shuts the door behind Kent and Seth, then turns the lock. He walks toward me, pulling his phone out of his pocket, and hits Play. Lonestar's "Amazed" comes through the speakers. "May I have this dance?" he asks, holding his hand out for me.

Without question, I place my hand in his. He pulls me close, and I rest my head against his chest as he softly sings the lyrics to me. We're not even moving, just standing still in the middle of our living room. When the song ends, he pulls away and lifts me into his arms.

"We're already home, so the bedroom threshold will have to do," he says, kissing the corner of my mouth.

In our room, he sets me on my feet. "Let's get you out of this dress." He spins me and lowers the zipper. His fingertips trail down my spine, following the zipper's descent. "Fuck, Pixie," he says, kissing my now bare shoulder.

The dress pools at my feet, and carefully, I step out of it, bending to pick it up. I toss it in the chair that sits in the corner of our bedroom. "You're overdressed, husband," I tell him.

His blue eyes sparkle. "I can fix that." With deft fingers, he unbuttons his shirt, and I help him slide it off his shoulders. Next are his jeans that get kicked off to the side.

"Take it all off." His deep demand causes goose bumps to break out across my skin.

"You too," I say, my voice thick with desire. Reaching behind my back, I unclasp my bra and toss it, before hooking my fingers in the waistband of my sheer white thong, and pull it over my hips. "I'm waiting," I say when he just stands there staring at me.

"Don't rush this. I'm making a memory." His gaze roams over me. "I'll never forget this day. I'll never forget this moment, the moment I make love to my wife for the first time."

I'm ready now. I rub my thighs together to keep from throwing myself on the bed and begging him to take me. I'm not against begging.

He steps forward and with our height difference, he has to bend down as his hand explores my pussy that's more than ready for him. "Damn, baby."

"Can we maybe move this memory-making along?" I ask as his lips trail down my neck.

"We can't rush this," he whispers.

"It's our wedding night. We can do whatever we want." I try to reason with him.

"Is that what you want? A fast fuck?" He slides one of his long thick fingers inside me.

"Y-Yes."

"That's not very romantic," he counters, his voice husky.

"Our life is full of romance. Look at today. You give me romance every day. Tonight, I want you, hard, hot, heavy." I reach out and palm his cock, stroking him gently from root to tip.

"Fuck," he moans, resting his forehead against my shoulder. "Wedding nights are not supposed to be dirty."

"Then we change the rules. We're good at that. Just ask our daughter." We've learned to take things as they come, and that includes this. I want him inside me. I love Daisy with everything I am, but the thought of not being interrupted when he slides inside me, well, I'm glad my new in-laws offered to watch her. I miss her, I love her, but I miss wild, hot, sweaty sex too.

"I don't want slow-and-quiet Mark, I want wild-and-sweaty Mark," I confess.

"Who am I to deny my wife anything?" He pulls his hand from between my legs and brings his fingers to his mouth, slipping his fingers past his lips. "On the bed," he growls.

I don't wait for him to tell me how he wants me. I know how I want him. Crawling on the bed, I stay on all fours offering myself to him.

"Jesus, Pixie. You're not holding any punches," he says, climbing on the bed and settling behind me. His hands grip my ass as I push back against him. "You're trying to make this end before it starts."

"It won't take long," I confess.

"Fuck." He moves away from me.

"Where are you going?" I ask him.

"Condom."

"Mark," I say, turning to look at him over his shoulder. "We're married now."

"I know, but I wasn't sure, so…" He shrugs. This man is always putting me first.

"We don't need those. Not anymore." To be honest, I started to tell him to toss them the night he proposed, but then I thought about this night and the fact that we get to feel each other for the first time with no barrier, celebrating our marriage.

"Babe, you pick our wedding night to tell me I can go bare? I'll be lucky to last a minute," he says, abandoning his mission for a condom as he takes his spot behind me once again.

"We have all night, and I'm so worked up, it's not going to matter." I push my ass against him and feel his cock—long, hard, and thick. "I mean, if you need me to do it myself," I say and he growls. I knew that would spring him into action.

"Not my wife, and not on our wedding night. Your pleasure belongs to me." He runs his cock through my wet heat. He gives me no warning as he thrusts inside me.

"Yes," I say breathily, letting my head hang and the feeling of being stretched around him wash over me.

Slowly, he pulls out, then slams back in. Over and over he does this. Each time his thrusts grow faster until he's pounding inside me. The bed is bouncing off the wall, my moans fill the room followed by his grunts, and I never want it to end.

"Baby," he says through gritted teeth, "I'm close."

Pushing my hips back, I grind into him until I start to unravel. "There," I pant, and he gives me what I need without asking.

Thrust after thrust.

His hands gripping my hips.

I scream out his name as my body shakes and my pussy convulses around him. I'm just coming down from my orgasm when I feel him still and release himself inside me. It's erotic and sensual. I can feel the hot spurts as he finds his release. It's new and exhilarating, and tonight was the perfect night for it to happen for the first time.

His body shudders with aftershocks before he pulls out and falls onto the bed next to me. His arms wrap around me and he kisses me sweetly. A complete contrast to what just happened. "You're trying to kill me on our wedding night," he says as he sucks in air, trying to even out his breathing.

"Wh-When can we do it again?" I ask, making him laugh.

"Give me a minute to recover, then we're going to shower, and I'm going to make love to you like I was supposed to."

"Oh, yeah?" I ask, rolling over to climb on top of him. My hips straddle his waist, and his cock that's still half hard twitches at my touch. "What if I wanted to make love to you?" I ask, stroking him.

"Baby, I'm yours. You can do with me as you wish." He sits up and kisses me, fusing his mouth to mine. "But first, we shower." He moves to the edge of the bed, me still in his lap, and places his feet on the floor. Never missing a beat, he carries us to the shower.

We take our time cleaning up and exploring each other's bodies. Which sets the tone for the rest of the night. Sex, shower, repeat. Not that a shower was necessary, but ours is huge with a bench that we've been meaning to get more use out of. I'm happy to report that tonight, we gave it a workout.

# Chapter 28

## MARK

Married life is fucking fantastic. I'm not sure why that is. All that has really changed is her last name, the title we have in the eyes of the law, and the rings on our fingers, but it's bliss. I love her more today than I did yesterday, and to me, that's all that matters.

"You ready for today?" I ask my wife.

It's our annual Friendsgiving and we have some big news. Not just that, but it's the one-year anniversary of her parents' death. The actual date was yesterday. We drove to Mason to put flowers on the grave, and drove past the house. It finally sold a week after we were married. A younger couple with two small girls. Dawn cried and said it was perfect. I happen to agree with her. Give the house life again and a new family to build memories within the walls.

"Yes. Besides, it's about celebrating life, theirs and Miss Everly's. I can't believe that she's two already."

"And this one," I say, bouncing Daisy in my arms. "Six months," I say, and she giggles when I make a funny face. "You can stop growing any day now," I tell my daughter.

"You can't stop it." Dawn laughs.

"I know." I sigh. "However, we can make another one." I shoot her a wink.

"We can do that." She smiles.

"So, does that mean we're going to?" I ask.

"Let's let her get a little older before we start adding to our brood."

"I want them to be close in age."

"Fifteen months is too close," she counters.

"Fine," I say, tickling Daisy's belly. "Mommy says we have to wait," I say theatrically.

"Oh, hush. Did you load the Pack 'n Play?" she asks.

"Yes, and the diaper bag is all packed and ready to go. All we need is the dish you made."

"I was on desserts this year. I made cookies for the kids, and then three pumpkin pies."

"Um, make that two pumpkin pies."

"What did you do?" she asks.

"I was hungry and they smelled so good," I confess.

"When?"

"I got up with Daisy in the middle of the night."

"When?" Her voice turns suspicious. "I didn't hear her."

"Okay, I got up to check on her, and I had to walk past the kitchen, and I couldn't resist. I just ate one piece. We can still take it."

"How big of a piece?" she asks.

My wife knows me so well. "Umm, a big piece," I say, not wanting to tell her it was half the pie. I very easily could have eaten the entire thing. I had to tap into my self-control. She should be proud.

"Lucky for you I made four." She grins.

"What?"

"I know you and pumpkin pie. I just hid the one I made for you. I was going to give it to you when we got home."

"Damn, I could have eaten the entire thing," I mutter, and she throws her head back laughing. Daisy laughs too just because her momma is.

"I'll grab the other pie and the cookies. You get the munchkin strapped in," she tells me.

"Did you know about the fourth pie?" I ask my daughter as I carry her out to the garage. I lifted the door and started the engine earlier, so the car would be warm and ready for us. "You have to let Daddy in on this kind of information." By the time I have her strapped into her seat, Dawn has the pies and the cookies loaded, and we're off. This year, even though it's Everly's birthday, Tyler and Reagan are hosting.

"Everly is going to be so excited," Dawn says once we're on the road. "We turned Ty and Reagan's place into a princess fairy tale."

I chuckle. "I'm sure Ty and the boys loved that."

"The boys actually did, much to Ty's dismay. It was pretty comical actually. He kept telling them that the men needed to stay together and that they couldn't let the women rule. The twins laughed so hard they had us all smiling. He's really good with them."

"Is that a dig at my daddy skills?" I tease.

"Never, you know better," she says adamantly.

"I know. I was just giving you shit," I tell her.

"You need to watch what you say. Our daughter is going to be the little girl who cusses like a sailor if you don't."

I shrug. "There are worse things she could do." I don't say anymore. I know that we're both thinking the same thing. She could turn out like Destiny. Her birth mother.

"This is true," she agrees, and the rest of the ride we chat about Christmas shopping and what to get my parents this year. We like to get them bigger gifts because no matter how many times we offer, they refuse to let us pay them for watching Daisy.

We're all sitting around the many foldout tables at Tyler and Reagan's, getting ready to dive into our plates that are overflowing with delicious food when Reagan stands. "This year, we thought"—she glances over at Ty—"that it would be a good idea as a family to say what we're thankful for. I tried to convince Ty we could do it individually, but he said that would take too long and the food would get cold."

"My man," Seth says, and we all laugh.

"So, we'll start. Ty and I are thankful for our boys. They're happy and healthy and that's all we could ever ask for."

"We'll go next," Kendall says, standing. "We didn't plan for this." She looks down at Ridge. "But without discussing it, I know Ridge would agree that we're thankful for our support system. Life is messy and unplanned, but having all of you in our corner, it makes things easier. So we're thankful for each of you."

"I'm thankful for the women in our lives that feed us like they do," Seth says, not bothering to stand. I swear if I looked hard enough, there would be drool on his chin as he eyes his plate.

Kent stands and clears his throat. "Pumpkin pie," he says, and I hold my fist out for him.

"My man," I say.

"I guess it's my turn," Amelia says, standing. "All the moments. I'm thankful for every single one of them. I've missed you all, and I cherish all we've had and those we will have," she says, looking around the room at all of us.

I look over at Dawn and she nods, so I stand. "The list is too long," I say, looking around at our family. "We'd be here all day, and for the sake of my stomach and yours, Dawn and I would like to narrow it down this year." I look down at my wife and her smile is blinding. "This year, Dawn and I are thankful for our daughter. Daisy Elizabeth Adams," I say, not sure if they'll get it, but I should have known better.

"It's official?" Kendall asks.

"She's yours?" Reagan questions.

"Did you get the final word?" Amelia asks.

"Yesterday." I nod. "We had our court hearing, signed the papers, and it's official. We're her parents," I say proudly. I thought when we got the letter that our application was approved and that was the end. However, it wasn't. We still had court hearings and classes we had to take. That letter basically just told us they were willing to let us adopt her. Regardless, it made the day special.

Chairs are pushed back, and full plates temporarily forgotten as we accept hugs of congratulations. My face hurts from smiling. I was pretty sure that the adoption was going to go through with Dawn being the only living relative, but in the back of my mind, there was always this fear the sperm donor, whoever he may be, might find out and fight us for her. Unlikely, I knew this, but it didn't keep me from worrying about it. She's my little girl after all. I suppose there will always be worry when it comes to her. That's what dads do.

"I'm sorry, I know I shouldn't bring this up, but you found out yesterday? On the anniversary…," Kendall asks, letting the anniversary hang there for interpretation. We all know what she means.

"Yeah." Dawn nods. "I know it sounds crazy, but could it be possible?" she asks.

"I say you believe what you feel," Reagan says.

"It's them," Amelia adds. "I'm not super religious, but…" She shrugs.

"Daddy, I'm so hungry my belly's mad at me," Knox says, breaking the tension and making us all laugh.

"Dig in," Tyler tells him. He picks up a piece of ham and shoves it into his mouth. Ben, Beck, and Everly, wanting to be like their big cousin and brother, mock him.

The adults follow suit as we enjoy the food, but more so the company. Me, I enjoy my wife and my daughter. I soak up every moment of each day, locking those memories up tight.

"What's the plan for New Year's?" Ridge asks. "Kendall's parents offered to keep the kids."

"Mom and Dad offered to keep the boys," Reagan tells him, and he nods.

"Your mom offered to keep Daisy the other day too."

"I think the grandparents are up to something." I laugh.

"Yeah, stealing our kids," Tyler retorts.

"I think it's sweet," Amelia says. "They just want to give you all time to be married couples without the kiddos." She raises her hands in defense. "And before you say it, I know you don't mind your kids being around. Trust me, I know this, I don't mind it either, but you have to admit being able to cut loose a little sounds enticing," she says.

"You did this," Reagan says.

Amelia shrugs. "Maybe. I just thought we could all hang and wanted everyone to have a carefree night."

"Where is this going down?" Kent asks.

"We can do it at our place," I offer before thinking twice about it. "We have three extra bedrooms, and the basement," I say as reasoning. When in reality, it's because I want my wife in our bed. I'm a greedy bastard when it comes to her.

"Sure," Dawn says. "We have plenty of space. If you drink you have to stay," she says.

"We're all drinking," Amelia informs us. "Wait, unless one of you is knocked up again, then the entire plan is shot to hell." She grins, not meaning it in the least.

"Not me," Dawn says, much to my disappointment.

"Not me. The boys need to be out of diapers first. I can't imagine three in diapers at once," Reagan says.

"Watch it, sister," Ridge warns. "You might get triplets next time."

"Bite your tongue." She points at him, giving him the evil-eye.

"I don't know, Reags. My swimmers seem to get the job done. I wouldn't rule it out," Tyler boasts.

"I want to go swimming," Knox says.

"It's too cold, buddy," Kendall tells him. "Uncle Tyler was talking about the summer."

"Oh." His little shoulders deflate. "That's okay. Grandma lets me swim in the bathtub," he says, and goes back to playing with the others.

"Mark and Dawn's place. The ladies can take care of the food, because let's face it, we'd starve otherwise," Kent says.

"Hey," Ridge argues. "I can cook."

"Yeah, but not like they can." He points to Kendall. "Ladies, you take care of the food. Gentlemen, we'll take care of the booze."

"We have the sectional downstairs, and then a queen in two of the spare bedrooms."

"I say the couples take the beds. I'll take an air mattress in the basement bedroom, or even in Daisy's room. I'm not picky," Amelia says. "Seth and Kent can duke it out for the chaise on the sectional and the recliner."

"Sounds like a plan," Dawn says.

218

"Who wants dessert?" Reagan asks. The women groan. The kids raise their hands and so do the big kids, meaning us guys.

"Don't hog all the pie. You have some at home," Dawn scolds playfully.

"Yes, ma'am."

I grab me a piece of pumpkin and share it with Daisy. She loves every bite. "That's my girl," I say when she opens her little mouth for more.

"Spoiled," Dawn says, taking the seat next to mine with two cookies on a napkin.

"So are you," I say, pointing to her cookies.

"You going to feed them to me?" she asks sweetly.

"You ready to go?" I ask her, and she throws her head back and laughs.

"No, she's not," Kendall says, her hands on her hips. "You're just going to have to wait."

I pretend to be put out, but I'm not and we all know it. I wouldn't trade this time with our family for anything.

# Epilogue

## Dawn

"How much time do we have?" Mark asks. His parents just left with Daisy for the night.

"Like thirty minutes if that."

"Let's go." He grabs my hand and starts leading me toward our bedroom.

"What are you doing?" I laugh.

"You said I had thirty minutes. I only need fifteen." He puts his hands on the button of his jeans.

"Slow down there, crazy man. If that. I said *if that*. We're not getting caught with our pants down, literally," I say, trying to hide my laughter.

"Pixie, we have no baby. It's go time," he says, and this time I lose the battle as I sputter with laughter just as the doorbell rings.

"I told you. That's probably Kendall. You know she's always early."

"Damn," he grumbles, kissing me quickly before leaving the room. I follow along behind him as he opens the door for Kendall and Ridge. "Hey, let me help." He takes a crockpot from Kendall's hands.

"Sorry if it took a minute to answer the door. My wife can't keep her hands off me," he says.

"You've been spending too much time with Seth," Kendall jokes, knowing damn well he would be the one causing us to delay in opening the door. Not that I don't ravish him, because I do when I know that we're alone. I would be mortified if they caught us, married or not. My best friend knows me all too well.

"I'm going to take our bags back to the room. Does it matter which one?" Ridge asks.

"Nope. Make yourself at home," I tell him.

Kendall and I are in the kitchen setting up the food when Reagan and Amelia join us. The four of us work together to get everything set up. "Ladies, we have way too much food," I say, looking at the spread.

"Nah, the guys will graze all night. They'll put a dent in it," Reagan says.

"Speaking of the guys, it's way too quiet. We better go see what's up," Kendall says.

"I thought this was a kid-free night," Reagan quips, and they both laugh.

I hang back with Amelia. "Hey, you okay?"

"Yeah." She plasters on a fake smile. "You know New Year, lots to think about. I'm good."

"All right, well, you know I'm here if you need anything."

"I know." She wraps her arms around me in a hug. "I'm glad he has you. Mark has always been the one who stays to himself more than the others. He needed a strong woman to bring him out of his shell."

"I don't know about strong, but I like to think we complement each other. And don't for a second think I didn't notice you changing the subject."

"I'm fine. Now, let's go. Kendall and Reagan might need backup."

I drop it for now, but even more so I feel as though something is up with her. I wish she would share the burden and let me be there for her. She helped me so much when Daisy was in the hospital. I make a mental note to reach out to her next week and invite her to lunch or even dinner. Something in me tells me she needs a friend. What's worse is she's surrounded by them and not willing to let us in.

She's being stubborn, but that's okay. I've learned to not give up that easy. I'll be here when she's ready.

# Epilogue

## MARK

My wife is drunk. She's drunk and cute as hell. I can't keep the smile off my face as I watch her dance around our basement as if she hasn't a care in the world. We've been through hell and back, so seeing her like this makes me happy.

"You know when we talked about this at Friendsgiving, I was thinking a night without the boys, some uninterrupted sexy times with my wife," Tyler says from his seat beside me. "Looks like that won't be happening unless I cut her off, and I can't seem to find it in me to do that."

"They're having a good time," I agree.

"I've had maybe four beers," he says. He tips his bottle up and drains it. "Want another?" he asks me.

"Nah, I'm good. Thanks." He nods and heads to the refrigerator to grab another.

"I want that," Seth says, slurring his words.

"Want what?" I ask, confused as hell.

"That." He points to the women who are putting on their own little dance party. "I want a woman in my bed at night. I want to stand off to the side with a love-sick expression on my face." He points to me.

I take no offense because he speaks the truth. "Make it happen."

"I really like her," he mumbles.

"Who?" I ask. It's a dirty trick, but he's been tight-lipped about this mystery girl for months.

"I want to be somebody's daddy," he slurs.

"Where's your girl tonight?" I ask.

"Don't know. Only seen her once."

"I thought you were texting her?" I reach out to keep him from falling to the floor.

"A few times, but it's not like that." He points again out to the women in the room. "I want it to be. She lives too far away. She's so sweet, and she's one of those." Again he points to the women dancing. "One of the ones I'd want to take home to my momma."

"Why don't you let me have this?" I reach for his beer.

"N-Nope," he says, popping the p. "This is my woman tonight. I'm going to drink until I forget."

"Give me your keys."

He digs in his pocket and hands them over. "I'd never do that," he tells me.

"I know, brother, but sometimes the alcohol makes decisions for you." It's been a hell of a long time since I've seen him or any of the guys this wasted. Hopefully soon, he'll pull his head out of his ass and tell this woman he's into her. Until then, he's safe here, and he can drink until his heart's content, and then suffer the consequences tomorrow. I, for one, am all for pacing myself. He stumbles off just as Dawn breaks away from the group and heads toward me.

"Hey, Pixie." I kiss her lips.

"Hi." She peers up at me. "This was a good idea," she says.

I chuckle, tucking some crazy stray hairs behind her ears. "You've been hitting it hard."

"I have a lot to celebrate for this New Year."

"Dawn!" Kendall calls out and motions for her to join them again.

"Gotta go. Bye, handsome." She jumps, kissing me on the cheek, and races back to the makeshift dance floor.

I watch her go, enjoying the smile and her laughter. I can't wait to see how time changes her, changes us. There is one thing I am certain of. I love her more every day.

Life has thrown me some curveballs, and there have been times when the unexpected changes have literally knocked me on my ass. I had to learn to live one breath, one second, one minute, one house, one day at a time. I've learned that the best things in life are truly unexpected. I've embraced it and learned to live with my unexpected fall.

*Thank you for taking the time to read*

# Unexpected Fall

*Want more from the Beckett Construction Crew?*
*Seth's story is next.*
*Sign up below to receive updates about the release.*

*Never miss a new release:*
http://bit.ly/2kMltRu

*More about Kaylee's books:*
http://bit.ly/2CV3hLx

# Contact
## KAYLEE RYAN

**Facebook:**
http://bit.ly/2C5DgdF

**Instagram:**
http://bit.ly/2reBkrV

**Reader Group:**
http://bit.ly/2o0yWDx

**Goodreads:**
http://bit.ly/2HodJvx

**BookBub:**
http://bit.ly/2KulVvH

**Website:**
www.kayleeryan.com

# Other Works
## BY KAYLEE RYAN

**With You Series:**

*Anywhere With You | More With You | Everything With You*

**Soul Serenade Series:**

*Emphatic | Assured | Definite | Insistent*

**Southern Heart Series:**

*Southern Pleasure | Southern Desire | Southern Attraction | Southern Devotion*

**Unexpected Arrivals Series:**

*Unexpected Reality | Unexpected Fight | Unexpected Fall*

**Standalone Titles:**

*Tempting Tatum | Unwrapping Tatum | Levitate*
*Just Say When | I Just Want You*
*Reminding Avery | Hey, Whiskey | When Sparks Collide*
*Pull You Through | Beyond the Bases*
*Remedy | The Difference*
*Trust the Push*

**Co-written with Lacey Black:**

*It's Not Over*

# Acknowledgements

*To my readers:*

Thank you for supporting me on this wild ride of publishing. I am so thankful to each and every one of you for giving my words a chance.

*To my family:*

I love you. You hold me up and support me every day. I can't imagine my life without you as my support system. Thank you for believing in me, and being there to celebrate my success.

*Eric Battershell:*

Thank you for another cover worthy image.

*Corey Mortenson:*

Thank you for doing what you do and bringing Mark's character to life.

*Tami Integrity Formatting:*

Thank you for making the Unexpected Fall paperback beautiful. You're amazing and I cannot thank you enough for all that you do.

*Sommer Stein:*

Time and time again, you wow me with your talent. Thank you for another amazing cover.

*My beta team:*

Jamie, Stacy, Lauren, and Franci I would be lost without you. You read my words as much as I do, and I can't tell you what your input and all the time you give means to me. Countless messages and bouncing ideas, you ladies keep me sane with the characters are being anything but. Thank you from the bottom of my heart for taking this wild ride with me.

*Give Me Books:*

With every release, your team works diligently to get my book in the hands of bloggers. I cannot tell you how thankful I am for your services.

*Tempting Illustrations:*

Thank you for everything. I would be lost without you.

*Julie Deaton:*

Thank you for giving this book a set of fresh final eyes.

*Becky Johnson:*

I could not do this without you. Thank you for pushing me, and making me work for it.

*Marisa Corvisiero:*

Thank you for all that you do. I know I'm not the easiest client. I'm blessed to have you on this journey with me.

*Kimberly Ann:*

Thank you for organizing and tracking the ARC team. I couldn't do it without you.

*Erica Caudill:*

Thank you for all of your help and support!

*Bloggers:*

Thank you, doesn't seem like enough. You don't get paid to do what you do. It's from the kindness of your heart and your love of reading that fuels you. Without you, without your pages, your voice, your reviews, spreading the word it would be so much harder if not impossible to get my words in reader's hands. I can't tell you how much your never-ending support means to me. Thank you for being you, thank you for all that you do.

*To my Kick Ass Crew:*

The name of the group speaks for itself. You ladies truly do KICK ASS! I'm honored to have you on this journey with me. Thank you for reading, sharing, commenting, suggesting, the teasers, the messages all of it. Thank you from the bottom of my heart for all that you do. Your support is everything!


With Love,

Made in the USA
Columbia, SC
03 March 2021